Totally Bound Publishing books by Jayce Carter

The Omega's Alphas
Owned by the Alphas
Shared by the Alphas
Saved by the Alphas
Protected by Her Alpha
Caught by Her Alphas
Tamed by the Alphas
Claimed by the Alphas
Exposed by Her Alphas
Trained by the Alphas
Reclaimed by Her Alphas

Ready or Not
Fake It 'til You Make It
Opposites Attract
Third Time Lucky
Enemies Closer

Grave Concerns
Grave Robbing and Other Hobbies
Hell Raising and Other Pastimes
Saving the World and Other Bad Ideas

Dark Sanctuary
Bound by Fear
Trapped by Doubt
Buried by Despair

Nemesis
The Corpse Princess
The Resurrected Queen

Larkwood Academy
Silenced
Whispers
Screaming

The Devil's Luck
A Devil of a Time

Collections
Sun, Sea and Sinful Delights
Secret Santa: To Catch a Fox
Cupid's Academy: Stolen

The Devil's Luck

A DEVIL OF A TIME

JAYCE CARTER

A Devil of a Time
ISBN # 978-1-80250-515-3
©Copyright Jayce Carter 2023
Cover Art by Kelly Martin ©Copyright March 2023
Interior text design by Claire Siemaszkiewicz
Totally Bound Publishing

A DEVIL
OF A TIME

Dedication

To all the girls who want to bang the villains —
you're my kind of people.

Chapter One

My name is Loch Lacey, and I am sexually attracted to red flags — the more of them shoved into a vaguely man-shaped form, the hotter and dumber I get.

I'd say that trait would end up killing me, but it already had. Five years ago, I'd let some fuckwit tell me pretty lies and sold my soul for his benefit, which left me spending my afterlife here in the Chasm as my punishment.

And even though I should have known better, a part of me saw the man across the bar, Tyrus, with a flashing neon sign above his head saying *death two here*. I didn't believe in love at first sight but fuck if 'my future bad decision at first sight' wasn't a thing.

Tyrus sat at his normal table in the back. He ran this place — much like he ran many of the businesses here. Whereas most bosses, especially ones with as much on their plate as Tyrus had, would half-ass the actual day-to-day headaches, he never seemed to. He was *always* here.

Right now, he was talking to someone else, his arm out on the back of the bench as if to prove himself in charge. *Talk about posturing.*

Of course, Tyrus was all about his posturing. He liked to play the game and from what I'd seen, he excelled at it.

"Another?" The bartender, Koya, put a new drink down in front of me before I got the chance to answer. Then again, my empty glass suggested I needed more. I didn't have a whole lot of talents, but I could drink most people under the table while staying on my feet. Call it a gift from a life spent trying to escape the ugliness of my reality.

I nodded in thanks, then brought the new glass to my lips. The liquor burned, but I didn't so much as flinch as I swallowed down a gulp.

"Hey there, pretty thing. You new here?" The unfamiliar voice made me struggle to resist the urge to roll my eyes like a petulant child.

I turned on my barstool to find a damned behind me, his body already twisted beyond recognition. He had horns that curled back from his temples and bright red eyes, his face having shifted into a muzzle. When I'd died, five years ago, the thought of talking to something as terrifying looking as him would have sent me screaming. Now, however? I was used to it.

Fangs, feathers, claws, scales? *Big fucking deal.* So long as they didn't drool or spit acid on me, I didn't much care.

"Nope," I answered before taking another drink and peering out at the dim bar again.

The Chasm was *always* dark. Even inside, even with lighting, it never got bright enough. Trying to do puzzles here was a fucking losing battle. It made me wonder if the very air here absorbed the light.

Wouldn't surprise me. Seemed yet another way to remind us all that we were the bad guys and this was our punishment.

"But you still look human—you can't have been here that long," the man added on.

I gave him a side-eye because I'd heard this shit before plenty of times. People showed up in the Chasm in two forms—as damned or as demons. They all looked human at first, but the damned quickly twisted into monstrous forms. They grew fangs and claws and became animalistic. Demons, on the other hand, kept their human body. They had another form, a demonic one, but they didn't have to take that. Demons were rarer and more powerful, putting them above the damned.

I still appeared human because I'd been one of the few who arrived as a demon rather than damned.

"Nope," I assured him. "Been here in this depressing paradise for five years."

"So why haven't I seen you?"

"Because I've been really fucking lucky so far?"

He narrowed his eyes until they looked like some cheap Halloween decoration, nothing but a red spotlight staring out from his not-at-all human face. "You're mouthy for someone who just got here."

"Again—didn't just get here. Why don't you go look for someone who might actually find you charming?" *Like there's anyone who would…*

He leaned in closer, bringing his face just in front of mine. His breath was hot and smelled of rotting flesh. "You need to learn how this world works. People survive by clinging to someone more powerful. You'll lose those looks of yours before you know it, get twisted into something just like the rest of us, so why not sell that pretty little human body while it's still worth something?"

My stomach didn't even roll. Was that how far gone I was already? That even this disgusting thing whispering into my ear in the middle of a bar, suggesting things I'd *never* take him up on, didn't even warrant any stomach churning? Not at least a rumble or threat of vomiting all over him?

I really am jaded, aren't I?

I'd suffered with assholes like him plenty of times, damned who took one look at my unmutated form and wanted to own and break me. I knew what I looked like, which was exactly the same as when I'd died. I didn't have to dye my hair green anymore, since it was like that when I'd taken the bullets that had killed me. I still had the small tattoo on each of my cheeks, hadn't grown more than my pathetic five feet in height and didn't put on or lose weight. Basically? In death, we ended up stuck. It made me feel bad for those who died with not-so-great trends like shaved off eyebrows or shitty tattoos.

On the plus side, I'd shaved the morning I'd died, so no worries about body hair! I had to find the silver lining where I could, or the dreariness of this place would get to me.

"Hard pass." I brought my drink to my mouth again, letting the heavy glass smack him as I did so.

At least that caused him to lean back and give me a bit of space.

"Who are you bound to? I'll just buy your soul off them."

The name caught on my lips. Talk about an answer I hated to give. Then again, that was how the Chasm worked. People didn't wind up here because they were bad people — though, to be fair, most of us were — but because we'd all sold our souls. Just admitting that I didn't own my soul made my mood plummet.

And given I was this far into a bottle on a...Tuesday night? Yeah, my mood was already dragging ass.

"I'll find out," he assured me. "And I can be *extremely* persistent. You'll be mine by the end of the week, and I can't wait to fuck up all that soft human skin. Bet you won't look so pretty when I'm done with you."

"I would personally advise against that," said a deep voice that made the man freeze. He turned slowly, as though if he took long enough, he'd find something other than what he expected behind him.

Except it didn't change. No matter how long the man took, Tyrus still stood there, his dark eyebrow lifted in an obvious challenge.

"She yours?" the man asked, a waver in his voice that made it clear he wasn't rising to that challenge.

"No."

"Then why do you care? Unless you're enjoying her right now, in which case, I'll fucking wait. I don't want to step on any toes."

"Hardly," Tyrus said with so much disgust in his voice that I was pretty sure I should feel insulted. I might not be sultry or sexy, but he didn't need to say that as if I were some rotting carcass. "She belongs to Gorrin."

And there went the color from the man's cheeks. In fact, forget some parting snarky shot—the man was lucky to stay upright as he fled the bar just as fast as his little legs could carry him.

"Coward," Tyrus muttered as he watched the man leave, then turned toward me. "Why didn't you tell him about Gorrin? Mentioning his name would have resolved this instantly."

"Somehow, it bothers me to admit being owned. Imagine that?"

Tyrus leaned against the bar beside me, giving me the chance to see him up close. How was it that someone could look that dangerous, even dressed in a suit, as civilized as a man could appear? He had tan skin and dark features, with deep brown eyes and black hair slicked back in true gangster style. He had facial hair that rode the line between being well-maintained still looking like he had a five-o'clock shadow.

He was terrifying in a wholly unusual way, and when he stared at me, I felt as if he saw me naked.

No, *worse* than naked. I could deal with people seeing bare skin—what did that matter? Plenty of people had seen my tits and I wasn't conceited enough to think they were special in any way. The left was better than the right, but neither were real superstars. Tyrus saw deeper than that, though. He peered into my soul—what a shitty turn of phrase since I'd sold that already—and saw things I wanted to keep hidden.

"You wouldn't deal with people like that if you gained your own power and made your own name," Tyrus added on.

It's always back to this, isn't it? Seemed it was lecture time yet again.

I took another drink, hoping the burning liquor would dull my senses and the conversation. "I'm fine."

"No, you aren't. In the Chasm, the only things that matter are power and connections. You need to obtain both to survive here."

"I'll do that about when hell freezes over, which it hasn't in five years, so I think I'm safe."

"This isn't hell."

"Close enough. I'm not about to go around stealing souls just to make myself more powerful."

"It isn't stealing — it's bartering. When you were still alive and human, did you not exchange money for goods and services? You do the same here. The only difference is that we use souls as currency."

I thought back to how I'd ended up here, to when I'd sold my soul, to that crushing regret when I'd realized it had all been for nothing. The memory threatened to close my throat, but I shut my eyes and took a deep breath to push it all away.

The Chasm wasn't the sort of place to show weakness, and certainly not in front of a Demon Lord like Tyrus.

The four assholes who ran this place — Tyrus, Gorrin, Hale and Yazmor — held the souls of nearly all the damned between them. This gave them the power to stand mostly unopposed. They ruled the Chasm through fear, threats and a good old heaping of violence just to really flavor the whole recipe.

"Thanks for the completely unsolicited advice, but no thanks. I'm good."

"You really aren't. You have stagnated here for five years. You've survived this long only because of your connection to us — that won't save you forever. It is an imperfect defense that chips away each time you use it. Eventually, it will crumble, and you will have to stand against threats on your own. You can either be moral or you can be strong. You will have to choose between the two." With that, he peered at Koya. "That is her last drink. She does not need to be drunk on her way home."

"Didn't think the devil cared."

"I am not a devil."

"Could have fooled me," I muttered as I gulped down the rest of the liquor and slammed the glass down on the bar top.

Tyrus said nothing else before he turned on his heels and headed back to his table. The other man still waited there patiently, telling me Tyrus had left his meeting to intervene on my behalf. It made his words sting more and irritated me worse than the cheap liquor.

And yet that annoyance didn't stop me from noticing the way he filled out his suit. Most men I'd known who wore such outfits mixed different colors. They'd have a black suit with a white shirt and red tie — something to create a balance. Not Tyrus, though. He paired a black suit with a black shirt and a matching tie.

It wasn't how he looked that garnered the fear and respect of others, though. It was his power, his demon form, his absolute ruthlessness that had earned him his place at the top. I'd yet to see that other side of him, and honestly? I never wanted to. Seeing my *own* demon form had shocked me enough when I'd first arrived here.

I peered back at Koya, who offered me an apologetic smile. "Sorry, Loch. If it were anyone else, I'd say fuck it and give you another, but I'm not about to piss the boss off."

"Thanks anyway, Koya." I shrugged and slid from the bar stool, the world shifting as I moved for the first time in a few hours and more than a few drinks.

Guess Tyrus hadn't been wrong about cutting me off.

Koya set something on the bar, and for a moment, I smiled. Had he given in to my meager charms?

Of course not. Instead of more alcohol, a cup made from a small skull sat there, the dark liquid inside no doubt coffee. "Should help clear your head a bit," Koya said.

"Thanks." I picked it up and took a drink. When I'd first arrived, the idea of drinking from a skull would have grossed me out. Funny how quickly things can become normal for people.

Demons and damned and skulls had been nothing more than Halloween jokes for most of my life, but now? Totally average. In fact, a day where I didn't see anyone brutally murdered would strike me as odd.

I headed toward the door, coffee in hand, ignoring the weight of Tyrus' gaze. Something about the way he watched me always let me know it was him even if I wanted to pretend otherwise. No matter how distracted, how busy, I always felt the weight of his gaze.

But I refused to look backward and acknowledge it, because men who were bad for me had already fucked up my life *more* than enough.

I could fuck it up all on my own now, thank you very much.

* * * *

The sound of someone crying was like background music in the Chasm — so normal most of us ignored it. Much like screams, we preferred to mind our own damned business.

However, some part of me had always found a soft spot for women and children, so when *that* sobbing was higher-pitched, I turned to find a female damned backed against a wall, another with his hand on the wall above her, caging her in.

"You're working, right?"

She nodded, though the motion screamed that she wasn't happy with the answer. Then again, one look at her body told me all I needed to know.

She was twisted as all damned ended up, her limbs so thin that they had a child-like quality. In a lot of ways, she really had an ethereal beauty to her that was rare. Of course, the barely there clothing, location and her words said she was a sex worker — and not because she wanted to be.

People in the Chasm did what they had to do, just like back on Earth. In fact, it mirrored the surface a whole lot more than most people liked to admit. Any vice that could be found there was replicated here, because we were all the same.

"So what's the problem?" the male asked as he pressed in closer.

"Last time..." The woman's voice drifted off.

"You look fine now. You healed up, so why're you bitching?"

Oh fuck that. I found my feet moving about all on their own. The woman kept going with weak denials, but each one only seemed to egg the man on.

"If you refuse me, you think that'll make Tyrus happy? You think that'll go well for you?"

"Enough," I said, breaking into their little back and forth.

The man twisted to look at me, but no recognition flashed in his eyes. I tried to keep my head down for the most part and not make too many waves. The benefit was that I didn't have a ton of people who had reason to hate me — the negative was that I didn't have a ton of people who respected me, either.

Not that the odds had ever really stopped me. Even when I made calculated risks, I tended to do the math horribly.

"This doesn't concern you," the man snapped, then turned back to the woman as though he were done with me.

"Sure it does. Doesn't seem like she's falling for your sales pitch, so why don't you back off?"

The man stepped away from her, but only to take a big, aggressive step my way. Instead of showing any fear, I took another drink of the coffee Koya had given me.

"She's working, isn't she? My money spends like anyone else's."

While souls were the main currency used in the Chasm, we still traded crystal shards as well. It was a more convenient way to keep track and people seemed to like the jingle from carrying them.

"She still gets to decide what clients she takes and which she sends packing. You seem to be in the second category."

The man approached until he stood just before me, his eyes narrowed. He'd been tall, but his time in the Chasm had twisted him so he hunched forward, and tusks came up from his bottom jaw. "Tyrus owns her, so the only person who gets a say is him. Last I checked, you ain't him."

"I don't have to be him. Go find someone else."

A throat cleared behind me, and I didn't need to turn to know who stood there. *Saved by a devil again.*

The man peered over my shoulder, made a sound of frustration, then stormed off the other way.

I didn't bother to turn around—the person behind me would wait as long as I wanted. Instead, I focused on the girl in front of me. "What's your name?"

"Kelly," she whispered. "Is Tyrus going to be mad? What if—"

I could spot the downward spiral she had just plummeted into, one I needed to break.

"It's fine," I assured her. "It'll be fine, I promise."

"But—"

I shook my head and took out a few shards from my pocket. I handed them over to her, enough to pay for whatever that man would have given her. "There we go. You earned, so you're good."

I doubted Tyrus would have been okay with anyone hurting the girls who worked for him anyway, but Kelly seemed to feel better once she had the shards in hand. "Just to be on the safe side." I held my hand out to her. When she put her hand into mine, I pulled a pen from my pocket and wrote on her arm.

Give her the night off and deal with your own problems yourself – Loch.

She looked at the words, her eyes widening. "You can't order him around!"

"If he has a problem with it, he'll complain later, I'm sure. Now, go on."

Kelly peered behind me, at the shadow waiting for me to pay attention to him, before she nodded and took off toward Tyrus' bar.

"She shouldn't be here," I muttered.

"You don't think anyone should be here," the man behind me said.

I turned finally, struck yet again by the Demon Lord who stood there, his arms crossed and a permanent scowl on his otherwise handsome features.

Hale. The tattooed and pierced bad boy of the Demon Lords. He had light brown hair, shaved on the sides and longer on the top. His throat and chest were covered in tattoos, the designs all weaving together until it would take close study to figure them all out. A curved silver barbell went through his right eyebrow, above one of his shockingly blue eyes, and a horseshoe shaped ring hung in his septum. He had a lip ring, and the glint of light at his chest showed off his pierced nipples as well.

Of course, that was also because he thought an open leather jacket should function alone, since he hadn't paired it with a shirt.

Show-off.

"I think you should be here," I said with a sickly sweet smile.

He snorted. "One of these days your mouth is gonna get you into trouble that you can't talk your way out of."

"Probably." I took another sip of the coffee, then turned to stare up at the walls of the Chasm, the dark cliffs that surrounded our little bit of hell on every side. Light came from one edge, the sky always glowing softly as if overcast, but never making it down to us. "What do you think the Plains are like?"

Bits of gravel groaned beneath Hale's boots as he walked up to stand beside me. "Fucking perfect, I figure. If it wasn't, what'd the point be? Probably boring, though."

"Boring isn't that bad. There's an old saying about 'May you live in interesting times,' that's really a curse. I think I'll take boring over that."

"Boring doesn't sound bad when you've been here five years, but take a look at the older damned, the ones who've been here way longer, and you'll find the biggest enemy is boredom. People don't do well when they ain't occupied. Fuck, maybe the Plains are just a big joke, nothing but bored-ass goody-two-shoes who off themselves after a year because they can't stand waking up another day there."

"Sounds like sour grapes." At his look, I went on. "It means since you can't have it, you decide it's not good anyway to make yourself feel better. I wish I could see the Plains," I admitted.

"Yeah, well, our kind doesn't get up there. Closest you'll get is when one of those fucking angel assholes comes down here."

Which wasn't all that common, given it hadn't happened in the five years since I'd been here. I'd heard about them—apparently the white wings weren't just a fairytale—but I'd never actually seen one.

"Stop looking so fucking forlorn," Hale snapped. "Angels don't come down here unless they got a really good fucking reason, which usually means they got reason to end someone big. In other words? You don't *want* to see 'em up close."

"Maybe," I said, even if I didn't feel that way.

Sure, I might just be smitten with what I couldn't have, might just think about how wonderful life would be if I were in the Plains because it wouldn't ever happen. I'd traded that away when I'd traded away my soul, which shackled me here to Gorrin and to the Chasm.

Which meant staring up at that glow, at the place where the impossibly high walls of the Chasm met the sky, was as close as I could ever hope to get.

And that really wasn't close enough for me.

* * * *

I walked into Gorrin's quarters, skull cup still in my hand. I'd left Hale without a thank you—not like he expected one—and had come back home. An underling had found me as soon as I'd arrived back at Gorrin's residence and ordered me here.

Gorrin could summon me on his own, but the feeling was...*unpleasant.*

Which was a nice way of saying it felt as if my brain were melting. Having one's owner call them was an order impossible to resist. *Any* order was impossible to ignore, but summons sat at the top.

Thankfully, Gorrin rarely used the method unless I was avoiding him and he'd grown tired of waiting.

When I entered his private quarters, the man I belonged to stopped me in place. He was impressive in an entirely different way from Tyrus or Hale, though no less powerful or intimidating.

Gorrin always dressed the way I imagined an old soldier would from a military and civilization that no longer existed. He had a dark blue jacket on with gold buttons and embroidered symbols I didn't recognize. He had matching pants on, and I'd yet to see him wear anything else. Despite living in the same place, I'd never caught a glimpse of him dressed down. No walking around in a towel or putting on comfy pajamas for a movie night for him.

He had wavy, shoulder-length black hair pulled into a short ponytail, but with bangs that fell forward and over one eye. Despite his power, he appeared young if I could look past all the menace and scowling.

Which was hard as fuck to look past…

Gorrin turned toward me and narrowed his eyes at my cup.

"Coffee." I held it up.

"Koya cut you off, I take it?"

"Technically, Tyrus did. Koya was just nice enough to give me the coffee."

"Well, I may have to show my gratitude. Attempting to have conversations with you when you are drunk is…*unproductive.*"

The way he said that made me laugh, even if I should have known better than to laugh at one of the most powerful beings in what was essentially hell.

"I haven't gotten *that* drunk in a while," I argued, thinking back to when I'd first arrived, when the pain of my situation had been greater than my ability to deal with it. I hadn't drunk at the bar back then, instead taking full bottles to my room and inebriating myself to the point of passing out.

Or, from time to time, enough to walk here, to Gorrin's quarters, and yell at him.

And Gorrin, for all his *many* faults, had simply crossed his arms and listened, as though I were a child having a tantrum.

Though, compared to him, I was.

He was a Demon Lord, the oldest from the rumors, likely the most powerful, and what was I?

A fresh demon who had yet to secure even a single soul of her own. Just a girl who had traded her soul in a bad deal and now found herself in the Chasm, unsure of her place, unable to move forward but unable to go backward either.

In short?

Trapped.

"You called?" I took a seat on the sofa in his quarters, the one that hadn't been here the first time I'd come. Had he brought it in for me?

The idea was strange, but he was impossible to read. I never knew what he thought.

"I did. I have a job for you."

"Lucky me," I muttered softly, then took a sip of the coffee as if that would hide what I'd just said.

"I ask little of you, all things considered."

Which wasn't entirely wrong. Gorrin owned my soul. He could ask me to do anything. Many others in such a position took advantage of that power, asking for the unthinkable, but the errands he sent me on tended to be rather simple.

I delivered messages, either here in the Chasm or on Earth. As a demon, I could go back to the living world at will. That was useful since damned couldn't, not without possessing a human, which wasn't the easiest of tasks.

I'd already pushed Gorrin far enough, so I kept quiet and waited for his orders. Even I could keep my mouth shut when I needed to.

Sometimes.

"Jay."

I frowned. "Is that name supposed to mean something to me?"

"She wishes to sell her soul. You will make the deal."

Gorrin had *never* asked me for this, probably because he knew I never would.

The very idea of trapping someone else as my choices had trapped me made me sicker than the threats of that man in the bar.

"I can't," I whispered.

"This isn't a request—it is an order."

I forced myself to look him in his honey-colored eyes, something I rarely did. It felt too close, too personal, like showing too much. Now was the time for that risk, though. "I *can't,*" I repeated, trying to make him understand. "I don't mean I don't want to—I mean that I can't."

"This is the way our world works. You will gain power or you will be the power someone else gains. Those are the only options. The fact that you ended up a demon has afforded you some amount of protection, but that will not hold. I have given you time, been patient, but I am through waiting. You will do as I command you."

I clutched the skull so tightly that the joints in my fingers ached. I went back to waking up here five years ago, after I'd lost my life, after I'd sold my soul to save someone who had never deserved it. I'd felt this aching emptiness as I'd realized I'd let what I wanted in the moment steal everything for all eternity.

Gorrin had been the one to offer me that deal, to trade my soul for his help.

And I *hated* him for it.

I hated him and the other Demon Lords and the entire Chasm.

No, more than that. I hated the world, the way it was set up, the way it seemed created to keep us all on our knees.

I'd grown up knowing just how violent the world was, learning far too early just what it took to survive and willing to do whatever that was. That same old ugliness stuck around even after death, as proven by Gorrin's demand.

I shook my head. "Please, don't ask me to do this."

I'd never asked him for anything before, not since I'd lost everything. I'd learned then how not worth it deals with a devil were.

Gorrin didn't soften at all. No, not him. He never gave an inch, never showed the smallest amount of weakness or doubt. He was brimstone—steady, unfailing, unmoving. "You may not believe me now, you may not see it now, but I am doing this for your own good. If you do not fall into line, you will not survive."

"I learned five years ago that survival isn't all it's chalked up to be."

He pressed his lips together, the only change in his expression he ever gave. "You are young and foolish still. You *will* do as I say. You *will* go to meet with this girl tomorrow, find out her terms and trade for her soul." Each of his last statements crashed into me with the force of a wave.

It was a command. No way to resist or ignore him. He gave me no wiggle room to interpret his meaning as I pleased. Instead, a pain in my head intensified until I dropped my coffee to slide my fingers into my hair and press my palms against my temples.

It didn't ease that pain, didn't make it so I could draw in breath. He'd never had to use this to force me to do anything before, which I guess showed just how serious he was about this now.

I stood, stumbling, unable to help it. I had to do this. Resisting wasn't possible.

The moment I decided that, the pain lessened. It seemed thinking about doing it, moving toward the command would appease the order enough.

I blinked, looking around once my head cleared enough to do so. Gorrin had left, but his orders remained in my head.

After everything I'd already given up, everything I'd sacrificed, everything I'd lost, it seemed the Chasm wasn't satisfied yet. It wanted more than my soul, more than my life. It wanted the last part of myself I could still stand, that bit that said I could still be a good person.

And I didn't see a way to get out of it.

It didn't matter what people kept telling me—the Chasm really was hell.

* * * *

I woke up and grasped at my stomach, pain radiating through me, my chest hurting from the way my heart raced.

That same damned dream.

Once I looked around to find myself in my room, when I realized it was just a nightmare, I collapsed back on my bed and tried to slow my breathing.

The nightmares didn't come often anymore. My first few months in the Chasm had had me waking in tears almost nightly, my throat sore from my own screams. At first, I'd tried to ignore the dreams, to pretend they hadn't happened and just close my eyes again after waking up.

I'd learned leaning into the memory was the only way to clear it.

So instead of trying to make myself forget and fall back asleep, I grabbed my stuffed whale, Bubbles, and pulled him against my chest as I let those old feelings wash over me.

I remembered the pain in my stomach from the bullet I'd taken, the blood that had covered my hands as I'd tried to hold the wound closed. I sure hadn't expected people to break into my apartment and start firing first thing in the morning.

Then, as I'd teetered on the brink of death, four people had appeared before me.

No, not people—devils.

The four Demon Lords who ran the Chasm had each offered me my life in exchange for my soul, drawn to me personally by a pull none of us understood.

And me, the lovesick idiot, had rejected that. Instead, I'd offered up my eternal soul and freewill in exchange for saving my boyfriend, the man the attackers had actually been after. I gave up my own future to save someone I loved, thinking it a worthwhile trade.

Until I'd woken in the Chasm to discover that the man who I'd sacrificed that all for hadn't given a damn about me. He'd made his own deal for power and revenge—not for me.

I held Bubbles closer to me, missing the way he used to smell of lavender when I'd first gotten him fifteen years ago. I remembered holding him back then and burying my nose in his side, breathing in that calming scent when I couldn't sleep.

I'd kept him with me through all the mess that my life became, moving him from place to place with me no matter how crazy my life got.

A laugh escaped me as I recalled my first week in the Chasm, when I'd gone to Earth to get him. Nothing else had drawn me from the safety of my room, but I'd ventured out to get Bubbles because I couldn't picture a life in the Chasm without him.

When everything else changed, when I lost everything else, the fact that I still had the same stuffed animal I'd had when alive had helped me adjust.

At least, as well as anyone adjusted to dying.

"What am I going to do?" I asked Bubbles on a sigh. "I can't do what he wants but I can't ignore him, either."

As usual, Bubbles gave no useful advice. I didn't know what advice I wanted, anyway. It was like standing on a one-way-street with no exits and wanting to know what to do.

There weren't any options, so I had to go forward, no matter how much it hurt.

I buried my face in Bubbles and tried to imagine the old lavender scent, to pretend time hadn't passed, that I was back in my old life.

Instead of that familiar scent or feeling of home, I only smelled ash and smoke, as if the Chasm wanted to make damned sure I knew exactly where I was.

It wouldn't even let me pretend I was free for a moment.

Chapter Two

Traveling to Earth sucked a big one.

It always did, no matter how many times I did it, no matter how used to it I got. The sickness in my stomach made me swallow slowly to keep down food, my body not enjoying the switch from the Chasm to Earth.

It happened through the soil, something that had thrown me at first. To move between the Chasm and Earth, I had to touch actual dirt then choose where I wanted to go. Yazmor had once tried to explain it to me, but I'd stopped paying attention part-way through. Listening to Yazmor was like a bad acid trip, and it never wrapped up nicely. I usually ended up more confused by the end of it than I'd started. All that mattered was that it required a connection to Earth and a place to appear on the other side. A general idea of where I wanted to go was enough, but when I actually started to move from one place to the other, I could narrow down an exact place based on where soil was on the other side.

The world came into view around me, moving from the dark to a brightness that made me squint. I found myself in a large room with huge windows, the sun shining and warm and impossibly painful to my unaccustomed eyes. My fingers pressed into the potting soil of a shrub, making me want to laugh for a moment.

I never figured I'd travel via houseplant.

And there, on a large canopy bed, sat a teenage girl. She had blond hair pulled back in a French braid and wore a pair of high-waisted leggings with a crop top. None of that was what I noticed the most though — instead it was the absolute hopeless sorrow on her young face. Well, that and a pull to her that told me she was ready to deal.

It was a strange sensation, this draw that happened when a person was willing to trade their soul. I'd felt it before, but this was the first time it was my job to do anything about it.

"Jay?" I asked softly.

The girl jerked her gaze up, her blue eyes red and swollen. "Who are you?" Even as she asked, fear across her features, she didn't yank back.

Her toughness made me smile. Then again, surviving as a young girl in this mess of a world toughened a person.

"My name is Loch, and I'm not here to hurt you." Even as I said that, I struggled to say it with any real conviction. Perhaps, 'I don't want to hurt you,' was a more honest statement. Instead, I added on to it, "You need help."

"You heard me," she whispered, then swallowed hard as if my presence suddenly made sense.

"You know why I'm here?"

She nodded. "My dad told me a story a long time ago about how, when he really needed it, he made a deal for help. I didn't know if I believed him, but I didn't know what else to do. If you're here to help me, then he must have been telling the truth."

No. Selling someone's soul didn't help anyone except the person who bought it. The person selling never ended up better off—I'd seen that time and time again.

However, I couldn't say that. Gorrin's order compelled me to work toward making the deal.

Instead, I looked at her. "What do you want?"

"Please, save my brother."

Another girl willing to sacrifice her future for a man. As much as I hated it, I understood it. At least this time it wasn't a lover though, right?

I waved her on, wanting to hear more. I needed to understand the situation before I could make any deal to solve her issue.

Jay rose from her bed and paced the length of the room as she told me the story. "Someone abducted my brother, Brendon. He's only five, and he has to be terrified."

"What do they want?"

"My father is a powerful man, and he has a lot of enemies. They're asking for a ransom."

"Who's your father?"

"Charles Kannor."

Well fuck.

The name felt like a kick to my solar plexus. That made this girl Jaymie Kannor, the daughter of the man who led the largest crime family in this damn town, the same crime family I'd dealt with far too many times in my human life.

Why was it that fate liked to screw with people? After avoiding the remnants of my human life, here I was, forced to confront them.

Was this why Gorrin had insisted that I do *this* deal? Probably. The manipulative bastard was the sort of man to do that exact thing, who would rip off scabs and just make a person bleed for his own entertainment and gain.

I'd never personally met the family, of course. When alive, I'd been as far down on the power structure as a person could get. I'd run errands and handled drops and tried to stay off the radar of anyone powerful or important. People like me ended up crushed if we ventured too close to the giants.

And here I was, supposed to make a deal for the soul of the only daughter in order to save the male heir. My actions here could shape the entire family and, in turn, the entire criminal underworld.

Which was exactly what I'd never wanted.

And yet, Gorrin's words left no room to just back out.

"Are you sure you want this?" I couldn't come right out and tell her no, but if I talked her out of it, I couldn't help it if she reconsidered.

At least, I told myself that. I'd take whatever little loophole might get me out of this, even though Gorrin would end up pissed if I failed him.

I could deal with that problem later, though.

"I have to," she said, an echo of the words I'd said five years ago when I'd made the same deal. "It's my brother. Even if my father agrees to pay, there's no guarantee that will work or that we'll get Brendon back."

"Charles didn't get where he is by being stupid. I'm sure he's working on another idea. You need to think about this—"

"I can't do anything else!" Jay stopped her pacing to stare at me and it was like looking into a mirror at my younger self. The helplessness, the anger, the frustration—I understood it all. "I wish I was my dad, who has the power to send men out there to search, or my uncle who could pick up a gun and fight himself, or anyone else but I'm not. I can't do anything to help my brother or my dad except *this*. This is all I have to give. Our mom is gone and it's just been us for a long time and I can't lose anyone else." Tears ran down her cheeks, sure signs of how far she felt pushed.

And I got it—I did. I remembered when I'd met the Demon Lords the first time, when I'd bled out on a floor after getting shot, knowing I'd die, knowing I couldn't do anything to help the person I loved. I'd been willing to sacrifice *anything* to save them.

Gorrin had known it, had capitalized on it, and now he wanted me to do the same to someone else.

Fuck that.

A slight pain in my head warned me that I walked a dangerous line, but I'd lived in the gray area my entire damned life. I'd survived by juggling what I wanted to do and what I had to do and somehow finding my way between the two.

I couldn't tell Jay no, but I *could* delay, right? Just putting it off wouldn't magically fix anything, but who knew what could happen over a couple of days?

"When is the pay off?"

"Two weeks. It's set for Friday the fifteenth."

Two weeks wasn't much, and I still had no clear plan, but it gave me time. "What if we wait? See what happens?"

She nibbled at her bottom lip, the torn-up skin suggesting she'd done it a lot recently. "I can't risk him like that. What if he gets hurt before then?"

"He won't be. They need him as leverage, which means they'll keep him safe until it's time for the handover." That pain pinched behind my eyes, and I could almost *feel* it as Gorrin's glare.

It wasn't, of course. He couldn't read my mind—at least, I didn't think he could. Instead, it was the order he'd placed on me warning me not to fuck it up.

"What's going to change in two weeks?"

"I don't know," I admitted. Maybe I should have lied and told her I could fix it, but something about giving her false hope felt wrong. Before she could second guess too much, however, I went on. "But if you make the deal now, that's it. It's done forever. I don't know what will change in two weeks, but you can't take it back later so take a few days to think and see what happens."

Jay took a deep breath then nodded. "Okay, I'll wait."

This wasn't much, and I still had no idea what I could do, but at least I had time to think. A delay was better than nothing. This was too important to screw up.

Maybe by saving her soul, I could save some small part of my own.

* * * *

I sat on the patio of the small coffee shop and remembered how much the food and drink in the Chasm sucked. It wasn't anything like what I could get up here.

It meant sipping at the sweet mocha with the sun beating down on me was a heaven I didn't think a damned person like me could ever really have.

After talking to Jay, I'd left the large mansion and headed for the coffee shop I'd spent time at back when still alive. It hadn't changed much, or perhaps I was so nostalgic that I could ignore any changes. I hadn't expected to ever return to this area of town, yet here I was.

Someone took my cup from my hand, and I frowned as I tipped my head backward to find a familiar man standing just behind me.

He lifted the cup to his lips and took a drink, then grinned, a bit of whipped cream stuck to his lips. "I knew you were a sweet drinks sort of girl."

"You shouldn't steal people's coffee. That's grounds to get shanked."

Yazmor sat across from me, seeming to have no desire to give me back my drink. Instead, his dazzling smile made him look every bit as young as he acted. "Who doesn't enjoy a good shanking?"

"What are you doing up here?"

"There was a concert."

"It's two in the afternoon. What sort of concert is over by two?"

"That band with the TV show. You know, the one with the bunny that sings with that shark."

I frowned, wondering what sort of freaky shit he was into until the pieces fell together. "Are you talking about *Meadow Fields*, the children's show?"

"Are you a fan too? I love the song they sing about the spider being water boarded in the spout."

I rubbed my temple with the fingers of one hand. "That's a song about perseverance, not torture."

He didn't appear put out at all about my statement or the way I looked at him. Then again, if people mocking him bothered him, he'd never have a free moment. Between his violet hair and matching eyes, his

I don't give a fuck attitude and his constantly odd behavior, Yazmor couldn't fit into normal society if he tried.

Neither on Earth nor in the Chasm.

I was about to bitch about my drink again when a waitress approached and set a cup in front of me. A pile of whipped cream sat on top of the drink and beside it, she put a plate with a cookie.

Sorry for stealing, was scrawled in frosting on the top of the cookie.

After the waitress walked away, I gave Yazmor my best glare, even if he made it hard to hate him. "You could have just ordered your own stuff instead of stealing mine and ordering an apology cookie."

"Would you rather have an apology cake? I also could write it on the side of a car for you." He paused and tapped his finger against his chin. "Oh, a boat! Everyone loves boats…"

A few years ago I would have laughed him off, but now?

I knew him well enough to know he was serious. If I didn't rein him back in, I would receive a boat with poorly written spray-painted letters in the form of an apology on the side.

"It's fine," I told him because it was far easier to just deal his nonsense than to tell him it was nonsense, especially because it never mattered. And what would I even do with a boat? That was a headache I sure as fuck didn't need.

Yazmor did as he pleased all the time, full stop. Where the other Demon Lords in the Chasm worried about their images, about retaining power by playing games, Yazmor never seemed to give a fuck. He dressed like a broke-ass college student, talked like an escaped mental patient and routinely got thrown out of every aquarium and zoo for petting the animals.

Usually animals who did not care for being petted.

In short?

The man was a walking, talking headache.

I picked up the drink he'd ordered me and sipped it, surprised to find it was even better than the one he'd stolen.

"White chocolate mocha," he said. "Even sweeter than a regular. Did you know that since they invented this, the overall glucose levels in America have increased by twenty points?"

"You're lying," I guessed.

"Possibly. It's hard to tell anymore." He reached out and stole a piece of my apology cookie before sitting back. "So what are you doing here? You don't normally spend time on Earth and never around here."

"Gorrin gave me a task."

"You should have made the deal with me. Can you imagine the fun we would have had? I'd get you a costume so you could dress up as my sidekick. We could have made a theme song." He stared off wistfully.

"You know, you have the same expression that eight-year-old girls have when they talk about their wedding day."

He let out a long sigh then cast me a smirk. "Just like them, my heart is broken. You picked another."

Even as he spoke, I shook my head. Yazmor was dramatic but rarely serious. He enjoyed life to the fullest, never seeming to think more than about five minutes into the future—if we were lucky.

Which was probably the reason we got along, at least as well as anyone got along in the Chasm.

There were times when I wished I'd made the deal with someone else, when I regretted picking Gorrin. I regretted selling my soul all the time, but to who was more of an every-once-in-a-while sulking I indulged in.

I struggled to imagine obeying Yazmor, though. We were friends — in a strange way — but trying to keep up with his never-ending nonsense made me suspect I'd have an aneurysm if I had to follow his orders.

Which brought me right back to the topic at hand, to the reason I sat at the cafe wasting time. "When was the first time you made a deal for a soul?" I stared at my drink instead of into his face.

I preferred seeing Yazmor as a clusterfuck joke — I didn't like getting a glimpse into the part of him that was just as powerful as Gorrin, Tyrus or Hale. Still, I had to ask.

I needed to hear it. If I asked the others, they'd only scold me. They'd tell me it was no big deal, to just do what needed to be done, that the person would sell their soul if they wanted, so why not sell it to me?

Yazmor was the only one who didn't seem to have the same darkness inside him, the only one who might understand.

"It was a *very* long time ago."

"Who's older — you or Gorrin?"

"I am," Yazmor said. "*But* he's been a Demon Lord longer, so he wins there." After a moment, Yazmor asked, his voice uncharacteristically soft, "Do you really want to know about this?"

"Want? No. But I need to. Everyone keeps telling me how I need to start collecting souls to protect myself, but they don't get it."

"And you thought if I told you my story, that would make it easier on you?"

When he said that, I realized he had a point. Hearing how he'd done it wouldn't really make a difference, would it? It wasn't like hearing how someone else went sky diving would make it less scary to take that first step.

But I didn't know what else to do.

Instead of calling me on my lack of an answer, he started to speak. "It was a man. He was nearly dead, his leg infected, no food or water, no chance of pulling himself anywhere. It was just a matter of a few hours before he either died from the injuries or something else happened on by to finish the job."

And the story reminded me of what I'd already known. People sold their souls because they had no other choice, and others preyed on that. We took advantage of it, using their souls and their inability to turn us down as a way to get what we wanted.

It was a despicable system.

"So you saved him? Why him?"

"I never liked the whole selling-of-souls thing before that. It struck me as distasteful."

"Didn't you sell your soul, though?"

"Nope."

That made me frown. The only people who ended up in the Chasm had sold their souls, and the only people strong enough to take out a Demon Lord—thus taking their position—would be demons who had gathered enough power to stand against the old one.

Humans could trade their souls to other humans, but it was rare. To make a deal, a person had to understand the gravity of what they did, they had to be informed enough to truly desire that trade. Without that, they couldn't hand over control to another. Few humans understood the worth of a soul, so few were capable of securing such a deal.

"If you never sold your soul, how did you end up in the Chasm?"

He shrugged, swirling the mocha in his cup as he stared at it rather than at me. "Maybe I'm just not the sort of soul who should end up on the Plains. I can't imagine I'd fit in there well." He let out a soft chuckle, and I could almost see the way he pictured himself on the Plains, the place where unencumbered souls went after death. If the Chasm was hell, the Plains were heaven.

"But that doesn't make sense," I pressed. "You can't just say you're special and have that be the end of it."

"Of course I can. Why did you become a demon and not a damned? Why is one person born into a rich and loving family and another thrown away at birth? If there is a reason for the mess that occurs in this world — or any other — then it is far too complex for even me to figure out."

"So why did you take that man's soul? What made him different?"

"He said please. He looked at me, eyes bloodred, breathing stuttering, and he said please. He said he'd give me anything for a little more time. I figured, why not? Why not help him? If he wanted to trade, who was I to deny him that? I dragged him to a healer and used some of my power to keep him alive."

"So it was just a whim?"

Yazmor widened his grin, showing his teeth that somehow managed to look dangerous despite being flat and blunt. A part of me wondered if I could catch a glimpse of his demon form like that, if something from his other side bled through for me to see. "You want to know the secret? Don't let others dictate your life."

"Easy for you to say — no one owns your soul. You're at the top of the tower here, so you get to say no."

"Oh, I never say no. No is like yes—far too clear cut. Never back yourself into a corner by saying anything so specific and hard-lined. Always give yourself an out by being vague, by twisting facts to whatever you want them to be."

His words made me pause. Gorrin's exact order was to make the deal, but he didn't say when. He didn't give me a timeline. That gave me some room, didn't it?

What did that room offer, though? Giving Jay time didn't change the position she was in. It didn't fix the problem. If nothing happened, if nothing changed, she'd make that deal.

Unless she doesn't need to anymore…

I shot up, out of my seat. The chair knocked backward, clattering against the tile of the coffee shop patio.

Yazmor smirked, staring at me with his unnerving violet eyes as if he knew I'd worked something out.

Which I had.

If I wanted to save Jay, if I wanted to make it so she didn't feel the need to sell her soul, I had to fix her problem.

That meant that to get out of this, I had to rescue her brother myself.

So after five years, after this world had gotten me killed, I'd have to walk right back into it.

I really am an idiot…

Chapter Three

Gorrin looked mad, but to be fair, Gorrin *always* looked mad. In fact, if I ever walked in and saw him smiling, I'd probably turn right back around and walk out, figuring him an imposter.

Given this was his normal attitude, I didn't hesitate as I walked up to him.

"You have yet to complete the task I ordered you to do." Gorrin crossed his arms. "I thought I made myself perfectly clear."

"She wasn't ready to make the deal," I said, my words not a lie. "I can't force her to agree, right?"

"She seemed ready when I sent you."

"She's young, and since you're old as fuck, let me remind you, selling one's soul is scary. Sometimes it takes a few days to take the plunge."

"So she's willing to risk her brother's life?"

I shrugged, drawing on all my past experience with both outright lying and bending the truth. Some people were bad liars, but not me. Surviving in the world I'd grown up in had required good skills with telling a tale.

"The ransom is supposed to get paid two weeks from now. I think she's hoping for a miracle before then."

Gorrin's gaze dug into mine, giving nothing away. It felt as if he peeled my skin from my body, as if he peered beneath everything I hid to find the truth.

And me? I didn't give him a fucking inch. I stared back, not flinching, not hesitating, not doing a thing but standing tall. If he didn't believe me, he'd send someone else, someone who might convince Jay to take the plunge now.

Eventually, he let out a soft, unhappy sound and broke the staring contest. It felt like a petty win, but in the Chasm, petty wins were all I could hope for.

"You need to think about this," Gorrin warned me. "You should remember your place here *carefully*. After five years, you should have a good grasp of how this world works, of where people sit in the power structure. Where am I?"

"At the top," I said without the least bit of sass. It was the truth. He might share the top spot with three others, but that didn't change that he was there, looking down on the rest of us.

"That's right, and I have been at the top for a very long time. I did not achieve nor keep my position by being foolish enough to allow others to deceive me." He approached me, but I didn't back away or let any fear show on my face.

It wasn't that I didn't fear him—only a fucking idiot would try to say he wasn't terrifying—but fear wouldn't do a damned thing for me. If he wanted to kill me, he could whenever he wanted.

So instead, I held my ground, tilting my head to keep looking into his expressionless face, even when he stopped a breath away from me.

"You always struggle against the order. You did it when you were alive, failing to bow to the system in place. You have done so since you came here. Why?"

I swallowed in an audible gulp before closing my hands into fists. "I have no idea what you're talking about."

He snorted softly, the sound telling me he didn't believe me in the least. "You can resist all you want, struggle as you wish, it will not change a thing." He wrapped his hand around the front of my throat, the threat clear. "You are a little fish in a river. You can swim all you want against the current, try to go a different way, to make your own path, but it will only wear you out. Eventually, it will overwhelm you, and you will follow the current as all things do." His golden eyes burned into me as if he wanted me to truly understand something.

But I couldn't.

"You're a Demon Lord. You took out whoever ruled before you. Doesn't that mean you didn't just swim with the current?"

He tilted his head as if my words surprised him. Still, he didn't loosen his grip at all. "Are you telling me that you plan to do the same? That you will kill me to claim my position?"

"Would you kill me if I said yes?"

"Why would I do that? It would be like going out of my way to step on an ant because they wish to take over the world. The threat does not exist, so why concern myself with a response?"

His words chilled me, especially because he was right. He was so far above me in terms of power that even if I stood there and told him exactly how I planned to murder him, he didn't need to lift a finger to prevent it.

"I'm not as weak as you think."

Gorrin tilted his head, then pulled away. Had he finished this little talk? Was he done threatening me? It seemed not when he returned just as quickly.

He grasped my wrist and pulled my hand out, his strength something I couldn't hope to fight against. "It is not a matter of weakness. If you were weak, you would never have become a demon in the first place. Instead, it is a matter of you not being willing to do what needs to be done."

He pressed something into my hand, and it took a moment for me to realize the item was a dagger with an ornate golden handle and engraved blade.

"What's this?" I asked, unable to understand why he would give me such an item.

"This is a very old dagger, one capable of delivering wounds that do not heal and leach the lifeforce from anything—dead or alive, damned or demon or angel. This is the dagger that gave me my position as a Demon Lord."

"So?"

"So, use it." He released my wrist and folded his hands behind his back, his head held high, his gaze harsh but steady. "If you are so certain you wish to change things, then use the dagger."

I moved my gaze between the dagger and Gorrin, going back and forth as his words settled, as I made sense of them. When I realized what he meant, I opened my fist, the warm metal falling from my grasp. It clattered to the floor, the sound loud in the otherwise silent room.

Gorrin didn't move, didn't break eye contact. "You tell me that you will not bend, but you are unwilling to take the steps to make that happen. I did not just wish for change—I used this dagger to ensure it. Now, it is your reminder of the same."

"I don't want it."

"That matters as much as you wanting to follow my orders. I have given you that dagger, and it now belongs to you." He gestured at my wrist, which made me flip that hand over to find a new tattoo there—a line drawing of that very dagger.

And the actual dagger, which had fallen, now was nowhere to be seen. I brought my other hand to that wrist and scrubbed at the mark. "What the hell did you do?"

"The dagger binds itself to its owner. Should you decide you are willing to actually use it, it will appear."

"And why would you give me something like that?"

"Because it is easy to spout such large ideals. It is so simple to claim some moral high ground when a person has no ability to carry out the actions needed to obtain it. So I have given you those means." He turned away from me as though he didn't care about me, as if he hadn't just handed me a weapon that could harm him. "I can only hope you learn not to struggle against the inevitable."

I stared at his wide back, my hands still held in fists, my teeth aching from how tightly I ground my molars. My throat was warm, as if his hand were still there, a warning against defying him.

"My mom called me Salmon when I was a kid," I said.

Gorrin stopped but didn't turn back around, the action enough to tell me he heard me even if he didn't acknowledge my words.

So I went on. "My mom told me I was always fighting against the way things were, that I was always making things harder on myself even if I didn't have a shot in hell at winning or changing anything. She started to call me Salmon, always swimming upstream, against the impossible."

Gorrin didn't twist back toward me, but he did turn his head so I could see his face in profile. "If you are a salmon, then you should think of me as the bear waiting for lunch."

And probably no words ever said were any truer than that.

* * * *

Charles wasn't at all what I expected.

I'd thought the head of the Kannor family would be stuffy and full of himself.

Well, there *was* some of that, no doubt. Charles was in his late forties, dressed in a suit that cost more than my first car. He sat at a large oak desk in his office in a building downtown, the huge windows overlooking the cityscape.

It was one hell of an 'I'm in charge' power move to be here.

Then again, Charles Kannor was high enough up the ranks in the criminal world that even the cops didn't dare touch him. Why not put himself up in an office like this?

"I'm afraid I don't know what this meeting was for," Charles said, folding his hands on the top of the desk to stare at me.

If he thought he could intimidate me like that, he'd end up horribly disappointed. After dealing with the four Demon Lords over the past five years — along with an entire Chasm full of the worst of the worst — some human was hardly worth an eyeroll from me.

"I'm here to talk about the abduction of your son."

His expression hardened, giving me a glimpse of the man others feared. "And how exactly did you hear that?"

"I'm well connected," I hedged. "Information like that doesn't stay quiet for long."

He pressed his lips together, staring hard at me as if he could figure out why I was here and what I wanted just by looking at me.

Good luck, buddy. If Gorrin can't dig into my brain, you sure as fuck can't.

After a moment, he leaned back in his seat and tapped his fingers on the armrest of his chair. "That's true. Enemies of mine managed to get my son, Brendon. I've kept the information quiet for obvious reasons. I wouldn't want others to try and use this as reason to cause more chaos in my life or to doubt my place or power. You aren't here just to tell me about the rumors, however. I suggest you get to your point—my patience is thin."

I leaned in, meeting his gaze head-on. "I want to help."

"Why? And who are you that you think you could do anything more than I can?"

"Call me a friend of a friend."

"People in my line of work do not have *friends,* and those who wish to stay alive never trust anyone who claims to be one."

"Are you certain? I would call anyone willing to make a deal with you a friend of sorts."

That got his attention. He sat up straighter, the first true expression on his features. Surprise? Fear? Hope? They all mixed together so quickly that I couldn't tell where one ended and the next started.

"You mean, you know *him?*"

Nope, not a fucking clue. Jay's words had told me what I needed to know—Charles here had sold his soul already. Given his position, I had no doubt he'd dealt with either one of the Demon Lords or someone close to them. I had no idea what he'd asked for, what they'd given him or who had made the deal, but none of that mattered.

I only needed him to believe I had a connection to said person.

So I nodded. "That's right."

"He cares about this? I thought he wouldn't show up again until..." Charles trailed off, his voice losing the strength it had had before. Then again, after selling one's soul, fear of death was a pretty fucking natural reaction.

"He prefers to keep important connections strong."

"So he can just save Brendon?"

"No. You've already given up all your leverage, so he can't act directly. Rules, you know?"

Which was an absolute lie. If one of the Demon Lords wanted to intervene in anything on Earth, they could. No such rules existed to restrain them from playing around to their hearts' content. The only real line was that they couldn't directly force a human to enter into a deal. They couldn't hold a blade to a human's throat and demand their soul, but anything short of that?

No one gave a damn. Who was there to give a damn? Whoever ran the Plains? The angels I'd heard about but never seen? Those assholes didn't care.

The Demon Lords just lacked a reason to interfere most of the time, which explained the position Charles found himself in. Gorrin could easily snap his fingers and fix this problem himself, could save Brendon without a second thought, but he had no good reason to. Instead, he'd use this mess for his benefit to get Jay in his pocket.

"So why are you here?"

"Because I work with him, and he's asked me to look into it and see how I can help. He can't do anything directly, but he can call in favors from those who owe him."

Charles took a moment to look at me more carefully, though I couldn't tell how he felt. No doubt he saw me and didn't think much of me.

That had been my place in life.

I had always been short and rather thin. I had that hated pear shape, and as a teenager had stuffed my bra for years wishing I had some actual cleavage. Even when I'd grown up, when I couldn't pass for a teenager anymore, I wasn't exactly a looker. My dyed green hair and the tattoos on my face made me memorable, I supposed, but nothing about me screamed capable or dangerous.

"You seem familiar," he said.

"I get that a lot." By which I meant that dying and becoming a demon had the small benefit of having most people not recognize me. I'd asked Yazmor once why that worked, and he'd explained that humans saw both physical and spiritual, though they didn't realize it.

I looked as I had when I'd been human, but I wasn't the same. It meant humans struggled to see me and connect that to the woman I'd been before. Close friends and family would recognize me, but outside of that, I'd just seem familiar.

"You really think you can do anything?" Charles asked.

I nodded. "I'm going to do whatever I can to bring Brendon back." *For Jay.*

"I have two weeks before we're supposed to pay the ransom. If you can't find him by then, I'll have no choice but to give them what they want."

"You know it could be a trap, right? Or that they might not give Brendon to you even if you pay."

"Of course I know that. Things like this often don't go smoothly, especially if everything is left in the hands of the enemy."

"But you're still willing to do the trade in person?"

"He could die if I don't."

"Like that would stop most people."

Charles furrowed his eyebrows, and I never expected to get a look like that from a man like Charles. I didn't care for him looking at me as if I were the monster without a soul.

Well, I mean, I didn't have a soul, but…

Focus, Loch!

"Most men in your position would look out for themselves," I tacked on.

"Brendon is my son. I'd do anything to keep him safe."

"But if you show up, they might kill you."

"I know that. I still hope it won't come to that, but I'm prepared for the sacrifice if it does."

Which made *no* sense to me. It felt like a bird telling me how afraid of heights it was. People didn't change, they didn't act out of character, so I didn't appreciate Charles here going all selfless and screwing with my preconceived notions.

"And if you're gone, who's going to keep your family safe?"

"I have plans in place for that. If it comes to that, I've made sure that my children will be safe. I lost my wife already, so I do not risk my children, not when I can avoid it." Even as he spoke, I got the sense he didn't quite believe it.

Then again, from his point of view, he didn't have a lot of options but to do the best he could and play it off as confidence.

"However, if you could resolve this for me," he said slowly, "I'd make sure it was worth your while."

Which was a pointless offer to me. I didn't want or need his gratitude. He was a crime lord on Earth, and I was a dead demon who lived in the Chasm. What exactly could he offer me? He didn't even own his own soul.

It meant that in a few decades, if he were lucky, he'd end up in the Chasm. I almost laughed, thinking about when he showed up to realize I'd outsmarted him, that I hadn't worked on anyone else's behalf.

"Sure," I said. Let him think he could be grateful all he wanted. "What can you tell me about what happened?"

"I know the Sand Snakes took him, because they gave me the ransom information."

"How did they get him? I'd think a kid of yours would be under pretty tight guard."

"He was. I thought I could trust all the guards I put on my family, but it seems I missed one rat. One of my men betrayed me and took Brendon to one of the Sand Snakes' men. The only solace in the whole thing is that they weren't about to trust a snitch, so they slit his throat. I only regret that I couldn't *personally* pay him back."

I nodded, knowing exactly what he meant. Trusting people seemed easy enough, but I'd seen over and over in my life how rarely people stayed loyal. Betrayal was a sure thing if the prize got high enough. It was a hard lesson, but one everyone eventually had to learn.

"What can you tell me about the Sand Snakes?" I'd heard about them before, but I'd been out of the loop for a long time. If they were facing off against the Kannor family, they'd grown a lot from the ragtag collection of bikers they'd been when I'd died.

"Let me call my second. He'll be at your disposal until this is resolved — one way or another." He took out his phone and typed into it, then set it on his desk. "We've found little to go on. I don't know where they're keeping Brendon and because they're a nomad group, nailing them down is challenging, since they have small places all over and their numbers are harder to pin down. My second has been looking into it, but maybe if you two work together, you'll come up with something better."

The door opened, and I twisted, ready to find some old timer there, the sort of OG who a man like Charles would trust all his security to.

Which was why it startled me as much as it did when I knew the man who walked in. I rose and stared, unable to think of a damned thing to say when faced with the very man I'd loved, the one I'd sold my soul to save, the one who had betrayed me...

Gunnar Thompson. My ex-boyfriend.

Chapter Four

I had no damn idea what else Charles said. Seeing Gunnar was enough to completely blank my mind and make it impossible to keep up.

I was pretty sure I nodded and responded but fuck only knew what actually came out of my mouth.

Before I knew it, I was in the elevator with only Gunnar, the first time I'd seen him in person since that morning when everything had changed.

The memory threatened to swamp me, to pull me back, to remind me of the pain in my stomach from the gunshot, the fear as my blood had poured out of me, the anger when Gorrin had later showed me Gunnar selling his soul in exchange for power and telling the other person that I had only been 'convenient' for him.

"What the fuck are you doing here, Loch?" Gunnar asked the moment the doors closed us in.

I turned around, keeping my face blank—at least, I hoped it was. I could lie as well as I breathed, but somehow facing Gunnar made me feel as if I'd plunged deep under water.

Breathing and lying were suddenly much harder.

"Have we met?"

"Don't give me that bullshit. I *saw* you die."

"You must have me confused with someone else. Clearly, I'm not dead." I held my arms out to sell the story.

Gunnar came close, forcing me back until I pressed against the wall. He reached out and hit the Stop button, the elevator shuddering to a hard stop. "Don't fucking joke around with me, Loch. You should know better. How. Are. You. Here?"

I stared up and into his dark eyes, hating how familiar they were. How many times had I lost myself in those eyes? Whispered, '*I love you,*' as I stared into those eyes? Being dead for five years should have been more than enough time to rid myself of these lingering feelings, but it didn't work like that.

This asshole had *betrayed* me. He hadn't given a damn about me, and yet I'd given up everything for him.

How dare the fucker look at me with eyes that made me *miss* him.

The desire to pluck them from his skull hit me so strongly that the stirrings of my demon form crept through me, made me wish I were in the Chasm where it could take over and tear him apart piece by piece.

I shook my head, trying to shove that desire away. I had a job to do, and I couldn't allow Gunnar to fuck up my life *again*. That meant I had to focus on what mattered, which was Brendon.

"You heard Charles—I'm just someone here to help."

Gunnar narrowed his eyes, but a voice through the intercom halted us both. "Is everything okay?"

Gunnar hit the Speaker button but didn't move away from me. "It's fine."

"You hit the Stop button."

"Yeah, I did, so shut up and leave me be."

No one responded at first, then a quiet, terrified voice answered. "Understood, Mr. Thompson. I will notify the fire department that there is no emergency."

The idea of Gunnar having that sort of power was fucking hilarious. Gunnar, who was lucky to remember to wash his underwear, had people scurrying around him like he was a bigshot?

What a pompous asshole.

"I know I saw you die," he said, his voice as sharp as ever. It wasn't a question, which said I couldn't convince him he'd gotten it all wrong. "So if you're here, that means you sold your soul, right?"

I set my hands on his chest and shoved him backward. He stumbled, probably because the action surprised him. I'd been tough before, but I'd never once stood up against him. "I'm here to find Brendon. Whatever you *think* you know doesn't matter."

"I don't need to think—I know."

His confidence pushed me too far. I jammed my finger toward him. "How fucking *dare* you take that tone with me."

He snorted and crossed his arms over his chest. "There's that good old temper. Guess even dying didn't change that."

"Is this some big game to you? How long did you wait after I bled out before you replaced me?"

"We're both too smart to think mourning means shit. We've seen the worst fucking people cry all the tears over someone that they put in the ground. Life is way too cruel and way too short to spend time feeling sorry for ourselves. I didn't kill you—I got nothing to apologize for."

"I loved you!" I yelled the words so loudly that my throat stung. Thankfully, I was much too far gone to think about all the people outside the elevator on whatever floor it was stuck at who would hear that outburst.

Let them hear! These words had ricocheted inside my heart for five years, and I'd be damned if I softened them now that I was forced to confront the man responsible for it all.

"Thought you were smarter than that," Gunnar said as if I'd just told him I believed in Santa Claus. "Love is bullshit. It's just convenience and lust that we pretty up so we don't feel so bad about it. I didn't fill you with bullets, didn't hire the men who did, so save your little temper tantrum for the person behind it."

"You could have saved me," I told him, rewarded with him at least looking surprised. Then again, he probably figured no one knew about his deal—surely not me. "I saw you in that bar, drinking afterward. The person offered to bring me back, and you turned it down. You picked power over me."

"You would have done the same. Anyone would have. You were gone, and if I brought you back, so what? We end up in the same fucking mess down the line? What would the point be in that? I did what I had to, same as you. The fact that you're here says you traded your soul to survive, that you picked your life over mine, so who the fuck do you think you are lecturing me?"

I opened my mouth to tell him the truth, but nothing came out.

It gave me a moment to realize the colossal fucking mistake it would have been to admit. It was bad enough that the Demon Lords knew the truth, that I'd traded my life to save his, but I didn't need Gunnar to know it, too.

Let him think I'd traded my soul for a few more years, that I'd somehow gotten saved, that I was just as selfish as he was. Better than him knowing everything I'd given up for him, for the fantasy that wasn't real. I could just about see the way he'd stare at me as if I'd disappointed him, and I didn't need to see that shit.

So instead, I crossed my arms. "That's ancient history," I said. "I'm not here to rehash it."

"So why are you here?"

"I told you—to save Brendon. Charles has friends who want to keep him in power, so I'm here to make sure it happens."

Gunnar snorted. "And you think you can do shit about that?"

Boy, did that attitude take me back. Gunnar had never thought I was capable of anything. He'd seen me as a willing body to warm his bed and an errand runner when he needed one. He'd never respected me for shit.

Five years hadn't changed that a bit.

"Charles told you to help me, so unless you want to defy him, why don't you shut the fuck up and do as you're told like a good lap dog?"

Gunnar stared hard at me, a look that might have scared me before. It didn't anymore. Let him be pissed—that didn't matter to me at all.

"Fine," he snapped. "You want to play the hero? You want to throw away your second chance on this bullshit? Be my guest." He reached out and hit the Stop button again so the elevator started moving. "But make no mistake here—you're in over your head."

And wasn't that the story of my life—and my afterlife?

* * * *

"I guess being a Kannor bitch has its perks." I glanced around the nice apartment Gunnar had taken me to in the same building as Charles' office.

Talk about moving up in the world after the places we lived. This place was a far fucking cry from that little one-bedroom he'd crashed at with me.

Gunnar locked the door behind us, then leveled me a warning look. "Be careful, Loch. Keep pissing me off and our history won't mean shit."

"Shit is about what our history means already." I walked over to the large window to gaze down at the city, the reminder of how disconnected from it all I had become.

I'd hidden away in the Chasm, not wanting to see any of this, to live through the reminders of the world I'd left behind.

And here I was, with life slapping me in the face like it was a dick.

"We both know that isn't true. I wouldn't let anyone but you say that shit to me and keep their teeth."

Which was true, I guessed. Gunnar wasn't the type to take insults lying down, which was no doubt exactly the reason we'd gotten targeted in the first place. He'd said the wrong thing to the wrong person.

Yet I didn't need to go down that road anymore, so I brought the topic back to why I'd come. "What do you know about the night Brendon was taken?"

Gunnar walked over to a wet bar in the living room and grabbed two beers. He opened them against the edge of the bar, then handed one to me.

It took me back, the feeling of the bottle in my hand, the scent of the familiar booze. Gunnar might have moved up in the world, but he still drank the same cheap shit we had back in the day, when we could barely scrounge up the funds to buy a six pack.

No matter how dangerous it was, I let myself tip the bottle back and take two deep gulps.

Gunnar let out a soft laugh, then did the same. After he swallowed, he held the bottle by the neck between two fingers and stared over at me. "I wasn't working that night. The asshole who betrayed us was named Morrin Ollie. He'd worked for the Kannors for eight years—never would have pegged him as someone to get bought out."

"What did they pay him?"

"Cold hard cash. He had a deposit of a hundred grand in his account a few days before it all went down."

I wasn't the sort of person who was shocked by that. A hundred grand could do a lot for a person. I'd be more shocked that anyone would choose loyalty over that sort of money.

"I didn't think the Sand Snakes were that big of a threat."

"They weren't, not five years ago. They were a motorcycle gang that hassled small businesses and sometimes hit people up for protection money."

"So what changed?"

"About four and a half years ago, they got themselves a hell of a scientist. They started cooking up a drug that people just loved, and the money rolled in.

Enough money and people start wanting power to go along with it. They're still nomadic—they don't like to lay down much in the way of roots—but they've made themselves a hell of a problem."

I frowned, the facts making little sense. "That doesn't explain why they'd go after the Kannors. It's like a Chihuahua suddenly deciding to take a chunk from a Doberman. That's the sort of heat only an idiot would bring down on themselves."

"Yeah, well, I'd never claim the Sand Snakes were all that smart. Get kicked enough and people decide they want to be the ones kicking. They probably figure if they can get one over on the Kannors, it'll raise their position. I doubt they give a damn about the actual money, but making the Kannors look bad would help them out."

"How did Morrin even get him out of the house?"

"A man on the inside does a lot. He turned off the cameras and escorted the kid out through a back door. Brendon knew Morrin, so he wouldn't have argued or made a fuss about going with him."

I thought for a moment about how Brendon must have felt when he realized the truth, when the man he'd trusted betrayed him. Had he seen the Sand Snakes kill Morrin? While most people would have been happy with that, he was just a kid.

"Do you have a picture?" I asked.

Gunnar left for a moment, then returned with a thin album. When he flipped it open beside me, it wasn't really a family album. Instead of happy photos of them on vacations and at reunions, it had images of each family member on a page with printed information on the opposite side.

He turned to Brendon's page to show a picture of the young boy. He looked older than he was, probably because as the male heir, a lot was expected of him. He had blond hair, like his father, but dark eyes.

It hurt to think about this child alone with people who had kidnapped him, people willing to kill him. Was he afraid? Crying?

That rare moment of feeling struck me, a time when I had to admit that the world we lived in really sucked. Even a Kannor heir deserved to feel happy and safe as a child.

I turned slightly to realize just how close Gunnar was. Since we stared at the same album, I hadn't realized that his arm brushed against mine. For one long moment, I let myself forget everything.

I forgot how much this man had hurt me, how angry I was, how little I could trust him. Doing that allowed me to forget that I'd died, that I'd sold my soul, that I didn't belong to even myself now.

Gunnar reached out and set his hand on the side of my face, twisted and came closer. His warm breath teased my lips and took me back to when I'd deluded myself into thinking we were meant to be, when I thought we were some ride-or-die, Bonnie-and-Clyde bullshit.

When his lips actually touched mine, however, that fantasy shattered. I felt *nothing*. It seemed some lies were too far, and my brain rebelled against it.

So I bit down on his lip — hard.

The album fell to the ground and Gunnar jerked backward. I let him go, releasing my bite.

He ran the back of his hand over his lip, his eyes wide. "The fuck is your problem?"

I met his gaze head-on, not giving a fuck if he liked my answer or not. "Let's be clear, huh? I'm not 'convenient' anymore for you. I'm not the same weak girl who trailed along at your heels for years begging for a little of your attention." I touched the tip of my tongue against my lip, clearing the copper tang of his blood away. "So keep your fucking hands to yourself from now on or lose them."

I left him standing there, confused and more than a little pissed, judging from his expression.

And somehow, walking away from him let me hold my head high.

Chapter Five

I forgot how much I fucking hate dive bars.

I'd spent so much time at Tyrus' place that I'd gotten used to the niceties. Sure, people got murdered there all the time, but it was the little things that made it special. Koya kept the bar tops clean at Tyrus' bar, the skulls cups were deep and — I kept in the gag when I nearly stepped on a used condom on the floor — people didn't need protection so sex didn't leave behind trash.

The loud music thundered through me, making my heart speed as if to match the rhythm. Still, no matter how much I hated this place, the sight of men in leather vests with a snake on the back told me I was where I needed to be.

Murphy's was a bar Gunnar had told me about where the Sand Snakes spent time — at least the higher-ups. Charles knew about it, but he wasn't willing to attack it directly because he knew better.

He'd sent people in — quietly — but since there was no sign that Brendon was there, attacking would only end up endangering the boy. The higher-ups would no doubt bolt, probably before anyone could grab them, and Charles would end up in a worse position. Dealing with abductors was a tricky situation, since pushing them could end up endangering the hostage.

However, I wasn't about to go in loud like that. It wasn't my style, and I lacked the ability.

Here I was, entirely on my own, and without the powers or ability to launch some sort of assault. It meant my best plan was to extract information and ingratiate myself to the right people.

Which I could do.

I'd survived this world—at least until Gunnar had gotten me killed—by understanding people. I knew what they wanted and could make them believe whatever I needed them to. At least, I used to be able to.

Five years was enough time to get rusty.

I ordered a bottled beer from the bartender since I wasn't about to trust the cleanliness of the glasses in a place like this. Plus, bottles were harder for people to drug. I had a higher tolerance to alcohol and drugs than I'd had as a human but give me enough and it still could land me on my ass.

And from the look of the people around me, I didn't want to be on my ass here.

God, it's been a long time since me or anyone else has been on my ass.

Then again, I didn't have a lot of great options. Trusting any demons or damned was stupid. Everyone in the Chasm was looking to move up and were more than willing to take out anyone they needed to to do it.

That for sure included me.

No orgasm was worth a knife in the back, after all.

I took a drink of the beer, using the chance to survey the bar. It wasn't the sort of place where people came without good reason. It didn't have the normal drunks, the random people who just wanted a beer or a place to make friends. Those sorts of people would walk the fuck out the moment they saw the bikers in here.

Some clustered around a few pool tables while others drank. The women wore revealing outfits and suggestive smiles. A couple of the women seemed pinned to the sides of men — the sort of men who clearly held a position of power — but most of them struck me as free agents.

They moved around, looking for anyone who could give them what they wanted. I didn't blame them — that was the position of women in many places. We had to play the hand we were dealt, which was often a shitty hand.

I'd never played that game exactly, the one where I buddied up to men just to get what I could. It had never seemed worth it. Don't get me wrong, I'd traded sex for money or safety in the past, at times when I didn't see any other options, but I'd never made it into a career.

Still, I had to use what I had, which to the men in this bar was a set of tits and a pussy. The idea that they might get to see those things could get me pretty far, even if mine weren't that great.

"Ain't never seen you here before," came a rough voice from just behind me along with the stroke of fingers down my bare arm.

I stopped myself from reacting like I wanted — by hitting him with the beer bottle in my hand. Instead, I pulled my lips into what I hoped was a convincing smile as I turned to face him.

The man was in his forties and had long black hair pulled into a low ponytail. He had the expression of a man who had spent all his life in places like this, who felt at home here.

It meant he wasn't a bad first target.

"I've never been here before," I said before tipping my beer back and taking a swig.

He smiled wider, then slid his hand around my waist and pulled me closer. "I got a thing for virgins who need a steady hand to show 'em the ropes," he said as he pulled me toward the back of the bar where a cluster of men and women sat at a large table. All signs pointed to that being the VIP room.

Which was exactly where I needed to go.

I giggled at his words even though they weren't funny or charming, all while I allowed him to guide me that way.

"Pretty," one of the men said as the man who had his arm around me sat and pulled me into his lap.

"Yeah, she is."

"You sure swooped her up fast."

The man whose lap I sat in chuckled as he wrapped an arm around me as if to keep me close. "I got an eye for fresh meat. If you wait around, someone else'll get the first bite." He picked up a drink from the table—not a beer but something dark in a glass. "What's your name, sweetheart?"

I kept my tone soft when I answered despite the sickening nickname. "Loch."

"Loch? Well, ain't that cute? Guess that makes me your key." He pressed his lips to my bare shoulder, to the skin not covered by the spaghetti strap tank top I wore. "I'm Clint. You don't much look like you belong here." His words weren't a threat so much as a question.

In other words, he knew I wasn't the normal bar fly who frequented biker bars. He didn't think I was doing anything shady, just that I wasn't used to this.

I can work with that.

"I met someone who invited me here," I hedged. "I thought it might be fun. The normal bar I go to is just so boring — the boys are all the same."

He laughed, his breath hot against my skin. "Makes sense. You won't find boys here, sweetheart, I can promise you that. We're men." The use of the nickname again made me suspect he'd already forgotten my name.

Which was fine by me.

"I've seen vests like yours around," I said. "With a snake on the back, I mean."

He let me shift so I could see him along with the rest of the table, so I sat sideways in his lap. He smirked as he responded, pride in his voice. "Yeah, we're all part of the same group — the Sand Snakes." He said it as if I was supposed to know that and be impressed.

I furrowed my eyebrows, playing the part of the innocent girl who had no idea about their world. For some men that would annoy them, but I suspected Clint here would get off on that power imbalance.

He laughed and wrapped his arm tighter around me. "You're fucking adorable, you know that?" *Bingo.* "We're pretty well known. Trust me, you won't find yourself a tougher group. I can show you a real nice time. Forget whoever it was that you came here to meet — they ain't me."

I kept my smile plastered to my lips, playing the part of the idiot who had wandered in here. "A group? Do you mean like...*bikers*?" I dropped my voice to a whisper as if it were a secret.

"That's right. Does that excite you?"

Not really. I'd grown up around men like that. They were cowards, just in their own way, all too willing to fuck over the weak for their own benefit.

Instead, I pressed my luck. The last thing I wanted was to keep going with this game and end up on my back without learning anything useful.

"So, are you like, the leader?"

Clint's smile fell a bit, but his words came out strong as if trying to prove a point. "Nah. Hopper there, he's boss." Clint nodded toward a man across the table, who didn't acknowledge the greeting. Then again, to them, I was just some floozy. I wasn't worth introducing to. "I'm an enforcer—means I deal with problems that come up." Clint's words reeked of self-importance, as if he wanted to prove that while he wasn't *technically* in charge, he was still a bigshot.

Handling men's egos was a full-time fucking job.

"That sounds scary," I said, trying to draw Clint back in.

"Maybe for others. I don't feel fear, not anymore."

I could almost picture the man pissing himself in fear if he ever made it to the Chasm, if he saw the damned there or came face to face with someone in their demon form. That image helped me to stay in character. "Wow, I wish I could be like that."

Clint shifted, then set a pistol on the top of the table with a loud thud. He had a smirk on his lips as if he had just unzipped and dropped his cock on the table rather than the gun. "You ever been this close to one?" he asked.

I shook my head, ensuring my eyes were peeled wide.

In reality, I'd shot something like that before I'd hit five. I carried daily from the time I was ten, after my father had given me a talk about how men only wanted one thing and how a gun was about the only way to keep it from them.

Clint grinned, seemingly reassured by his imagined increase in power. He wanted to prove he was scary, to make me afraid, to make me want to cling to him. They were all stupid games, but ones I recognized enough to play.

"Have you ever used it?" I asked.

"Course I have. Anyone who hasn't used one shouldn't carry one." He slid his fingers over the top of my thigh, the jeans I wore keeping him from touching my skin directly.

Thank fuck for that. I was glad I'd decided to go with jeans and not a skirt, because I had no doubt he'd have tried to sneak beneath it already.

More fabric gave me more time to maneuver.

"When was the last time?"

He pressed his lips together as if thinking for a moment, the hum of conversation around us disappearing as I focused on him. "Couple days ago. Put a bullet through some snitch's brain, then left his worthless body in an alleyway."

Which sounded a hell of a lot like Morrin, didn't it?

Did that mean Clint had been the one to kill him? It would mean he was high enough to know about Brendon, too, wouldn't it?

"Shut up," Hopper snapped from across the table.

Clint turned to look at the boss, his expression something between annoyance and submission.

Clearly, he didn't want to take on Hopper but didn't care for him ordering him around, either. "What?"

"You talk too much, especially about things that don't need to be talked about."

"You really think she's gonna say shit? Come on, look at her." Clint caught my chin and held it as if showing off a new pet.

"Maybe, maybe not, but you don't need to go spilling secrets just to get your dick wet. If you can't get into a girl's pants without that, then you deserve the blue balls you get." Hopper's tone said he didn't care for Clint or his loose lips.

Clint's fingers dug into my chin, taking his annoyance out on me. Then again, it was far safer to do that then egg Hopper on any more.

"Besides, she doesn't look nearly afraid enough," Hopper added on, his gaze meeting mine.

"What? Look at her—she's terrified."

"Nah. She's just good at looking afraid. I saw her when she walked in here—didn't look around, didn't jump when you walked up to her, didn't even pull away when you just grabbed her. Girl ain't nearly as afraid as she pretends to be."

Clint jerked my face his way to stare into my eyes.

Fuck. This wasn't good... Hopper was far smarter than I'd given him credit for, which sucked. I preferred my criminals to be dumb as shit. It made it far easier to deal with them when they were.

Clint pressed his lips together, a sure sign he took Hopper's opinion as fact.

Just as I tried to decide if I could reach Clint's gun first, as I worked out in my head a way to get out of this, another voice rang out and increased the tension in the bar tenfold.

"You want to let my girl out of your fucking lap? Or you want me to take her?"

I turned to find Hale standing there, and his angry smirk said I really wasn't any better off…

Hale

This girl is fucking trouble.

That much was obvious with a single look at Loch, her green hair like a beacon that let me spot her even in this crowded bar. I'd sensed her here, on Earth, the power and pull of a demon impossible to ignore.

Of course, I sure as fuck hadn't expected to find her perched in the lap of some asshole biker. She'd been in the Chasm for five years, and she'd never cozied up to anyone this way.

Even when it would have made her life easier, when garnering favors would have made her safer, she never went that way.

Fuck knew *I'd* tried to get her into my own lap. Still, she'd always resisted, and I wasn't asshole enough to force a girl. Wasn't any fun if she wasn't just as into it as I was.

And go fucking figure, I didn't care for her in his lap. It took all my very limited control not to break the bastard's fingers for touching her. No one would think twice if I set this whole fucking bar aflame.

Why do I even care?

Just asking annoyed me, mostly because I didn't have an answer. Why did Loch dig her way into my brain? How, in five years, had she become so entwined with all four of us Demon Lords that she was damn near an honorary lord?

Just what the fuck was she?

Trouble, that's what.

Which was no doubt part of my draw to her. I'd made a place for myself in the Chasm, but fuck knew I hated rules. I hated doing what anyone said or falling into anyone's expectations, so maybe seeing a girl so dead set on doing her own thing got to me.

Not that she'd ever given me a sign that she reciprocated. Loch was nothing if not stubborn, but that was one of the few benefits of being dead. It wasn't like either of us was getting any older.

No matter if she wanted to give in yet or not, though, I had no plans to just ignore her perched in some fucker's lap, especially with the way Hopper and the others at the table stared at her.

Never much figured myself for the white-knight type, but why the fuck not? Wouldn't mind a bit if Loch wanted to play damsel in distress for me.

And if I got to kill someone during? Well, all the better.

Loch

"Your girl?" Hopper spoke instead of Clint, which told me they had to know Hale. Otherwise, the boss wouldn't get himself involved in the bickering of underlings.

"Yeah, *mine.*" Hale said that in a possessive way that could excite a frigid girl.

"She's asking too many questions," Hopper said. "Figured a girl of yours would know better than that. Even a pretty face doesn't excuse that shit."

Hale snorted as if Hopper were an idiot and he didn't mind making that perfectly clear. "I ain't got time for girls who are nothing more than a pretty fucking face. Loch there's got smarts enough to be useful. I'm getting sick of your hands on her, though." Hale directed that last part right at Clint.

Clint opened his mouth as if to argue back, but Hopper's voice cut him off. "Let her go, Clint. You can find another cunt for the night, can't you?"

Clint pressed his lips together but obeyed, releasing me.

I scooted off his lap and slid beside Hale—mostly because I didn't have any other good option. I didn't trust Hale, had no idea why he'd shown, but he *had* just saved my ass.

"She was asking a lot of questions," Hopper said. "I was starting to think she was a cop."

"Nah, not a cop, just a girl with more curiosity than good sense."

"Girls like that cause problems."

"And men like me don't mind problems, not if the girl is worth it." Hale set his hand on my waist and pulled me against his hard side. "This one's more than worth it."

The claim said what he needed it to—he'd defend me.

It was a gauntlet Hopper wasn't willing to pick up. I had no idea what they thought of Hale, how they knew him exactly, but they seemed to know enough that they refused to fuck with him.

"Well, enjoy your night," Hopper said, his tone totally different than the one he'd used with Clint or me.

I guess that said what he thought of each of us.

Hale nodded, then turned and walked away, his arm still wrapped around me. He leaned in, his lips brushing my ear as he whispered to me, "You are in *so much* fucking trouble, Loch."

And the way my heart sped agreed with him.

Chapter Six

Hale didn't ask me why I was there. Whether that was because he didn't care or he didn't think it was the right place for that conversation, I had no idea. Instead, he just played the part of boyfriend.

Well, *boyfriend* as far as this world went. Things like romance were a lot more iffy here. Mostly, it meant he wouldn't let anyone else fuck with me—figuratively or literally.

He handed me a glass with liquor in it that he'd gotten from the bartender.

"This didn't seem like a good place for that sort of drinking," I said without taking the glass.

He didn't pull it back. "They give me cleaner glasses than they give others, and no one here would dare to try and drug it, not when you're with me. Something stronger will help you fit in, though."

I sighed but took what he offered, unable to argue with his reasoning. He still had his other hand on my waist, our bodies so close as we stood at the bar that we could almost be screwing. Each time I took a deep breath, my chest brushed against him, a reminder of our nearness.

And my pulse raced in a way it hadn't when I'd been in Clint's lap, or when Gunnar had tried to kiss me.

Why was it then that Hale looked entirely unruffled by this all?

Not fair.

"What are you doing here?" I asked when I wasn't sure what else to say.

"I like to spend time in this area. Heard a rumor of a green-haired girl sniffing around Sand Snakes' territory. Figured it had to be you."

"So you came just to check in on me?"

"You attract trouble, and these people are the kind of trouble you don't want to fuck with. Thought I might be useful. Looks like I was right."

I huffed when I couldn't deny his words. He *had* been useful.

"It's normal to say thank you," he pressed.

"You want me to thank you?"

"I saved your ass. I'm wasting my night playing the part of your boyfriend. I deserve a lot fucking more, but I'll take a thank you for now, at least."

I leaned in and kept my voice low. "For now? If you want, go ahead and hold your breath until you get something more. Bet you'll pass out before I give in."

He made a soft, amused sound deep in his throat before taking his own glass and downing the alcohol in one big gulp. "Never figured this was your sort of place."

"What can I say? I like the ambiance." Just as I said that, a fight broke out beside us. It ended quickly when one man broke a pool cue against the face of the other, a splatter of blood falling to the floor next to my foot. The man who got hit fell and would have knocked into me, but Hale pulled me against him to hold me out of the way.

I looked up and into Hale's blue eyes, then tried to keep my voice playful. "Yep, wonderful atmosphere."

Hale laughed and shook his head, but he didn't release me. When I went to pull away, he tightened his grip. "Play the part, Loch. You're selling a story, right? Can't imagine this is worse than sitting in that fucker's lap."

I lifted my eyebrow at his tone. "Are you jealous?"

"Jealous of you cozying up to some two-bit human enforcer like that? Why would I be?"

And yet, even as he said that, his actions betrayed him. The way his fingers held me tightly, the way his voice was all possession, it suggested the same thing.

That for whatever reason, Hale was jealous. I wasn't some romantic idiot who thought it was love. Instead, I had a feeling it was nothing more than selfishness. I was a toy he'd enjoyed screwing with over the past five years, and he didn't appreciate someone he considered beneath him toying with me.

He was nothing but a kid mad about someone else touching his shit.

Telling myself that didn't stop my body from reacting, though.

I tried to focus, to stop my pulse from racing. "Hopper seemed to respect you."

"Everyone respects me. If they didn't, they'd be six fucking feet under." Hale spoke in a way Clint no doubt wished he could. Hale said it with absolute confidence, and it made it easy to believe him.

"I didn't think you spent enough time on Earth to get recognized."

"I prefer Earth. The Chasm is dark and depressing."

I couldn't argue that point. Maybe what the Chasm really needed was an anti-depressant business. Maybe counseling for the damned? We could start up deep breathing and yoga to try and counter pesky things like eternal damnation and enslavement.

"You're thinking something stupid," Hale said, then pressed his thumb against the center of my forehead. "You always get lines right here when you drift off in that head of yours."

I glared at him despite it holding no real anger. He wasn't wrong—I much preferred whatever was going on in my head most of the time.

"So how long do we have to play this game?" I asked, gesturing at where his hand still held me tight.

"Depends. If you want to come back here, it'd be good to carry it on a while. The bigger a claim I put on you, the longer people will remember it." He dropped his gaze from my eyes down my front, the look nothing short of a leer. "Wouldn't mind putting a pretty big claim on you. Pretty sure they'd all get the point if I sit your pretty ass up on this bar and have you coming on my tongue."

The way he stared at me said he expected me to be embarrassed, to blush and stammer in return.

Too bad.

"That might work, if we're pretending that you had the skills to actually do that."

"Oh, Loch, you're playing with fire."

I rolled my eyes and brought my drink to my lips. Fighting with Hale had no real purpose. I'd learned that early in my time in the Chasm. He enjoyed it too much, so we never came to any understanding. He wanted that back and forth, the push and pull, and each time I engaged, it only spurred him on.

I still recalled the first time I'd met him in the Chasm, when he'd shoved me against a wall, threatened my life, then kissed me. He'd said it was only a matter of time before he fucked me.

That 'matter of time' had lasted five years thus far. Five years of picking at each other but never anything more.

Which was fine by me. Just like Tyrus was a bad bet—so was Hale.

In fact, all four of the Demon Lords might as well have been on a poster showing women the sorts of men to avoid.

They were selfish, violent, possessive and manipulative. Nothing about them implied they'd make good romantic partners.

They were after eleven and before seven men at best. Good for a reckless, drunken night of sex that led to aches and regret the next morning, but nothing more.

He pulled in a deep breath, as if breathing me in, before he smiled again, his facial piercings glinting as they caught the light. It made him look even more dangerous and made me worried I might just be in over my head. "Well, guess we better play our part, huh?"

Don't fall for it, Loch. You know what men like him are like — don't make that mistake again.

If only I felt confident that I could remember that…

* * * *

I peered around the room as if it were a prison.
Might as well be…

The door closed behind me, and one glance at Hale showed me the man who would be doing the waterboarding.

"You don't need to be so fucking jumpy," Hale muttered, a bottle of Scotch in his hand as he set all the locks on the door.

"Well, I wasn't expecting a sleepover."

"Me either, but if we turned Hopper down, he'd have gotten suspicious. While I don't give a fuck whether or not he trusts me, seems like you want him to buy your story."

I turned away from him as I peered around the small studio apartment Hopper had set us up in above the bar. After blending in best we could, playing pool and drinking and talking to others, the bar had given last call. Hopper had come up and offered us a room in the building as an apology for Clint's behavior.

We had to either accept it or insult him by rejecting it.

Which led us to accepting it and me somehow sharing a room with Hale.

"I survived hell for five years. I can survive a night with you."

"Told you before—the Chasm ain't hell."

"Might as well be. Pain, suffering, damned souls. I'm not seeing a difference." I caught sight of the single bed that sat at the far end of the room and chose to ignore it. Even at two a.m. I didn't need to think about the sleeping arrangements.

Hale set the bottle on the counter, seeming not to think we needed to drink anymore. To be fair, I'd had more than my fair share already. I had a nice buzz going, one that loosened my tongue.

Not enough to use it on Hale, thankfully.

"One bed," Hale said as he stared at the single sleeping place.

"I'll take the floor."

"I wouldn't recommend that. Place like this probably has pests."

"There *might* be pests on the floor, but if you're sleeping in the bed, I know for a fact there's one there."

He snorted before opening the cabinets in the small kitchenette. "I'd say I don't bite like they do, but that ain't true. In fact, I bite a hell of a lot harder."

"Not a fan of moderation?"

"If you're gonna bite, might as well make it hurt." He pulled a box from the shelf and tossed it to me.

I caught it, then glanced down to see what it was. Breakfast cereal?

"Nothing fancy, but you haven't spent much time on Earth. You need calories while you're here."

I went to argue, to tell him I wasn't hungry, when my stomach growled. *Huh, seems like I am actually hungry.* I muttered a grudging thanks before reaching into the box and taking a handful of the cereal. It was slightly stale, but the moment I started to chew, I realized just how much I'd needed it.

Even better, it settled my stomach, which hadn't appreciated me pouring alcohol on top of nothing.

The apartment was set up with a small bathroom off to the side, a closet with mirrored doors, a bed that didn't seem any bigger than a twin and the small kitchenette with a sink, a short counter, and a hot plate and microwave.

In other words? It was on par with a cheap motel. Clearly the room wasn't intended for long stays, but rather for people who needed to crash for a night or two after drinking themselves into a stupor.

Hale glanced at the locks as if to check, then nodded. "I'm gonna go shower. You hear anything, you come get me."

"I don't need a babysitter or a bodyguard, you know."

He pointed at me as if I were a child spouting nonsense. "You ain't collected any souls yet, so you might be tougher than some of the damned, but you ain't got much power. Don't be stupid and forget that."

I pressed my lips together, not offering him anything until he turned around and walked into the bathroom. Him being right was the worst part. When it came to the Chasm, I was near the bottom. The fact that I'd made my deal directly with a Demon Lord was nothing more than a stroke of luck. It didn't offer me much in the way of tangible benefits.

Unless I gave in, unless I started to play their game, I'd never move up in the world. I was a little stronger than a human when on Earth, but not enough to make much of a difference. It meant Hale wasn't wrong when he'd told me to come get him if anything happened.

Not that I would.

Fuck that. I'd rather face pissed-off bikers than admit to Hale that I needed him. He'd take that shit and run, and I'd lose the upper hand forever with him.

The sound of water from the bathroom let me take a deep breath, since it meant I didn't have to be on edge. So long as Hale was in there, I had a minute to myself.

Days had passed with no luck, with me getting no closer to my goal. I hadn't made any real progress with the Sand Snakes, still had no idea where they might be keeping Brendon, had no idea how to find him.

Hale had helped me infiltrate that world, but it didn't mean they'd talk to me. They had no reason to —

I was just some woman who belonged to a man they didn't want to piss off.

I ran my fingers through my hair, pushing it out of my face, wishing I had a clearer idea.

Instead, each hour that ticked by reminded me that I was running out of time. Each minute I wasted here was another minute Brendon was terrified, another minute closer to Jay making the ultimate sacrifice.

The alcohol, which normally dulled my senses enough to ignore my problems, only managed to make me feel more hopeless.

The door to the bathroom opened and when I lifted my gaze, all those thoughts dissipated.

Hale stood in the doorway, a towel wrapped low on his hips and another over his head as he dried his hair. It left his tattoos on display, the most of him I'd ever seen.

He sometimes wore a jacket without a shirt underneath, but I'd never seen him naked from the waist up.

And talk about that bad boy aesthetic...

His body was lean but toned, and damn near every inch I could see was covered in ink. The images were a mixture of subjects, but they were all in shades of black and gray. They covered his throat, his shoulders, went in sleeves down to his knuckles. He had more on his chest, his abs, and the images moved with each breath.

When Hale moved the towel on his head, when his bright blue eyes met mine, I struggled to draw in a breath.

What was this tension between us? Was I really so hard up for sex that I'd consider a man like Hale?

No, not a man. A Demon Lord... Talk about a bad bet. There was no winning if I fell into this bullshit with him, no coming out of it better off than before.

He didn't smirk, didn't mock me even though I had no doubt he could tell exactly what was on my mind. I might be a good liar, but even I had no hopes of hiding just how much I wanted him in that moment.

Five years suddenly felt like a century, and I missed that connection, that ability to go mindless with pleasure, to let myself go. I wanted to sink into the familiar motions of sex, into the way passion could erase everything else.

I was on my feet before I could think twice, approaching him, each step drawing me nearer to a cliff. He didn't come closer, didn't mock me, just waited.

He smelled like strawberries.

It was an odd scent to identify him with, but after a moment, my useless brain supplied that it was probably the shampoo left here.

His gaze was intense, but it wasn't until I saw a flash of red inside them, the smallest glimpse of his other form, that I woke from my lust-filled stupor.

Don't fuck the Demon Lords.

Such simple advice, yet here I was, ready to throw it away. To hide the fact that I'd gotten up, that I'd all but stalked him, I rushed past him and into the bathroom. I slammed the door shut—probably smacking him in the process—and turned on the shower to pretend that had been my goal the entire time.

Too bad I doubted even a long cold shower was going to let me get myself under control.

* * * *

I wished I could look as sexy as Hale did after a shower, but women got the short end of that stick. I looked more like a drowned rat than some sea goddess.

Of course, I used that—or at least tried too—as some sort of reassurance that I could control myself. If I looked like a pathetic dog after a bad trip to the groomers, that would destroy the whole sexual-tension thing going on, wouldn't it?

In the main room of the apartment, I found Hale stretched out on the bed, still in nothing but a towel, his phone in his hands.

He cast me a sidelong glance without turning his head or slowing his fingers. He held the phone sideways, tapping with his thumbs, making me guess that he was playing some game.

I peered around the room but could come up with no other idea. If I sat on the floor, he'd bitch and moan until sleep was impossible anyway. Giving in, I went over and sat on the edge of the bed, my towel wrapped tightly around me.

While in the shower, Hale had strolled in to take my clothing. He hadn't tried to peek in through the curtain, to steal a glimpse of me, which confused me more than anything else. Instead, he'd only said that he was tossing our clothes into the washer.

Of course, that gave me nothing to wear except for a towel that wasn't nearly large enough to cover everything I wanted it to.

"You're thinking too hard," Hale muttered. "You're going to give me a headache."

"I'm not thinking."

"You're *always* thinking. You should knock that off. If you ain't come up with whatever you want to figure out yet, you probably won't. No reason to ruin your night by running yourself in circles."

I twisted to glare at him, annoyed by how comfortable he appeared. "Not all of us can just go with the flow and expect shit to work out."

"Course you can. If you did, you probably wouldn't get into so much trouble." He dropped his phone to the bed and focused on me.

And I really missed him playing on the phone.

"Why are you here?" I asked when I couldn't stop myself. "I appreciate that you helped me out, but why are you still here? Even with our cover story, you've got no reason to spend the night in some little apartment here."

"You ever stop to think maybe I just like spending time with you?"

"With how I talk to you? I doubt it."

"I got plenty of people who are afraid of me. It's refreshing to have someone squawking at me."

"Squawking is pretty damned insulting," I pointed out.

"Then collect some fucking souls and get stronger. Once you are, maybe you won't sound so much like a parakeet just making noise." The harshness of his words didn't match the odd affection of his tone. When a smile spread across his lips, he only further confused me. "You know, that almost sounded like a thank you."

"Keep on dreaming."

"I plan to—course, my dreams usually have you naked and spread out for me."

"I know people say dreams do come true, but don't expect that one to."

He chuckled as if my rejection didn't bother him at all.

It probably didn't. I doubted he was the sort of man who struggled to get women. In fact, even though I knew better, he tempted me.

He rolled slightly to toss his phone on the windowsill, the action exposing his back to me. It was the first time I'd seen his back, and the sight stopped me entirely.

While ink covered most of his back, it didn't hide the gnarly raised skin from scars. They were deep and crisscrossing, some short and others running the length of his back. Worse, they overlapped in such a way that they couldn't have happened all at the same time.

I didn't mean to, didn't think about it, but before I knew it, I'd reached forward and traced one of the thicker scars with the tip of my finger.

And just as fast as I touched him, I found myself pinned to the bed, his heavy body above me, his strong hand at my throat. His eyes, always intense, seemed to have caught flame. A tremble in his arm screamed how close to the edge he was.

He pulled his lips back as if to snarl, his chest rising and falling in rapid, uneven panting. "Don't fucking touch my back."

"What happened?" I asked, forcing the words out even though he still had my throat gripped. The hold was more of a warning, not tight enough to fully cut off my air supply.

"You shouldn't poke at old wounds," he said.

"There are so many…"

He dropped his gaze down, over my front, which reminded me that I'd been in nothing but the towel.

And I no longer really wore it. The movement from him pinning me had undone where it had wrapped around me and now the edges hung open, exposing me entirely. And just like he wore his scars, I had my own. The one from the gunshot that had ended me remained there, in the skin over my stomach.

"Aren't there better things to talk about?" he asked, but the lust in his voice seemed forced. I had no doubt that he wanted me, but I suspected he went to that to hide what I'd seen.

And even though his back didn't face me anymore, I still couldn't get the image out of my head. There were so many marks on him, ones that all differed from each other. What had happened?

"Don't think about it," he whispered. Instead of the threat he normally had in his voice, it came out like a desperate plea.

How was I supposed to ignore it? It felt like a stupidly unreasonable request. There was no way for me to just pretend I hadn't seen it, to make believe, and yet he wanted me to?

He must have seen that in my expression, because his lips pressed together tightly. "You can't? Well, then I guess I'll make it so you can't think about a fucking thing except what I'm doing to you." He closed the distance between us and took my lips in a kiss that might have been able to do as he said.

What I'd tasted five years ago felt like a tease all of a sudden. Hale didn't kiss me slowly, didn't ease into it. He delved past my lips, and the hard ball of his tongue ring added yet another dimension to the kiss. He touched me as if consumed by flames, as if begging me to burn with him.

That sounded fine to me. It made me think that the Chasm was the hell I often called it, and this was me burning in hellfire. I'd worship at the altar that was Hale though, especially when he ran one of his large, strong hands down my body. He teased it over one of my nipples, then cupped my breast in a confident touch.

I moaned, but he swallowed the sound, stealing it from me, and all my thoughts of the marks I'd seen, of the reasons this was a bad idea, they all went away. I'd spent five years in a world I hated, there because of a choice I regretted, and now I was supposed to do what I didn't want to do just to survive. If Hale could make me forget that, even for a minute, I'd take it *happily.*

He was a bad bet, but I could deal with paying up later.

I reached up, wanting to wrap my arms around him, to pull him closer, but he jerked out of reach.

Right. His back.

As quickly as the fact hit me, before I could think much about it, Hale caught my wrists in one of his hands and pinned them above my head. It stretched me out beneath him, and while I should have been afraid of him — he was a Demon Lord after all — I couldn't get that to make me want to stop.

He pulled his lips up to one side in a smirk, the action making me want to run my tongue over the metal ring there. "I'm going to fuck you, Loch. You ready for that?"

He didn't ask me if I wanted to — what was the point in that? It was obvious. Instead, he just asked if I was ready, as if it happening was a foregone conclusion and the only question was when.

And there was only one right answer — I nodded.

His groan made my cunt squeeze down, the masculine sound like an aphrodisiac to me. He reached between us with his free hand and slid his fingers along my slit, letting out another sound that said what he found pleased him.

He didn't mention it, though. Instead, he grasped his cock and rubbed it against my pussy.

I peered down between our bodies, frowning at a flash of silver that caught my attention.

Hale let out a soft, breathless laugh. "What? You didn't think my piercings stopped at the waist, did you?"

Yeah, I did. Normal people didn't consider getting their junk pierced, did they?

"Didn't it hurt?" I asked, going for a slightly nicer response.

"Not much." He leaned back on his knees and stroked himself once, then lifted his cock so I could see the underside.

Or rather, so I could see the line of piercings that ran along the bottom of his shaft. There were four of them, all with curved silver barbells, and I had no idea what to even say about it.

Except... "Is that going to hurt *me*, then?"

Hale snorted softly, then used his free hand to tease my cunt as he spoke, as if he was willing to have the conversation but *not* willing to stop what he was doing. "Nah, Loch, it won't hurt a bit. Fuck, you might even find you like it. I've never gotten a complaint."

"You let someone put a needle through your penis — who is going to complain to you?" Even though I tried to sound tough, Hale's constant stroking of my clit made my words sound like some sexy whisper.

He stroked himself once more, then leaned back down. He didn't hold my wrists again, but I also didn't make the mistake of trying to wrap my arms around him. Instead, he went still and stared down, into my eyes. He didn't move again, not until I met his gaze, as if that were a conversation in itself. Then again, I could lose myself in the depths of his blue eyes.

When I gave in, when I didn't hide anything from him, he shifted his hips forward and plunged deep into me with a single hard thrust. He filled me nearly all at once, the sudden fullness almost shocking with its intensity.

But not painful. No, fuck that. I'd waited so long, been so wet, that even though it was overwhelming, it was only in the best ways. Just like he'd promised, the piercings didn't hurt at all. I had no idea if it felt better because of them or just because I was that hard-up for action. It didn't really matter one way or the other.

He let out a sound less civilized than his last one. It was deeper, hungrier, almost pained in its intensity.

And he gave me no time to adjust. Was that because he'd waited, too? Because he still wanted to distract me from my question, from the things he didn't want to talk about? He wanted this to be just sex and if I had any brains at all, I'd let it be just that.

He fucked me hard, his thrusts wild, before he leaned in and took my lips in another kiss, as if he wanted to own me in every way he could. I returned the kiss, stroking my tongue into the heat of his mouth, against the ball of his tongue ring, all the while giving him everything.

He grasped my thigh in a punishing grip, using it like another bit of leverage to take me deeper, to have more of me. I couldn't move, couldn't touch him, couldn't do anything but accept him.

It was like he used this to tell me *this* was the real him. He warned me that he had nothing else, that I should expect nothing else, and right now?

I wanted nothing else.

Hale was surly and dangerous and unpredictable. The only part about him he would offer me—his body—was the only part I wanted.

So I gave in to him and the moment that had been a long time coming.

I fell asleep at some point, after he'd worn me down to the point of exhaustion. The entire time, he kept my hands away from him, didn't give me the freedom to touch him, to ask questions, to even think. Eventually, my eyes slid closed, and when I woke up?

Well, the empty bed was hardly a surprise.

Men like Hale weren't the type to stick around. A good orgasm or two was the most I could expect, and I should be thankful for that much.

Chapter Seven

Three days since seeing Hale and *nothing* had changed.

No matter how much I tried to hang out around the Sand Snakes, how much I tried to catch some small detail to let me in, it didn't work. They saw women as expendable. It meant while they treated me with some level of respect due to Hale, they never said anything useful to or around me.

Which meant the days moved and time closed in on us and I found myself no closer to where I needed to be.

I let out a long sigh as I sat outside, trying to lose myself in the city's noise and busyness.

"You know, some cultures say that sighing is happiness escaping the body." Yazmor took a seat beside me on the bench, his hands tucked into the front pocket of his large hoodie sweater. He'd paired that with baggy shorts, making him look impossibly younger than usual.

I looked at him and let out another sigh just to be difficult.

"Not going well?"

"Not even a little bit."

Funny that the two of us could have a conversation without any specifics, where we didn't have to say anything that would make sense to anyone else, and yet even if we didn't understand, it helped.

I leaned back on the bench and stared off into the throngs of moving people. "Did I get dumber after I died?"

"Maybe?" At my sharp look, Yazmor grinned. "I didn't know you when you were alive so how would I know?"

He had a point, but I didn't appreciate it. "I survived a lot when I was still alive. I made my way through this world of criminals and rapists and murders and I managed it. Now, though? I feel totally out of my depth. Now I can't seem to figure anything out, can't see what people are doing or why."

Yazmor tilted his head, his violet hair shifting as he did it. "Well, you *did* die."

"And?"

"And that's a bit traumatic, isn't it? Unless you're into that sort of thing…" He pressed his lips together, then shook his head. "No, you aren't that type. So you died, you suffered the ultimate failure. Of *course* you're more unsure now—you've seen what happens when things go bad."

I blew a long breath out, considering his words. I touched my stomach, the scar left behind from when I'd finally lost that game.

He had a point, didn't he?

Except what was I supposed to do about it? How was I supposed to get myself out of my own head?

"Come along." Yazmor rose.

I stood without thinking about it, then paused when I realized just following a Demon Lord—even Yazmor—was a bad idea. "Where to?"

"I need a favor."

"But you don't own me. I don't have to do your favors…" While some of afterlife in the Chasm escaped me, that was a detail I knew for sure.

"We're *friends*, aren't we? Friends do each other favors." He lifted an eyebrow at me. "I've done you favors."

"Like what?"

"I gave you a birthday present!"

"You gave me a venomous snake!"

"You're welcome." He smiled widely, as if he'd just made his point.

And what was I supposed to say back to that? In his mind, we were evidently friends. Sure, the snake wasn't the best present I'd ever gotten, but it was the only one I'd gotten since dying.

And what he hadn't mentioned were the many times he'd given me advice—always while pretending not to—or when he'd cheered me up. In fact, when I'd first gotten to the Chasm, when I'd thrown myself headfirst into the pity party to end all pity parties, he'd been the one to come to my room and drag me out of that pit, to force me to interact.

Which meant, even though I was too smart to ever admit it, he was right. I owed him.

"Fine," I muttered, regretting it immediately when he smirked.

Yazmor smiling *never* meant anything good.

* * * *

"We're at an amusement park?" I rubbed at my temples while I walked beside Yazmor, the lights of the rides and loud music impossible to mistake for anything else.

Yazmor had called us a cab and had them take us to Boosters, a mini-golf and small amusement park in the city. It had all the classics—a short roller coaster that always threw out the backs of adults who underestimated it—go-kart racing and bumper boats. Inside a large central building they had a trampoline park as well.

Of course, coming at noon on a weekday meant the park was far less crowded than it would be on the weekends or evenings. We hadn't even waited as we walked up for our second trip on the log ride, ignoring the glare of the teenager who ran it.

I pressed in tight to Yazmor's side—there wasn't much room in the ride that was made for children. "Is this your favorite ride?"

Yazmor grasped the metal bar in front of us as if he were expecting the small log to suddenly jerk forward and he needed the grip. "One of. What's your favorite? Not just here, but *any* amusement park ride."

I bit softly at my bottom lip as I considered his innocent question. "Probably the gravity one that looks like a spaceship. I loved it because it gave me this ability to almost float, where everything changed, and I wasn't bound by the same rules I always had been." As I spoke, I went back in my head to that stupid ride, to all the times I'd ridden it over and over again, only to end up sick at the end of the day and puking in some trashcan.

Yazmor said nothing, which drew my gaze toward him. He stared at me hard, an oddly serious expression on his face.

After a moment, he blinked quickly and slapped on his normal smirk. "Maybe next time we'll go somewhere with one of those. We'll ride it over and over again, then make Tyrus come and pick us up when we're too sick to make it back home."

We spent the rest of the ride in silence, and I couldn't stop thinking that I'd said too much. Yazmor made it easy to forget who and what he was, to think of him as safe or weak.

People didn't become Demon Lords by accident, though. They didn't remain in power by acting sweet and kind. No matter if Yazmor made it harder to see, there *was* a darkness inside him, one that could swallow a person whole.

After the log ride, Yazmor got a candy apple and cotton candy, holding them out to me in question.

I took the cotton candy—I didn't want anything heavy.

A kid ran by, flinging themselves toward a trash can. They leaned over it, one hand pressed over their mouth. They heaved a few times but didn't actually throw up.

"You okay?" I asked.

The kid breathed slowly, then straightened up, giving me a look at them. It was a young boy who was nine or so. Spotting him said school had let out by now, which explained why there were more kids around.

He nodded and wiped his mouth with the back of his hand even though it didn't seem he'd actually thrown up. "Yeah," he said, his voice a bit shaky.

"Too many times on the tea-cups?" I asked. "Those things don't seem like a big deal but they sneak up on you."

Yazmor held his hand out. "Candy apple?"

The kid eyed it suspiciously for a moment, no doubt recalling all the many times he'd been told not to accept candy from strangers—and there weren't a lot of people stranger than Yazmor.

Still, the way the kid widened his eyes spoke volumes about how much he wanted it, and it only took a minute before he accepted the treat and rushed off.

I turned a glare on Yazmor. "Do you want to get put on a list?"

"Depends what the list is for."

Even after five years I could never tell when he was kidding or when he was seriously that clueless. That was why I usually assumed he was serious.

"You can't just give candy to children you don't know. Worse, he was already sick!"

Yazmor tilted his head before grinning. "Are you jealous? I'll go get you a candy apple of your own, if you want."

I rolled my eyes at him before taking another bite of my cotton candy.

We walked through the park, the sun having started to set, the lights of the rides shining brightly.

"What's your favorite ride?" I asked when I realized I'd answered but he hadn't earlier. I really didn't know much about Yazmor, did I?

Despite the time we spent together quite often, he never spoke about himself. Or, perhaps it would be more accurate to say he never said anything useful about himself. Often he'd speak, but the things never made sense. It always felt like he was talking in circles, in riddles that never got to a punch line.

"Ferris wheel. It's quiet in there. I can look over everything, but it can't touch me, like I'm in my own little bubble."

I peered at him, his words oddly clear... That was Yazmor, though. He always seemed to be in his own world. He smiled and laughed when no normal person would have a reason to, and he saw things in a way the rest of the world couldn't. Somehow, he seemed like a Ferris wheel, like someone far outside of everything else.

He paused when he realized I hadn't moved, turning toward me. He didn't smile at first, his eyes intense as he stared at me. He reached out, but something froze me. Even though I knew I should back away, that trusting him at all was stupid, I remained rooted in place.

He ran his thumb over my lip and to the corner of my mouth, then pulled back, a bit of cotton candy stuck to him. He slipped his thumb past his lips, the action incredibly sexy in a way *nothing* he did should have been. He smirked after eating the cotton candy and said, "Delicious," before turning his back to me and walking forward.

I stood there, frozen, my cheeks so warm I wouldn't have been shocked if they burst into fucking flames. What the fuck was *that*? It felt like seeing a part of Yazmor I hadn't even known existed, seeing him in a way that seemed impossible. Yazmor, who was forever absurd, was *not* sensual.

There were things I could tolerate—sleeping with Hale, lusting after Tyrus, even having dirty dreams about Gorrin where he scolded me and I, for some twisted reason, got off on it. Those things made sense.

But seeing Yazmor in that way wasn't okay. It felt like losing my good sense and falling into the madness of the Chasm. Staring at his back, noting for the first time that he was handsome in a very strange way, made me gulp and acknowledge that my bad taste in men truly knew no bounds.

The hours ticked by as we spent time there. The uncomfortable moment from earlier had dissipated, with Yazmor wiping it clear almost immediately when he decided to win all the goldfish at a game just to save them.

I had no doubts that he'd used his powers to win the game—he'd thrown a ping pong ball into a floating cup perfectly the first time—but he looked so damn happy when they'd handed him two bags with ten small goldfish inside them.

It reminded me of Gorrin calling me little fish, but I couldn't help a smile at how happy it made Yazmor.

A kid ran by, a boy around Brendon's age, and it brought me up short.

I was here, playing around, having fun, and for what? Brendon was terrified and Jay got closer and closer to a choice she'd never be able to take back.

And instead of working on the problem, here I was playing around with Yazmor.

It hit me harder than I expected it to, drawing a frown from me. Back when I'd been alive, I wouldn't have been able to just compartmentalize things like this, to know a child was suffering and just ignore it.

I'd watched so many of the damned be twisted by the Chasm, seen as more and more of whatever they had been drained away.

Was that happening to me?

My steps slowed until I stopped, until I found it hard to draw in a breath.

Yazmor twisted back toward me, the way he always did, as if it took a moment to realize he was alone. "Do you need to throw up?" he asked as if the obvious answer was me simply feeling sick from junk food and rides.

"What are we doing here?"

"I told you—a favor."

"What favor? I don't have time to waste like this."

He cocked his head to the side. "This isn't a waste."

"No?" I held my arms out to the side. "So what is it? Because so far, we've gone on rides and eaten fair food and that's it."

"We also spoke to people, bought things, and even our presence caused ripples for others. Those all change the course of events."

"I don't need any of that philosophical bullshit from you, the whole butterfly effect idea. I need more tangible things. I don't get to just sit back and hope things work out while I fuck around." Maybe yelling at him wasn't fair, but I didn't know what else to do.

Yazmor shook his head. "You don't understand. I don't know why I hoped you would, why I thought you might. The world is more complicated and so much simpler than people realize. It's all connected, all bound together, and if you step back enough to see it, you'll recognize that."

It felt like when a rich person explained that poor people are poor because they can't manage their money, like useless advice that doesn't actually do shit to help other than making him feel better.

Yazmor turned his head, the goldfish he'd been determined to win in his hand. He pointed his finger into the distance, and in that direction, the balloon of a young girl standing beneath the Ferris wheel popped.

Great, so we're here to make children cry. Why does that not shock me?

Except, the seriousness on Yazmor's face kept me silent and just watching.

The child sobbed, holding on to just the string of the balloon, while the mother tried to reassure her. They moved toward a cart selling more balloons.

Meanwhile, the boy who Yazmor had given the candy apple to rushed for a trashcan in that area, his hand over his mouth, but he didn't make it. He leaned forward, throwing up near where the girl had been. Clearly, the apple hadn't stayed down well.

Which meant, so far, Yazmor had made one kid cry and another throw up.

And *this* was the man I had hoped could help me?

The boy stumbled toward the bathrooms, leaving the mess there, but it had the advantage of forcing all the other people to avoid the spot.

I went to turn toward Yazmor, to tell him off again for all this, when a loud creaking made me freeze. From the Ferris wheel that sound continued, even above the music and noise of the park, with everyone going still and looking that way.

I jumped backward when one of the carts of the Ferris wheel broke off, plummeting toward the ground. It bounced off another cart beneath it, then went sailing down to the exact spot where the girl had stood, where the boy had thrown up, the spot empty because of the things Yazmor had done. Just beside the place sat the empty stall where Yazmor had won the fish, the worker standing back far enough to avoid injury, but the tank where the fish had been shattered.

I turned toward Yazmor, the pieces all falling into place, my eyes wide as his words finally made some horrible sense.

How could he have done that? How could he have seen all those tiny bits of information and worked them together into that? It was like looking at puzzle pieces and knowing exactly how they fit together before ever seeing the final picture.

He held the two bags with the fish and stared at me, his expression blank, and for the first time, I felt as if I really saw him. I saw how much he held at any one time, the way he saw the world, the reason it all felt like a game to him.

How could it feel real when he balanced so much?

"You need to take a step back," he said, his voice oddly careful, as if he tried very hard to sound normal. "When things don't make sense, you have to look at the bigger picture or you will never see what you failed to notice before." Yazmor didn't wait for me to respond. Instead, he held the fish tightly and turned, walking away, his pace making it clear he didn't intend for me to follow.

After a minute or two, I took off as well. Sirens in the distance said I didn't want to get caught up with this mess. The authorities would come to check out the scene, to ask questions, to interview people. No one had gotten hurt on the ground, though from the screams it sounded like there had been someone inside the cart. A strange sense of trust made me suspect the person deserved what they got.

Why I trusted Yazmor, I wasn't sure. I didn't get the sense he often cared what happened to most people, yet

I also didn't see him as needlessly cruel like Tyrus, Gorrin or Hale.

Whatever the case, I didn't want to get mixed up with the police, so I took myself toward the parking lot. I'd arrived in a cab with Yazmor, but motels weren't that far. A short walk and I could crash there for the rest of the night.

I went over the events of the day in my head as I walked along the dark side road. I thought about what had happened with Yazmor, with Hale, with the Sand Snakes. I tried to replay everything I knew, everything I'd heard, using the silence to try and work out a plan.

I was too close. I'd focused in on one plan and ignored all other options. *That* was what Yazmor had been trying to teach me. I needed to let go of what I thought I understood to find a new path, a new way to work through what I knew.

All the details swam around in my head, distracting me, blinding me to everything around me.

Which was the exact reason I didn't notice anyone approaching, why they got the jump on me, and why a severe pain in the back of my head was the last thing I felt before everything went dark around me.

Yazmor

I should never have brought Loch here. It was foolish sentimentality—something I had assumed I'd long ago lost.

Why was it, then, that my smile felt honest for the first time in...

I shook my head as I refused to do the math required to determine that. It wouldn't answer my question, either.

I thought about Loch's smile, about the enigma she was. I could normally take one look at any living creature and understand them perfectly. I knew what they wanted, what they valued, and how to twist them as I pleased.

Loch was a mystery to me, however. From the first time I met her, she was a blank slate, a living creature who posed a mystery to me.

Was that all she was? Just a life-sized puzzle for me to solve? Something to help pass the endless years that made up my life?

She sparked something inside of me I had never felt, as if she cured the crushing boredom that had spanned so many thousands of years. Living things were chaotic, and she represented pure chaos, and yet something inside of me *wanted* that.

It was dangerous — to both of us.

And yet as I held the fish I'd won, the ones I'd saved, I couldn't stop thinking about the way she had smiled at me.

It seemed, even at my age, life could still surprise me.

Chapter Eight

I woke with a gasp, then wrapped my hands around my head as if that could stop the throbbing that I worried might just split my skull in two.

My thoughts were scrambled, and it took a long moment of forcing myself upright for them to start stringing together into some semblance of consciousness.

I remembered walking toward the motel after the amusement park, then a pain in my head.

Which pretty much pieced it all together.

I peered around the dark room, blinking to try and clear my vision. I wasn't bound, but the room I was in didn't have any furniture in it. The more I looked, the less sure I was that it was even a real room.

Instead, a concrete floor and wooden walls with small gaps between the planks reminded me of a shed. It had no windows and only a single door. I stumbled over to it and pushed the door, which didn't budge.

Metal jingled on the other side — a padlock?

Which meant I was trapped in here, but by who?

Was I just unlucky? Had I ended up falling victim to what all women are warned about—walking alone in the dark? It seemed rather insulting to end up getting picked off by some serial killer after everything I'd been through.

Hell couldn't get me, the devils couldn't get me, but some pervert managed it? *Rude.*

I only hoped that I got an awesome true crime documentary by that Irish guy with the nice voice, and that my friends all lied and said I was a wonderful person who lit up a room in a non-arson way.

A shadow fell against the door from outside the shed and made me pull back. The metal clicked, then the door swung open.

Standing there was a face I easily recognized—Clint.

He stared at me with a sickening grin, one bathed in lust and violence. It made my skin feel too tight for my frame, as if bugs skittered across me.

"I knew there was something about you," he said before he pulled the door closed behind him. He took a lock from his pocket and hooked it to the latch on the inside of the door, ensuring I couldn't leave. No doubt he had the keys in his pocket.

However, that didn't do me much good. I wasn't much stronger than the average human, and given Clint's size and violent tendencies, I doubted I was a match for him.

Especially since my head was still sluggish from the hit I'd taken.

"Where am I?" I asked, trying to keep our conversation safe. I still had no idea what he wanted from me.

He could have figured out I wasn't who I said I was, or he might just be pissed that he'd gotten humiliated by Hopper, Hale and me.

I never thought that petty revenge would be the preferable option, but here I was. I'd rather he be pissed about that than pissed about realizing my true intentions.

"You're at a place we got here for conversations. Before you think about it, don't bother screaming. We're a long fucking way out of town."

Which was a *really* bad sign... People didn't take others out to the middle of nowhere for a nice little chat. They did it when they didn't want others to hear screaming.

"Why?"

"Because you ain't who you said you were."

Fuck.

"I don't know what you're talking about," I lied, digging deep for all my skills with spinning stories.

He crossed his arms, somehow making him look even bigger. "Course you do. Now, I gotta wonder if Hale knows or not. Is he in on this or is he just another fucking patsy for you?"

I swallowed hard, then smiled as if I was a vapid little thing. "You've got me confused with someone else. I have no idea who you think I am, but you've got it all wrong."

He approached me slowly, each step like another warning. "I knew there was something off with you when you showed up. You keep trying to buddy up to folks, but you don't say shit about yourself. Hopper, he probably knew it, but he didn't want to get on Hale's bad side. Now though? Too late."

I backed away with each step he took, trying to keep distance between us, but too quickly I found myself pressed against the wall. I didn't have to fake the fear as I stared up and into his face.

I'd spent enough time around bad people to read them well, to be able to tell just how far they'd go. Some people were like Gunnar, willing to do bad things if it really came down to it, but they didn't enjoy it. Others were like Clint here, men who got off on the ability to hurt others.

Which meant it probably didn't matter what I had to say, what explanation I had for whatever information they thought they knew, Clint was beyond listening.

He was ready to have his own brand of fun, and he didn't play nice.

His large, heavy hand caught my chin and lifted my gaze to his, as if he wanted to make damned sure I understood *exactly* what was about to happen and just how much he'd enjoy it. "You're working for the Kannors," he said, no doubt in his voice at all. "You're snooping around to find Brendon, hoping to steal him from under our noses."

I tried to shake my head, but it only caused his fingers to dig farther into my chin.

"Don't lie to me — ain't a point, not now that I know every fucking thing. Someone saw you leaving Kannor's office. Little disappointed that someone the Kannors sent could be this fucking stupid, though. You didn't even get close."

Ouch. Why I could find his words hurtful, I wasn't sure. No doubt he was going to do a *lot* worse, yet the truth of those words made them sharp. I'd gone into this so sure I could manage it, and yet I didn't have a fucking clue where they were keeping Brendon. At this rate, I'd either get myself killed — again — or I'd have to make the deal with Jay.

Of course, that was a problem for tomorrow me. For today me, the whole torture-and-murder threat was a bit more pressing.

"You going to keep telling me stories?"

"They aren't stories," I said, a last-ditch effort.

Clint released my chin, and it wasn't even close to a shock when pain sprang up in my cheek after he backhanded me. I wanted to stay on my feet, to take the hit like some champ, but physics being what they were won, and I ended up on the ground.

Clint crouched down, his lips pulled into a smile that said we weren't even close to done. "Keep lying all you want — ain't gonna change a thing. I was gonna be real nice to you, but you wanted to make a fool outta me? Well, now I ain't gonna play nearly so nice."

I spat blood at him, the last moment of resistance probably not worth it, but fuck it.

If I was going to get my ass handed to me here, I wasn't about to do it without making sure he knew *exactly* what I thought of him.

* * * *

Hours later, everything hurt. Clint had left me, probably because my consciousness had started to drift in and out. He was the type of person who didn't see a point in this unless he could hear my screams or see my tears.

And no matter how much I swore I wouldn't give him the pleasure of reacting like that, fuck knew I had. It was like telling myself to simply hold my breath underwater. I could do it for a while, but soon enough, the reality of my body took over and I would open my mouth and pull in lungfuls of water.

Just like that, I'd lost my resolve and screamed enough that my throat felt raw. My entire body felt heavy and useless, and blood covered me, some of it dried and some still sticky.

So I panted, lying on the concrete floor, wondering just how I'd ended up here.

Stubbornness.

Wasn't that the truth? I'd been so sure the system was flawed and broken that I'd wanted to do it differently. Then I'd assured myself that I could do what no one else had, that I could fix this all myself, that I could do it alone. I'd pushed away the people around me, the ones who might have actually been able to chip in, and it had all landed me here — bleeding and broken and just waiting for the end.

"Never thought I'd miss the Chasm," I whispered to the empty space.

I remembered when I'd first gotten there, how much I'd hated it. I'd hated the darkness, the gloom, the violence.

And here I was on Earth suffering just as much.

Maybe where a person was didn't matter — people sucked whether they were alive or dead.

I thought about the people I'd met in the Chasm. What I wouldn't give to see that all again. I wanted to crawl into my bed there, to fall asleep on the couch in Gorrin's quarters, to hear Tyrus cutting me off before I drank myself into a stupor. I wanted to listen to another seemingly pointless and confusing story from Yazmor, and I wanted to hear Hale come up with another odd and vulgar insult.

I slid my eyes closed, trying to conserve what little energy I had. Jay's face stared back at me, fear and anxiety clouding her features, making her look so much younger. I saw myself in her again, the desire to do *anything*.

Had I lost that?

I drew my hands into fists. I had been willing to sacrifice everything I had to save Gunnar. That might have gone badly, but I'd still been willing to do it. I'd had convictions and drive. Where had that gone? In the years since I'd died, had I really turned so complacent that I would just give up?

No.

I shook my head and pressed my hand against the ground to push myself up, but I slipped in a puddle of blood.

I had almost no energy, nothing left to give, but I refused to just roll over and die. Fuck that. I'd died once already and that was *more* than enough for me.

But I also had one shot at this. One chance to get one over on Clint, to get outside and free.

If I could just get outside, I could get myself back to the Chasm. I could dig my fingers into the soil and sink down, escaping from Clint and the others here.

"We'll be out of here by morning," came Clint's voice from outside the shed. Others were here, but I hadn't seen them. I thought it was less to protect their identity and more about Clint wanting to have all the fun himself. "Bitch won't make it another couple hours."

"You get anything useful?" the other man asked.

"She makes pretty noises, but none of 'em told me shit. I bet she's just a pretty face that the Kannors hoped would trick us." The lock outside clicked open just before Clint walked through the door.

He shut the door and put the lock on the inside, just as he had each time before. This time, however, I watched him slide the keys into his pants pocket.

I needed those keys.

Clint crouched down on the balls of his feet, meeting my gaze. He smiled, and it was the sort of smile that reminded me of how much evil could lurk in a person. It was the sort of smile that might have tricked someone when they first met him, one that almost made him seem friendly.

I'd seen the monster beneath, though. When he'd struck me, when he'd dragged a blade over my skin, when he'd wrapped a hand around my throat and squeezed until my vision had wavered, then released only for me to gasp and do it again.

Funny that I'd spent time with the Demon Lords, with the evil creatures who ran what humans would think of as hell, and they didn't have this level of darkness in them. Or, at least they hid it better...

"Look at you." Clint ran his fingers over my cheek, red covering them when he pulled back. His tone held a twisted affection in it, as if he liked me suddenly. "You were so tough before, huh? You talked in that bar like you were dangerous, but look at you now? This is where you belong—this is *how* you belong. Fuck, I even got half a mind to keep you. Could have you like my own little pet, my little songbird who screams for me whenever I want."

And here I'd thought dying was the worst thing that could happen...

I opened my mouth and whispered.

He frowned. "What was that? That you're even still talking is pretty fucking impressive."

I repeated the motion, my voice broken and quiet.

Clint leaned in closer, lines appearing in his forehead as he struggled to make out what I was saying. He brought the side of his face in so close, as if my words mattered.

No doubt, he saw them as something else he wanted to remember, my weak begging, my tearful pleas. I could picture the way he'd remember those later while he jerked off at night.

Well, I didn't plan on being a masturbatory aid for this asshole.

So I pulled together what little strength I still had, building it up with my determination to not die here, to not fail Jay, to keep moving forward. I didn't want this fucker to end me, not here, not now.

I whispered once more, now so close that my breath spilled on his cheek. "Fuck you." As I finished saying it, I threw myself toward him and bit down on the side of his face.

I ignored the warm copper taste that filled my mouth, the way my teeth bit into soft flesh. If I thought about it too much, I might just lose my nerve along with my lunch.

He let out the most pathetic scream, and I felt like I finally understood him better. I fucking *liked* that sound from him. This was how people made friends, right? Shared interests.

I didn't let myself get distracted, though. I kept my jaw locked as I moved my hands. I wrapped one into the front of his shirt so he couldn't easily shove me away while my other wormed into his pocket.

Got them! I grasped the keys and pulled them out just as he managed to land a hit to my stomach.

The pain was sharp—far sharper than any of his other hits. It knocked me away from him, his face a bloody mess, missing a large chunk of his cheek that I spat to the floor. He rose and stumbled around, one of his hands on his face as if to hold himself together, backing away while trying to reorient himself.

I took the chance to throw myself at the door, my hands slipping around the keys from the blood on them. I shoved the key into the lock, but a weight slammed into my back, knocking my breath from me.

"You fucking bitch," he growled into my ear and another pain, this time in my back, made my legs buckle.

At the same time, the lock snapped open. I slid it out and let it fall to the floor, only still on my feet because Clint's body pinned me to the door. I swung my head backward, slamming it into his face.

It hurt, aggravating the spot where I'd gotten hit the first time, but a crunching said I'd nailed my target—his nose. It didn't matter how tough a person was, breaking their nose would make their eyes water and render them fucking useless for at least a minute.

Sure enough, he stumbled backward, so I twisted the handle and fell through the door.

I hit the ground, thankful to find dirt beneath me. Ahead of me, two men stood by a log cabin, their eyes wide as if I was the last thing they'd expected. Then again, they'd thought I was almost dead.

A bit more than almost dead, really.

I nearly laughed at my own stupid joke when they rushed toward me. It probably wasn't actually that funny, and I thought it was only because I dangled so close to passing out. Right, I needed to stay on track, especially because those last two hits from Clint were still such sharp, overwhelming pain that I knew they hadn't been just punches.

He had to have driven a knife into me — twice. The world around me dimmed and brightened, my body stuttering and close to giving up the good fight.

So I buried my fingers in the dirt outside the shed, then closed my eyes. I could have pictured anywhere in the Chasm to go, but my short-circuiting brain made its own choice.

I sank down, connected to the soil, leaving behind the startled shouts of the men. When I pulled in a breath only to find that familiar and oddly comforting smell of brimstone and ash and smoke, I almost smiled.

"Loch?"

A startled masculine voice was the last thing I heard before I passed out.

Tyrus

The snap of power as someone transported into the Chasm just inside the backroom of my bar had me heading that way, prepared to deal with whatever the problem was.

I expected to find Yazmor, ready to tell me about his most recent problem. He often showed up out of the blue in order to drone on about things I couldn't care less about. He was also one of the few people who would dare to transport into my place.

What I didn't expect to find was a small, familiar body covered in blood on the floor, her hands buried in the dirt that Koya left there for when demons delivered goods from Earth to here.

Loch.

I would never fail to recognize her green hair, her lithe frame, not even bathed in red and wounds as she was now.

And yet, my body didn't move, as if frozen by the sight. She let out a whine, the sound so small and pathetic it didn't belong in the Chasm at all. That woke me up and spurred me to action.

I leaned down and lifted her, surprised to find her so light. I hardly noticed anything around me as I took her into the bar from the backroom, past Koya who stared, eyes wide, and into my private quarters at the top of the building. The elevator had never taken so long to make the trek up.

I set her down on my bed, unable to understand what had happened, how she'd been hurt, or why she had come to me. None of it made sense. She was owned by Gorrin, and through their link, he could have healed her far quicker.

Yet...she'd come to me?

"Who did this to you?" I asked, my voice soft as I tried to take inventory of her injuries.

And there were so many of them. I had never thought of Loch as weak, as fragile, but I did then. She had a deep knife wound to her stomach and another in her back, over her left kidney. She had bruises covering her face and her lip had multiple splits in it. Another cut on her eyebrow implied something large and very hard had struck her face.

Numerous small cuts dotted her as well, the marks even enough to tell me they'd been placed purposely. These had not happened from an accident or even from a quick fight. Instead, someone had tortured her, and if she'd suffered it any longer, it would have been the end of her.

And why did that bother me so much?

I'd watched many come through the Chasm, watched most of them suffer and eventually fall once again, and it had never mattered to me. What care did I have for weaklings? If a person could not stand and survive this world on their own, they deserved to perish, and the faster it happened, the better for all involved.

And yet, that normal cynicism was absent when I looked at Loch, when I watched her labored breathing as her body started to knit itself back together. Now in the Chasm, she'd heal faster, able to draw on this realm so her demon blood could restore her to health.

A knock on the door came a moment before Koya peeked his head inside.

"Is she…" He trailed off.

"She'll live." Though, looking at her, that felt almost impossible. How could a person survive what she had gone through? As weak as she appeared, it took great strength to pull oneself back from the edge of that void.

"What happened?"

"I don't know, but I intend to find out." I turned, ready to leave, to track down whoever had *dared* to lay a finger on Loch. She was my…

I didn't know how to finish that statement, wasn't sure there was a way to finish it. She was something, and the anger inside me at seeing her harmed woke an old part of me, one that had slumbered. I acted calmly and rationally at all times. I made my plans not out of anger or emotion, but out of logic.

Yet that logic escaped me now.

Koya stood in my way, blocking my path. "You can't just leave her."

"You think to direct my actions?" Even I heard the threat in my voice.

Koya flinched, but he didn't move. "Other damned might have gotten word about her or seen when you carried her. You think they won't take a shot at her if they can?"

"You're here, are you not?"

"I'm not enough to stop them if they want to get to her. Besides…"

I narrowed my eyes. "Besides what?"

Koya peered past me and to Loch's unconscious form. "I'm pretty sure I'm not the one she wants to see when she wakes up."

I stood tall, ready to grab Koya by his throat, to explain to him the folly of trying to order me about, when a broken whisper from behind me stopped me.

"Tyrus."

I turned to find her eyes squeezed closed, her body trembling as if freezing, and my name falling from her lips like some prayer.

And just like that, Koya won.

I shot him a glare that sent him scurrying out before I returned to her side. I sat on the edge of the bed and ran my fingers through her hair, brushing it from her face, noting the way the green of it mixed with the blood. "Why did you come to me, little demon? You should not trust people — certainly not me."

My warning fell on deaf ears, though, because Loch only seemed to relax at my voice.

I sighed, then went to get a bowl of water and a rag. I could do little for her, but she would certainly feel better if she woke not covered in blood.

And my control of my temper would be aided by the same.

Chapter Nine

"I'm never drinking again," I groaned as I came to.

Normally, I knew my limit. Sure, I occasionally miscalculated it, but I'd gotten old enough to have far fewer of these mornings when I woke up, pounding headache, no memory of the night before and a lot of questions about how I'd ended up where I was.

I opened my eyes, wincing against even the dim glow from a light on the nightstand. I didn't recognize the room at all. It was nice—really fucking nice for the Chasm. I was on a comfortable bed with expensive silk sheets and the softest comforter I'd ever felt.

Five years in hell without waking up in a stranger's bed, yet here I was. I tried to recall the night before, to remember who I might have made such a big mistake with—and given the pain in my body, it had to have been a really fun mistake—but nothing came back to me.

I sat up and turned my head to find the last person I expected.

Sitting in a chair beside the bed, his elbow on the armrest, his head leaning against that hand, Tyrus was fast asleep.

Please tell me I didn't fuck Tyrus...

All those times I'd told myself to forget any feelings I had for that man, each time I'd lectured my hormones to settle the fuck down, they all came back to me.

I moved, ready to walk-of-shame my ass out of there before he woke up, but a pain in my stomach stopped me. I let out a gasp, unable to stop it.

Tyrus snapped his eyes open, the intensity of his gaze making me freeze as if I'd been caught. "You're awake." His voice sounded like it always did, which made this all the weirder.

Then again, Tyrus didn't strike me as the sort of man who fell in love after one hook-up. It would have freaked me out more if he'd started talking to me differently and whispering sweet nothings into my ear.

"Why am I in your bed?" I asked, coming right out and saying it. I could have beat around the bush, acted as if I knew exactly what had happened and didn't care, treated it like an itch that had needed scratching and like I wasn't sorry at all about it.

But my body was too tired and in too much pain for me to carry that on for long.

"You don't remember?"

I shook my head, then realized I wore a large shirt that wasn't mine. It was black and buttoned up the front, and one good look at it made me want to hide my face in embarrassment.

It had to be one of Tyrus' shirts, right?

"You were injured on Earth, and when you transported back to the Chasm, you did so to my backroom."

I swallowed, my throat impossibly dry as I tried to make sense of his story. I doubted he was lying, but it didn't make any sense. I'd been injured?

I thought back. I remembered... The amusement park. I recalled Yazmor, and the way he'd saved that kid. I remembered walking toward the motel.

Clint.

The shed, the blood, it all hit me at once, as if a door had opened and it all poured back into me. I yanked the shirt up to find a large wound on my stomach, the skin already knitting back together, though it was almost black on each side of it from bruising.

I lifted my gaze to find Tyrus staring up at the ceiling, looking awkward.

What the fuck?

"Do you think you could cover yourself?"

His words made me glance down again, and this time I noticed that not only had I pulled up the shirt, but I had nothing on underneath.

Which meant I'd just flashed all my business to a Demon Lord like some drunk sorority girl.

Brilliant.

I yanked the shirt back down, though as soon as I thought about it, I narrowed my eyes. "How did I get into this anyway?"

"I dressed you." Tyrus glanced back at me as if to ensure I'd covered myself. Once he seemed convinced that I'd done it, he looked me in the eye. "You were covered in blood. I couldn't assess your injuries without taking off what was left of your old clothes, then I cleaned you and put you into that."

I tried to picture that but just couldn't.

"Why are you looking at me like that?"

"I'm just having a hard time picturing Nurse Tyrus. You don't strike me as a comfort and care type."

He snorted softly, which made me realize he'd removed his jacket. He still had on a black button up shirt and tie, so he hardly looked relaxed, but it was still more dressed down than I'd ever seen before. "If you'd have rather someone else perform that duty, you should have taken yourself to them instead."

I sat up straighter as I tried to make sense of that. "What do you mean?"

"You chose to come here, to me. Why?"

I thought back to those moments at the end, when I'd dug my fingers into the soil and forced myself back to the Chasm. My head had been a mess, my body in pain and barely moving. "I don't remember exactly," I said, the answer partially true at least.

"What happened?"

"Wrong place, wrong time," I lied.

He shook his head as if he heard the lie loud and clear. "You being targeted is hardly a surprise — your personality alone is enough to make enemies." He went silent after that, as if giving me an out.

Yet…I couldn't keep myself quiet. I considered his question, one I wasn't sure how to answer. In those moments when I transported, when I locked into where I wanted to appear, I picked *here*?

Why?

Sure, I didn't want Gorrin to know about it because that would bring up questions I didn't wish to answer. Still, if I'd gone to my room at Gorrin's place, I would have been safe. Tyrus had no reason to protect or help me, so why did I come here?

"A strange thing can happen during transport," Tyrus said, drawing my attention back to him. "You see, some of the time, if forced to transport when a person is hurt or frightened, they rely more on subconscious thoughts."

"That sounds like some 'manifest positivity' bullshit."

He didn't smile—no, not Tyrus—but his expression did soften just a bit. "I'm serious. From the state you were in, I am going to guess you transported out of instinct."

"So why would I come here?"

"Because somewhere inside of you, you trust me. You were hurt, frightened, knew that returning to the Chasm would expose you to danger that others might use against you, so you took refuge in a place you believed would be safe."

"And I thought *you* were safe?" Even saying that felt like some joke. In all the time I'd known Tyrus, of all the things I thought about him, never had 'safe' been one of them.

Tyrus gestured at the room. "Am I not? I cleaned you, treated your wounds and ensured you were protected from any who would do you harm. Perhaps your subconscious knows something your conscious mind has yet to accept?" With that, he stood, then slid on his jacket, which had been slung over the back of the chair.

As he buttoned it, it felt as if he were sliding back into a role I knew, the him I'd seen before, and the softness I'd witnessed when I'd woken disappeared.

Which was the real him?

* * * *

I woke with a gasp, the memory of that fucking blade dragging against my skin so strong that for a moment, I thought I was right back in that shed.

I sat up, and even the horrible tugging in my stomach where the healing injury was couldn't sink through the phantom pains.

"Easy." Tyrus' voice accompanied his large hand against my back, helping to support my weight.

I curled forward, hanging my head and taking a deep breath to try and calm myself. Tyrus went from just supporting me to rubbing that hand against my back, the touch far more relaxing than it should have been.

"Nightmare?"

I let out a hollow laugh. "Nah, not me. Do I look like the sort of person who thinks deeply enough to let things like trauma affect me?"

"Judging from that whimper you let out, I would guess so." His hand never stopped those gentle motions before he asked softly, "Are you ready to tell me what happened?"

"Nothing worth talking about," I said. "Ran into some trouble and was lucky enough to get outside to get back here."

"Outside?"

"Yeah, to soil…"

He let out a soft breath and the bed shifted as he sat beside me. "Yazmor told me a trick in the past. When I first became a Demon Lord, he said to always keep a handful of soil in each pocket, so if I were ever on Earth and found myself in a bad position, I would have a way out."

"You're telling me Yazmor walks around with sand in his pockets?" I paused, then let out an actual laugh as I sat up. "You know, as soon as I said that, I realized how stupid a question it is. Of course Yazmor keeps sand in his pockets. That's probably the least weird thing he keeps there."

"That is true. Once he pulled a squid from his pocket and told me it was named Bob."

"You're here all the time. Didn't think you ever went to Earth."

"I don't much anymore. I prefer to set up my affairs so others do such work. Still, I've always recalled that advice from Yazmor. In fact, I'm surprised he didn't tell you that himself."

"He probably did. He gave me a huge book when I first arrived, but after the first page which had crudely drawn pictures of all the Demon Lords naked, I decided I didn't need to venture any farther."

Tyrus snorted, the sound oddly unsettled from him. It wasn't with normal derision, but rather out of surprise. "I would ask if you were kidding but knowing Yazmor as I do, I am certain you are serious. Please tell me you destroyed the book?"

"Nope. It is safe and sound for future blackmail."

Tyrus made a soft sound in the back of his throat. "Isn't that cunning of you? I look forward to your negotiation in the future." He removed his hand from my back, then asked, "Are you feeling better?"

"Yeah, I am. Thanks." As soon as I said that, unease hit me. "But I'm sure you've got other things to do than babysit me. You're busy, after all."

"I have gotten my affairs in order so I have some free time. What sort of Demon Lord can't even take a few days off when needed? Don't worry yourself so much."

I swallowed hard at his kind tone, unsure how to deal with it.

"Unless you would prefer I leave? Perhaps my presence makes it more difficult for you to rest…"

Before he could pull away—and I was sure he would—I blurted out a response I hadn't really thought about. "Don't go."

Tyrus tilted his head, his dark eyes narrowed.

"I might have another not-at-all-a-nightmare."

Tyrus' cheek twitched, as close to a smile as I'd ever seen from him, and sat beside me on the bed again. "Then I will stay."

Silence settled between us, and my eyelids grew heavy again. However, I couldn't seem to quite fall asleep. "Tell me a story," I asked.

"I am not a bedtime story person."

"I'm sure you can come up with one."

He let out a long-suffering sigh, but it didn't sound like a no. "Fine, but lie down and close your eyes." When I did so, he went on. "Once upon a time, there was a princess who was supposed to wed the son of a distant king. The problem was that the girl was stubborn and wild and had no intention of bowing to her father's wishes."

Tyrus' words soothed me, and even as he told the story, it was his tone that really eased me, the steady rhythm lulling me back to sleep.

I never figured I'd feel this comfortable, and even if I wasn't sure I could trust him, even as I remembered every red flag crammed into him, I couldn't help but drift off beside him.

I really am fucking stupid, aren't I?

* * * *

That throbbing in my head started up, and this time, it wasn't due to Clint or what had happened. Instead, it was the familiar summoning from Gorrin.

I'd spent two days in Tyrus' room healing, and I finally felt back to my old self.

Well, mostly.

I wasn't as fast, and moving much hurt, but that was still miles ahead of the first day when Tyrus had offered to help me to the bathroom.

Tyrus had returned to bring me food at each meal and had spent more time than I expected in the room. In fact, I'd found an odd comfort in him being there, in him working at the desk in the room even if he didn't speak much to me.

I'd considered what he'd said, that I'd gone to him because I felt safe, and the more time I spent in his bed, the more I worried he might have had a point.

I groaned as the pain worsened, telling me I hadn't gotten moving fast enough.

Tyrus shifted his gaze to me, that intensity telling me he heard. "Pain?"

"Yeah, a pain in my ass." I pulled myself from the bed, wincing as I realized my abs still hurt. As it turned out, muscles didn't like knitting back together all that much.

Tyrus was beside me in a moment, a strong, steady arm around me. It made me send him a glare. How was I supposed to deal with behavior like this? Tyrus should know to behave like the evil devil he was instead of acting sweet.

He glanced down at my back with a frown. "Did you fall?"

Fall?

Him entirely missing my sarcasm was almost endearing as I realized his confusion. "The pain in my ass is Gorrin," I explained.

His face went carefully blank, but he nodded. "He's summoning you?"

"Yep. Guess my vacation is over." I pulled away from him, his touch too warm, too tempting. "I give this place four stars. Good food, good protection, but the screams of the damned in the middle of the night were distracting."

He turned around, giving me his back when I reached for the buttons of the shirt of his I wore. "Being upset about that while living in the Chasm is like living by the beach and hating the smell of the ocean."

"You could laugh just once, you know?" I stripped the shirt off, then reached for the outfit he'd gotten for me the day before that he'd left on the dresser. I never figured I'd manage to feel comfortable enough around Tyrus to strip naked, yet here we were.

Somehow, despite that serious way he could stare at me, and that I knew exactly how dangerous he was, he'd treated me almost kindly. Nurse Tyrus was alive and well as it turned out.

The clothing he'd gotten me wasn't what he would have *ever* picked out for me, and that fact made me smile. No doubt, if he'd gone with his wishes, he'd have put me in some fitted dress or a badass suit that made me look like some mafia queen. I, of course, would have hated those options.

Instead, he'd brought a basic loose T-shirt and a pair of gray sweats. He'd given me underwear as well, and I swore up and down that I wouldn't blush at how he'd not only gotten them for me but that he'd managed to pick the exact right size.

And these were *far* more his style. The bra and panties were made of expensive silk along with lace detail, and I couldn't deny the slight thrill of feeling that cool fabric against my skin.

Once I'd finished dressing, keeping the waist of the sweats low enough to not bother the still tender flesh from where Clint had tried to skewer me, I took a deep breath. "Decent," I said.

Tyrus turned back toward me, moving his gaze over me slowly. He peered at the now empty bed and his lips tipped down.

The expression was strange on his normally stoic face. It almost looked like…longing?

That didn't make sense to me, though, and if I said it, it would only piss him off. Instead, I opened my mouth to thank him for everything he'd done. Before I could say a word, however, another wave of that same old pain hit me, causing me to stumble.

And yet again, Tyrus managed to be by my side, his hand on my arm to steady me so fast, I didn't notice him moving. Was he really *that* tuned in to me?

And did I really want a Demon Lord like him tuned in to me?

"You should go," he said, though his tone implied he didn't perhaps love that idea. Still, he pulled away once I'd regained my footing. "He will only continue to summon you and the longer it takes, the more difficult walking will become. Let's go."

"Let's? As in, both of us?"

"I kept you alive these last few days — I won't allow you to get targeted now, on your way back. That would render all my work useless."

I wanted to argue with that, but he wasn't wrong. Judging from the slowness of my steps, I couldn't deny that I wasn't up to par when it came to dealing with any problems I might encounter, and no one would fuck with me if Tyrus escorted me.

The walk was quiet and more than a little awkward. Tyrus matched my pace, no doubt for my own benefit since his longer legs meant he probably walked faster.

When we approached the large building where Gorrin resided, the tension between Tyrus and I only grew.

What was I supposed to say?

We paused just outside the main gate—Tyrus wouldn't dare to enter Gorrin's personal residence without good reason. Things like that could get taken as insults and no one needed any more violence here.

"Thanks," I said but kept my gaze down, unsure how to face him. When he didn't speak, I kept talking as if that would make it any better. "For taking care of me and not killing me and not letting anyone else kill me."

His fingers caught my chin and lifted my gaze until I stared at him. "You should have chosen me."

Those words caught me off guard and I wasn't sure how to respond. Hadn't I chosen him when I'd been hurt?

He stroked his thumb along my jawline, the touch reminding me of a few times when I'd woken to find his fingers running through my hair, the touch oddly gentle. "You should have made the deal with me, not with Gorrin. I don't like that he has you, that you are bound to him. I find it…distasteful." The way he said the last word said he didn't care for admitting it, either.

Though, his words finally made sense. We were talking about five years ago, back when I'd had to pick one of them to make the deal with. I hadn't known any of them, had only met them for a few minutes before I had to make that far-reaching choice.

I'd picked Gorrin because he'd seemed the safest, like the one who considered a deal the most businesslike.

I hadn't known what I was doing back then, and I couldn't say I'd make the same choice if I had to today.

"We're past that, aren't we?" I asked. "There isn't much I can do about it now."

"Normally, I'd purchase your soul, but Gorrin won't sell. I've known him for too long to expect that. For whatever reason, you are in high demand, little demon. Still, I hate that he can summon you, that no matter what happens, you will always be connected to him, that he will always own a part of you I can't touch." Tyrus came closer, not releasing me, until his breath warmed my forehead. Was he going to kiss me? Would he cross that line?

What did I feel about that?

I had no idea…

I didn't need to know, however, because another wave of pain hit me, disturbing our conversation.

Tyrus sighed, then released me and stepped backward. "You need to go."

"Thank you for taking care of me," I said again.

"Don't thank me for that."

"Why not?"

He let out a sound that was almost a laugh despite holding no humor. "You are too trusting, Loch. You take a moment of selfishness from me, an attempt to get closer to you, to get under your skin, and you thank me for it. Do not forget that people only do the things that benefit them personally. Never mistake greed for kindness—especially from me." Tyrus nodded sharply at me, then turned on his heel and walked away, leaving me there in the darkness at the gate, unable to make sense of him or my own feelings.

Then that pain made me stumble again and I remembered that I couldn't exactly ignore Gorrin any longer.

Time to go face the devil...

Chapter Ten

It felt like I hadn't seen Gorrin in months.

It hadn't been that long, but so much had happened that it seemed longer. He looked the same as always—serious and rather annoyed.

Or maybe that was simply how he looked when he dealt with me.

He had his hair pulled back as usual and some strange part of me wanted to see him with it down, to see him let go and relax.

That's going to happen about fucking never...

"You haven't been in the Chasm in days." Gorrin didn't beat around the bush as he directly brought up his point.

"I'm still working on the deal you asked me to take care of."

"Really?" The way he asked that implied he didn't come close to believing me.

Still, I stood tall, holding in the way I hurt, the way the walk had jostled my still sore and healing body. I didn't want him finding out about that, didn't need him looking into any of it. If he realized I'd gotten hurt, he'd want to know how it had happened.

I nodded to sell my story. "Yep. I think she's close to accepting since we're nearing the deadline. Besides, you're always saying I should spend more time on Earth, aren't you?"

"Yes, I have said that, but I've suggested it so you can make deals of your own. You haven't done that, so far as I can tell. How exactly have you been spending your time on Earth?" His golden eyes locked on me, as if digging deep into me and picking my words apart.

"I've been reacquainting myself so I can be more useful. Five years is a long time away."

He narrowed his eyes, a sure sign he didn't come close to buying my bullshit. It was too bad Gorrin wasn't a lot stupider—it would make my life easier.

"Well, if that's it, I think I'll go rest." By which I meant I needed to get my ass to my room where I could stretch out and whimper in peace and quiet.

Except, when I went to turn, Gorrin moved forward so fast that I nearly stumbled in surprise. He pressed his hand to my stomach, somehow finding the exact spot where the knife had gone into me.

I cried out, the sound pathetic and weak but impossible to hold in. My knees gave in, but I didn't collapse to the floor. Instead, I found Gorrin's strong body holding me up.

"You thought you could hide this from me?" he asked, his tone vibrating with an anger I wasn't used to from him. He was always so calm and collected, which meant seeing that mask slip for a moment startled me.

I tried to pull away, to escape the intensity of his look, but that didn't help. Gorrin reached down and slid an arm behind my knees, then lifted me against his chest.

I was used to feeling small compared to the men I spent time around, but never had I felt *quite* so outmatched as I did right then.

"Be still," he snapped, the order like a warning in my head, one I couldn't stand against.

He walked slowly, so careful that he didn't jostle me. He didn't go toward the front door, the one that led to the hallway then my room. Instead, he went back toward a door that I had never gone through.

He flicked his fingers and the door opened for him automatically, then he kicked it closed with his heel after walking through.

A glance around let me know where I was.

His bedroom.

Which was the *last* place I ever wanted or planned to be.

He set me down on a huge bed, though the blankets were so perfect that I struggled to believe anyone ever slept on it.

Especially because the thought of Gorrin sleeping seemed impossible. He was far too wary and paranoid to let his guard down to sleep, right?

He didn't ask for permission or hesitate before he grabbed the hem of my shirt and pulled the fabric up and over my head. His gaze lacked any heat, surveying me as a vet might a dog.

That's better, right?

"What happened?"

"Nothing."

"Tell me what happened." He dropped his voice, the demand thundering against the insides of my skull as my entire being wanted to obey.

Except I couldn't. If I told him the Sand Snakes had done this to me, he'd figure out I was trying to save Brendon, and if he did that...

Well, Gorrin was ruthless when it came to those who stood in his way. I didn't want to receive that same treatment.

So I resisted, reaching up to grasp the sides of my head as if that might dull the pain.

Gorrin crouched in front of me and set his hands on the outside of mine, angling my face toward him until I looked him in the eyes. "Tell me," he pressed, though an odd hint of desperation wavered in his voice.

Still, I resisted. I refused to give in, not even to him, not if it meant Jay's future.

After another moment, he let out a low, angry sound and the pain disappeared. Had he stopped it? Had he removed that order? Why?

"You were seriously injured, and you didn't come back to me?" He didn't release me, his hands warm and large as they held me. "I could have healed you in a few hours, but you failed to even tell me?"

I pressed my lips together, not sure how to answer that. It was true, but I had a feeling he wouldn't like anything I had to say.

Gorrin released me, but he didn't back away. Instead, he moved the tips of his fingers over my face, the touch unfailingly gentle. "They have mostly healed, but I can still see each injury. Bruising here, a cut at the eyebrow, more at your lip. Your nose was broken, as well." He stroked over each place, deep lines etched into the space between his eyebrows as if my injuries hurt him.

He didn't stop at my face, though. Instead, he kept drifting down, over my throat, my collarbones, finding each mark I thought were nearly invisible now. "More bruising here—someone grasped your throat. Cuts from a blade, here and here and here and…" His voice trailed off for a moment, as if he realized there were more than he could point out easily. "Bruising here—internal bleeding." He shifted behind me, setting one hand on my shoulder to hold me still. I jumped at the touch of his fingers on my back, the feeling more intimate because I couldn't see him. "A stab here, damaging to the kidney. This would have killed you if you had been a human or even damned." He moved to the front again, to the last place, the one that still showed the most damage and discoloration. "And another stab wound here. It looks like two days' worth of healing here in the Chasm." He paused as his fingers drifted over the closed wound there. "Which means you did return to the Chasm, simply not to me. But to who?"

I didn't answer—I wouldn't repay Tyrus' help by throwing him under the Demon Lord-sized bus that was Gorrin.

Gorrin tilted his head, that gleam in his golden eyes betraying just how clever he was. "You would go to Yazmor for minor problems—you two are odd friends, after all. However, he is not the most trustworthy, so if you were seriously harmed, you wouldn't go to him. Hale is likewise problematic, because he runs on instinct, and if you were hurt, he would focus more on who had done it and retribution than you. You wouldn't go to a damned nor a demon owned by anyone else because that would be the same as going to the Demon Lord themselves. It leaves Tyrus as the only choice."

I didn't tell him he'd guessed right, but I didn't really need to, did I? He'd read the situation perfectly, able to figure it out without me saying a word.

He sighed when I didn't speak. "Am I so terrible that you would risk your life just to avoid coming to me for help? Have I mistreated you so badly that you believe I wouldn't heal and protect you?"

I opened my mouth, but nothing came out. I wasn't afraid of him exactly, but I also didn't trust him.

"Just say what you want to say." He kept his voice flat, as if not wanting to give me any additional reason to worry. "I will not be angry or punish you no matter what you tell me. Just be honest."

Honest, huh?

Yeah, it was easy to tell someone to just be honest, but that felt like a lion opening its mouth and asking me to floss for him while assuring me he wouldn't bite. *Easier said than done.*

Yet, his imploring look got me to answer. "You have an idea of what you think is best and you don't listen to me—you don't hear me. What I think doesn't matter to you because you're so sure you're always right."

"I am far older than you, have done and seen far more. Do you truly believe I might not know better than you?"

"Not always. You might be old as dirt but that doesn't mean you're perfect. And what's best for *you* isn't what's best for me. You've never taken the time to get to know me at all, to know anything about me, so how can you know what I want or need?"

"You believe I don't know you?" It was impossible to miss the frustration in his voice. After a moment, he rose but didn't look at me directly. "Lie flat, please. I'll finish healing your wounds."

The distant quality of his voice made me uneasy, but I did as he asked. It was when I realized how uncomfortable it was to wear so little in front of him.

He sat on the side of the bed, his gaze landing on my bra. "I don't like you wearing items from *him*." Even as he said it, he didn't ask me to remove the items, didn't tear them. Instead, he set his hand on my stomach and a warmth washed through me.

Just being in the Chasm had sped my healing, but since he owned my soul, he could do far more. At least, that was my understanding. It wasn't as if many folks in the Chasm would use their power to help those beneath them.

"You hate me."

I jerked my gaze up to his, but Gorrin didn't look at me. Instead, he remained focused on where he healed me.

Even still, he kept speaking, his voice quiet. "You like to drink, but you hold your liquor well. You sleep poorly, but you don't like to admit that, so you pretend that you don't suffer from nightmares. You sleep with a blue stuffed whale named Whalebert Von Bubbles, and you returned to Earth to get him your first week here. You want to be heartless, and you act as if you are, but the truth is that your compassion will likely end up killing you — again. I have spent every day since you came here in fear that that day would be the one when that softness you have ends you, and worse? The thing that draws me to you is the same thing that threatens you."

I stared up at him even as he avoided my gaze. Was he proving that he knew me? That despite my accusation, despite me claiming he knew nothing about me, he actually had been paying attention the entire time?

It made me frown as I thought back on all our conversations over the past five years, all the times I'd thought he'd paid me no mind. I'd treated him as my enemy from jump, assuming he saw me the same way. His words showed that to not be true.

But why? Why would he notice any of that? Why give a damn about what I drank or how I felt?

He pulled his hand back, which drew my gaze down to my front. All that discoloration was gone, my body looking as if the ordeal had never happened. I sat up to find no pain at all, none of that tightness or that deep ache.

Maybe he was right—I should have come here first. The two days I'd spent in pain suddenly seemed like pointless suffering now.

"You should rest," he said as he stood. "I healed you, but you still need time and sleep to recover all your strength." He turned to leave, as if we had finished our conversation.

But...I didn't feel finished. I wanted to remain in this quiet moment with him, a time when I could see a part of him I'd never noticed before. I couldn't say it wasn't there before, so much as I'd just never taken the time to look.

I didn't know what to say, though, so I let him go, sitting there in his room only to realize that while he might know about me—I knew nothing about him.

* * * *

I tried to sleep, but despite the exhaustion that hung on me, my rest was fitful at best. Within two hours, I gave up the fight. Maybe it was everything that had happened, or maybe it was my lack of a plan, or maybe it was my talk with Gorrin, but I couldn't get my brain to settle. So I gave up and pulled the shirt I'd worn before back on. Walking around in just my bra was generally a bad idea, but even worse given the awkwardness between Gorrin and me.

I left his bedroom, expecting to find him working as usual. There were few times I came here when I didn't find Gorrin engaged in some part of his work. He was usually staring into the well that showed him Earth or going through files.

Perhaps that was why not finding him right away caught me off guard. It took a moment for me to spot him on the couch where I usually sat. He had stretched out lengthwise with his head on the armrest.

Was he asleep?

I approached him slowly, my steps light to keep them silent. He looked different somehow, relaxed in a way I'd never seen before. Those far too intelligent eyes of his were closed, which instantly decreased his level of intimidation. His mouth was relaxed rather than pulled into the unhappy line he always wore around me. In fact, I'd had no idea he could look so…soft.

He'd removed his jacket, instead in just pants and a white shirt. He still wore his boots, which struck me as odd. Gorrin seemed like the type of person to get angry about shoes being on furniture. Was that a sign of just how tired he was?

I stopped when I was just beside him and he still hadn't moved, hadn't opened his eyes or said a thing to me. His chest rose and fell, which told me he lived, but the entire thing freaked me out. Seeing him downright vulnerable was beyond strange.

I reached out and poked him hard in the cheek, then jumped backward like teasing a snake.

He snapped his eyes open, taking in his surroundings quickly but without panic. It was the sort of thing I wished I could do.

He sat up, frowning as he spotted me. It took a moment for him to speak as if he worked through what had just happened. "Did you poke me?"

"Now that you say it out loud, I feel like I should say no…"

"Yes. Perhaps poking Demon Lords is not the wisest thing you have ever done. Or, knowing you, it might be."

"Were you sleeping?"

"I don't sleep."

"But you lie down? And close your eyes? And become unconscious?" When he nodded, I lifted my eyebrow. "But that's not sleeping. Sure."

He blew out a slow breath, then shook his head. "I don't sleep, but at times when my power is low, I do rest in order to recover more quickly."

"Why was your power low—" As soon as I asked, the answer became obvious.

He'd healed me. I'd never seen him do it before, had no idea what it entailed, but apparently it took a lot out of him.

"Why would you heal me if it hurt you?"

"It doesn't harm me—it simply takes a portion of my powers until I rest."

"But you have so many souls bound to you. How can that be worse than anything else you do?"

"Healing is not a normal use for the sort of power I have accumulated. It requires more of it."

Which meant he'd known it would weaken him like this? And he'd done it anyway? That made him seem like a person instead of the one-dimensional character I'd grown used to, the one villain I got to blame for everything wrong in my life.

Which meant I didn't really appreciate seeing him in a different light.

I frowned, unsure how to react. Should I stay here? Should I leave him to rest? Should I watch over him?

Unable to walk away when he was in this state because of helping me, I sighed and moved his legs until I could sit on the couch. He sat up straighter, peering at me as if unsure what to do.

"Stop making this weird," I snapped, then pulled at his arm until he stretched out again, this time setting his head in my lap. The position was strange, and far too comfortable with Gorrin, but it felt like the only thank you my emotionally stunted ass could come up with.

He'd taken the time and effort to heal me, to protect me, so this was the least I could do, right?

And, funny enough, when he didn't move, when he didn't tell me off for the overly familiar position, I started to relax. Before I knew it, my eyelids grew heavy and I drifted off, his even breathing like a sleep sound that relaxed me enough to finally rest.

Gorrin

Would I ever understand Loch? Five years into knowing her, five years since I'd won the rights to her soul, and she remained an unknown to me.

I stared up at her sleeping face, surprised that she'd let her guard down around me in this way. Was that proof of a budding trust between us or was it simply a sign of her own exhaustion?

I sat up, craving a better look at her. For once, she didn't stare at me with distrust, didn't pull away or flinch when I came near.

Why did I care about that? Why did this person draw me in like this and make me question myself?

I didn't understand—after all the time I'd spent unmoved by others, here I was with this pain in my chest, one that sat deep inside me and ached like a bruise that never healed.

Her green hair had soft curls in it, ones that made her appear younger than her actual age. The tattoos on her cheeks, though, they surprised me as they had that first day when I'd met her. The angel wing on one side and the demon wing on the other felt oddly topical now, like some piece of fate that had marked her before she'd ever known why.

I'd asked her why she'd picked those and there, but she'd gotten defensive and given me a lie. I stroked my thumb over her cheek, following the lines of that small angel wing. Her skin was warm and impossibly soft, which made me narrow my eyes.

This attraction was foolish and dangerous—for us both.

Despite knowing it was one-sided, that she would never feel the same affinity toward me, I had no idea how to break the chain.

Of course, if she ever realized the truth, if she understood everything I'd done, she would hate me even more.

I'd thought I'd grown used to that role by now. Unfortunately, I couldn't bring myself to view it with the disinterest I always had before. The idea of her looking at me with that same hate and fear I found intolerable.

"I'm sorry," I whispered, my voice low to ensure she didn't wake. She still needed more rest to finish recovering, to gain her strength back. A selfish part of me also wanted to hold on to this moment as long as I could, and it would shatter the moment she woke.

So instead, I admitted the truth to her, only now when she couldn't hear me, when I could let my guard down. "You have already gone through so much, suffered so much, but there is so much more yet to come. Rest now, little fish, while you can. I will keep the devils at bay, at least for a while."

She shifted, but I couldn't tell if it was because my voice soothed or upset her. Instead of worrying about it—what did it matter?—I leaned in and stole something I didn't deserve, something she'd never allow, but something I couldn't resist.

I brushed my lips against hers, so gently to ensure she continued to sleep, allowing myself to sink into that softness for just a moment. I didn't have to be a Demon Lord, didn't have to rule the Chasm, didn't have to be anything other than what I wanted to be. I indulged in this moment because I knew I could never have it again, never have it for real. There were no deals to be made to attain what I wanted, which made Loch the one thing out of my reach.

And the only thing I had ever truly wanted.

Chapter Eleven

"Surprised to see you here." Gunnar's expression—the widening of his eyes and the tightness in his jaw—backed up his words.

"Why? Aren't you supposed to help me?" I pushed past him and into his apartment. We'd known each other for too long and too well for us to stand on any sort of ceremony.

Besides, once a person is at fault for getting me killed, they lose the right to things like privacy.

"Heard some rumors—the Sand Snakes were all hyped up over catching some spy. Figured that had to be you."

"And you clearly cared so much." I waved Gunnar's false concern off. No doubt he'd heard about it and shrugged.

"What did you expect? For me to come rushing in to help?"

I snorted at his question. That was something, wasn't it? That I'd grown beyond the naive little girl I'd been before, the one who still thought people were generally good. I didn't expect shit from him or anyone else, so when he fell spectacularly short of basic decency, it didn't even hurt. "I know you way too well by now to expect anything like that. As you can see, I didn't need a rescue."

I could hold my hands out and show off like that because of Tyrus and Gorrin. Between the two of them, I was back to my old self—totally healed. In fact, due to the state I'd been in when I escaped, the Sand Snakes probably assumed I was dead.

Sure, the whole disappearing in front of them probably freaked them out, but people like Clint probably did enough drugs that they were used to seeing weird shit they couldn't explain some of the time.

"I can take care of myself," I told him. "I'm not the same girl I used to be."

"Clearly. Girl I knew could keep herself alive, but she liked to hide in the background. Never figured you'd show up here again, looking like you're about to take this on all by yourself. You were always the one telling me to stay out of this shit, to keep my head down, and yet here you are."

"There are bigger things at play right now than power. That was the problem before—all you gave a damn about was getting power. You played these stupid games for no good reason. It wasn't worth the risk back then."

"But it is now?"

"Now there are two kids at risk."

"Two?" He tilted his head, as if he didn't understand. Then he went still and let out a laugh. "That's it, ain't it? Took me a while to figure out why you came back, why you'd give a damn, but I get it now. Girl sold her soul to save her brother, right? And you're here to make that happen."

Wrong. How was it that Gunnar could manage to get that close to the truth but still miss it entirely?

Because he's always been a short-sighted idiot who never cared to really know me at all.

Still, it was as good an excuse as any. "You know how it works," I said. "I mean, you sold your soul, right?"

"Just how is it you know that? Been wondering since you said it before, since people don't go around admitting that shit or talking about it."

"I'm better connected than you think. Rumors spread fast where I've been."

"And where is that? Did you take your second chance and hide out in the middle of nowhere? Live some nice little fake-ass life until you got called back by whatever small-shot you made your deal with? I mean, they had to be small or why would they leave this task to *you*?"

His words might have hurt if I respected him or cared about his opinion in the least. Thankfully, I didn't, so his words were as useless as the rest of him.

I shrugged. "Just lucky, I guess." Silence fell between us, and eventually it got to me. As much as I hated asking him for anything, I needed to. The prize was worth even going to Gunnar. After a long sigh, I turned and faced him head on. "I need to look at that book about the Kannors again."

"Why's that?" The way his lips tipped up into a smirk said he enjoyed this *far* too much.

"I'm at a standstill, and I'm running out of time. I need a new angle, and to do that, I need more information." I lifted my eyebrow, then added on for good measure, "And Charles *did* order you to help me. I could always talk to him if you don't like that order anymore."

He made a sound that said he knew I was manipulating him before he left the room for a minute. When he returned, he had that same book in his hands. He gestured at the couch, then handed me the book once I'd sat. "Your whole 'cozy up to the Sand Snakes' not panning out?" The way he said it screamed that he knew I'd gotten nothing. He was the exact sort of asshole who would enjoy needling me about failure.

"They were a lot less willing to part with information than I expected." I kept it vague, not wanting to share anything I didn't need to. "Didn't figure some drunken motorcycle gang would have such diligent members."

"If you'd bothered to ask me, I would have told you that much. They don't trust outsiders, and they sure as hell don't tell shit to women."

"Like you'd have told me anything."

"Sure I would have. In case you forget, this affects *my* employer. If Charles gets himself into a bad place with this, it'll be my ass, too. I want this all resolved at least as badly as you do."

"So why haven't you done any of this? Last I checked, it doesn't seem like you've made any sort of progress. You've been sitting on your ass this whole time. Either you're inept or you're not trying that hard."

He set his arm over the back of the couch and stared at me, his gaze too familiar. Why was it that even after knowing exactly the sort of person he was, he could still make me question myself? Something about those eyes took me back to when I'd believed we had a future, when I'd thought we were meant to be like some fate-bound pair. Sure, I knew he was a fuckwit now, but back then?

I missed that certainty, even if it had been a lie.

I turned my focus to the book—that was the important thing right now. I opened it and flipped to the information about Brendon.

Again, I was hit by how normal he appeared on those pages. It was hard to think that he was afraid right now, that so many lives rested on his fate. He didn't look like that, though. Instead, the picture made him look like any kid, like the embarrassing school picture that parents liked to show off to aunts and uncles no matter how much the kid complained.

I ran my finger along the words printed neatly on the pages behind the image. They were far more extensive than I'd have expected, but given the power the family wielded, I suppose it shouldn't have surprised me.

He enjoyed playing video games—the sorts with lots of building. He didn't seem to have many friends, at least beyond those he interacted with for the sake of his father. The notes talked about him spending time on his own, about him reading and disappearing into stories instead of dealing with the rest of the world.

I frowned as I realized how blind I'd been. I'd walked into this, heard Jay's story, and thought only about her. I'd rushed into it all without taking the time to get to know Brendon at all.

Yazmor's lesson came back to me about not looking at the big picture, about getting focused on tiny bits so much as to miss the important stuff.

"Even if we get the kid back, he's got a rough life ahead of him," Gunnar said.

"What do you mean? Kid with his pedigree has his future all worked out already."

"Sure, but fitting into those shoes won't be easy. I've been around long enough to be able to take one look at a person and know if they can deal with the stresses of power. Charles can, for example. He can make the hard choices, do the things that normal people can't. Brendon, though? Kid is too soft, too gentle. This world is gonna chew that kid up until there's nothing left."

Looking at the picture and information in front of me, I struggled to deny it. "Weird to think that such a sweet kid could come from a man like Charles."

"Just happens that way. Honestly? His sister would be a way better choice for taking over. Too bad they're all still caught up with what's between a person's legs, as if that's all that fucking matters. Fuck, it'd be better if they just let her marry someone who can hold the family together and let 'em run it as a pair. They're gonna take the Kannor family down with this ass-backwards sort of thinking. Won't need any help from others."

"If you care, then why aren't you doing more to get Brendon back? Because I've seen you work hard before, and this sure as hell isn't it."

He exhaled slowly, the way he pursed his lips making me think he was imagining having a cigarette right now. He knew how much I hated smoke — was that why he didn't light up around me?

No. There was no way he gave a fuck about what I liked.

"I've tried," Gunnar said. "I've been working my contacts since it happened, trying to pick up a trail. I ain't the same idiot I once was who went off half-cocked. That's what got you killed in the first place. Now I take my time and do the work needed. Fact is that the Sand Snakes make this really fucking hard because they don't have set up places like most gangs. They ain't got the same roots to follow. It makes it a hell of a lot harder to track them down. Given you haven't had any more success than me, are you really in any place to question me?"

I wanted to argue that *I* hadn't been in this world for the past five years like he had, that I was entirely behind him in terms of information, but what was the point?

Maybe he was right. Maybe he did give a damn about Brendon, and I just didn't see any of it from the outside?

Or maybe Gunnar was the same self-centered asshole he'd always been, and he didn't think Brendon was useful and might even be a threat to the Kannors.

I couldn't put anything past Gunnar.

Instead of answering, I kept reading the information in the book. Brendon didn't seem to be a behavioral issue. I didn't see much in the way of trouble at school or big incidents. He seemed healthy, though in the medical area I frowned at how he had appointments every three months.

No one needed checkups every three months unless they had an illness, right? Of course, illnesses weren't the sort of thing a family like the Kannors would let people know about.

"What are these appointments for?" I pointed at the book.

Gunnar scooted closer so he could read where I gestured, but the action pressed him against my side.

He didn't notice it at all before he tapped at the line of appointments. "Asthma."

"He has asthma?" I noticed that part wasn't listed anywhere in the notes.

"Yeah—pretty bad case of it. We've got a shit load of purifiers in the house to help out—managed to get him to the point where he almost never needs his rescue inhaler."

"Did he have his inhaler with him when he was abducted?"

Gunnar paused, then shook his head once as if that hadn't occurred to him. "No, I don't think so. Because it's been so well under control, he doesn't carry it with him, especially at home."

I thought about that, recalling the Sand Snakes I'd met, the way they'd acted in that bar. Brendon had a great set up at home, but I highly doubted they had the same sort of purifiers wherever they were keeping him. Things like dust, mites and pollen could set Brendon off—along with the stress of abduction.

That would mean they'd need an inhaler, right? That wasn't the sort of thing they could grab at a corner store.

There were only so many pharmacies around that worked under the table, with pharmacists willing to break the rules for a bit of extra money.

I got to my feet, finally feeling energized again. If I could just find the right pharmacy, the right worker, I finally had a line.

"Did you just work something out?" Gunnar asked but didn't rise, just staring at me with that old intensity that made me feel as if he understood me better than I liked.

"I've got a plan."

"What's your plan?"

I shook my head. "Not a fucking chance. I don't trust you well enough to tell you anything."

"Ouch," he muttered as he rose as well, standing so close to me that I struggled to separate years ago from now. "We've got a long history, you and me. You really think you need to keep your guard up like this around me?"

His words might have melted me, but I remembered him in that bar, selling his soul for his own benefit while calling me convenient.

"I don't know what you're talking about," I said, my voice carefully blank. "I mean, I'm nothing to you. Just a convenient hole, right?"

His eyes widened a moment before I shoved the book at him. Clearly, he remembered his conversation, and now he knew I'd seen it, too. At least those words, mirrored back to him, silenced him as I turned around and walked out.

He'd broken my heart once. I wasn't stupid enough to give him a chance to do it a second time.

* * * *

"Loch!" The excited shout came only a moment before someone threw themselves against me, wrapping their arms around me and hugging me tightly.

The new me, the one who had spent the past five years surviving in the Chasm, wanted to yank away. Being this close to someone felt like an open invitation for them to drive a knife into my back.

Seeing as Clint had already done that recently, I was over getting stabbed.

However, the old me, the one who had known this woman, returned the hug.

"Kylie," I said, a surprising amount of affection in my voice. I gave in to the urge, to the way I wanted to pretend like no time had passed, that I was still the same girl I'd been before.

"I thought you were dead." She clung to me tightly, clear evidence of how much she'd missed me.

But that was the reality when someone died, I guess. Most people couldn't come back as I could, which meant those left behind had to handle the grief of loss alone. It was strange to think about it, given I knew dead wasn't *dead* the way people thought about it.

"Sorry," I said as I pulled back. I wished I could tell her everything, that I could explain what had happened and why, but I knew better.

Humans didn't deal well with the truth, with the reality of life and the afterlife and the hopelessness of it all. It tended to ruin their lives nearly as much as selling their soul did.

"What happened?" she pressed.

"I had some people after me." I used the lie I'd already come up with, hating having to tell it. "I needed to hide until the heat cooled a bit."

"You should have come to me." Kylie caught my wrist and peered right into my eyes. "I could have helped you, you know?"

"I know. It's just...I didn't have a lot of time to think or plan. It all happened so fast, and I didn't want you to end up in trouble, too."

Her expression softened, which I understood. Our world didn't spawn happily-ever-afters for many. We usually understood that, accepted it. When I stopped to think about it, though, it actually sucked.

"Well, since you're back, is it resolved now?"

"Mostly," I hedged. "I've got to watch my back, but no one is looking for me now."

Technically the Sand Snakes are. And I guess Gorrin would be if he knew. And if Charles knew I wasn't working for the demon who took his soul, I'd be in trouble there, too.

Life really was more complicated than it should have been.

"You didn't come back just to visit." Kylie nodded toward the couch in her high-rise apartment.

She was the sort of woman who always made me feel a bit bad about myself. Most of the time, I'd felt like I had the whole adult-female thing figured out. Kylie made me suspect I was doing a piss-poor job at it. She had a fancy apartment at the top of a building that normally wouldn't even let me in the front doors. She wore a suit that made it clear she was a badass.

It made me peer down at myself, at my ratty-looking white T-shirt and my ripped jeans. I tucked a lock of hair behind my ear as if *that* were the one change that would bring the whole mess of my outfit together.

"You're doing well," I said.

She smiled, though the edges reminded me that Kylie was a lot more than met the eye. She was an infiltrator — someone hired to go undercover and fit into any situation or role. I'd met her long ago, when she'd been looking into a club I frequented. She'd been the one to make me scurry off before a raid by the police hit the place.

"My skills pay well." She shrugged, and again it reminded me what I liked about her. She didn't boast, she didn't feel the need to rub her skills into anyone else's face. She was confident in what she could do and didn't take anyone's shit about it. Hell, I'd seen men who would kill someone without a second thought quake when they heard her name.

She was my *maybe someday* girl crush. She was who I wanted to be, who I wanted to live up to.

Not that I thought I had much of a chance.

And somewhere in my head I could picture Tyrus staring at me, his eyebrow lifted as he scoffed at me — a demon — envying some human woman.

"So, why did you come?"

"I need your help," I admitted.

And in true Kylie fashion, she offered me a smile that was her equivalent of 'of course! You don't even have to ask.'

It was one of the astounding things about the woman, how quick she had always been to help me even if I couldn't do a damned thing in return.

Well...I suppose I had given her information back in the day, before I'd gone through the whole dying thing. Still, nothing I'd said had been worth nearly as much as she'd given to me. That made me uneasy, since in our world no one did anything for free, but I'd never had it in me to actually ask.

"I need some information."

"That's pretty much my specialty. What can I do for you?"

I tried to think about how to phrase it. The last thing I wanted was to accidently say something that would end up drawing her into my problems. I spoke slowly to give myself more time. "If the Sand Snakes needed to get a specific medication without a prescription, where would they go? I know different groups have agreements with different pharmacies, so I need to know who they'd deal with."

Kylie tapped her fingers against the counter of her kitchen island as she stared at me, her eyes alight and *far* too intelligent. Getting one over on this woman was probably impossible. "I heard some rumors about the Sand Snakes looking for some girl with green hair. There aren't that many like you around. You really did come back with a bang, didn't you?"

"That was a misunderstanding," I muttered.

"Misunderstanding? Like when you accidentally took the money you were supposed to deliver to a thug and instead dropped it off at that foster home?"

"That was a misunderstanding also," I pressed. "They misunderstood that I wasn't going to do what they wanted." Just saying it made me grin and I recalled that tiny sense of accomplishment from screwing over an asshole. "And before you lecture me, the thug was on a hit list! I figured he'd be dead before he realized I'd screwed him over."

Of course, that hit had fallen through because he'd bought his way out of trouble, leaving him alive and me on his bad side.

"How did you end up raising the money to pay him back?"

I shuddered as I recalled all the jobs I'd taken and the less than pleasant things I'd done. "Let's just say I managed it and leave it at that."

She let out a soft laugh, one that showed she respected me in her own way. "Well, if you're looking for a pharmacy that works with the Sand Snakes, you'll want Priority One Pharmacy down on Fourth and Oak. They've got a good relationship with Hopper, and the pharmacist, Wayne Killor, regularly hands over what they need in exchange for protection and a good amount of money."

I nodded as I committed that to memory. If that was the pharmacy they used, I should be able to get information out of the pharmacist there. It was a lifeline, at least, a path to Brendon I hadn't had before.

And given we were only a week away, I was quickly running out of options here.

"Are you sure everything's okay?" Kylie asked.

When I looked up and saw her expression, I paused. She rarely looked really worried, but here she was, staring at me as if she were actually concerned, as if she gave a damn about what happened to me.

"Yeah," I said, even though I didn't quite feel that answer was totally honest. Something about the way she looked at me kept me speaking. "I just have something really important I have to do, something that actually matters to me."

"Something matters to you?" Kylie spoke those words as if they didn't quite make sense.

"Right?" I laughed even if it wasn't funny. "That's not like me at all."

"That's not it. It's just not like you to admit something matters. I mean, you donated that money because it mattered to you, and you did plenty of things because you cared, but you always pretended you didn't. I noticed when you walked in that you'd changed, but I guess I didn't realize just how much..."

Her words caught me off guard, especially with how true they were. It reminded me that she noticed far too much.

Yet the familiar moment, the fact that I felt accepted by someone from my past, it had me speaking. "If I don't do this, not only might a kid die but another will make a choice she can't ever take back. I don't want that—I want to do something to fix it. I guess I just underestimated how hard this all is. I thought I could step back into this world and navigate it like I did before, but it all feels so much more difficult."

Kylie nodded but said nothing, as if just giving me the chance to speak and work through what was in my head.

"I feel like I'm not getting any closer, like time is ticking by and I'm not making any real progress. What if I fail? What if I put all this in and I don't even do what I wanted to do? I've never given a damn about failing before, but it *matters* this time." I folded my hands in my lap, feeling pathetic that I'd just unloaded so much on her. Sure, I'd kept some of the details to myself—such as dying and turning into a demon—but the rest were the real facts of how I felt, the things I couldn't admit to anyone else.

Gunnar was just as dangerous as he'd ever been, so I knew better than to rely on him. I couldn't talk to the Demon Lords like this—none of them would understand. Gorrin would just stare at me as if disappointed. Tyrus would shake his head before trying to explain the world to me yet again. Hale would call me a fucking idiot and probably threaten me. Yazmor would be nice, in his own way, but offer up advice that made no sense and was ultimately more confusing than enlightening.

Which meant Kylie offered me the only chance to speak from my heart and say how I felt without fear of the reaction.

"The last five years have been hard, and I've been mostly on my own, and it feels like I came back here, and everything is different."

"It's not different," Kylie said, speaking softly. "This world doesn't really change—I know, I've been in it a long time. It feels different because you've grown."

"I feel like the same fuck up I've always been."

"Not even close. I remember the teenager I told to leave before the raid. You were afraid of your own shadow back then, afraid of anyone looking at you, of making waves. You've grown a lot, though. You're here, standing on your own, ready to do what you feel is right. That takes courage, and it's courage you didn't have all those years ago."

I thought back to everything I'd done and none of it felt all that courageous.

I sighed, then got to my feet. I couldn't just sit here and bask in old memories. Each hour that passed put me closer to a deadline I couldn't change, closer to complete failure.

"Thanks for the help," I said, feeling vulnerable and on display in a way I didn't much care for.

Too much had happened recently, too many times I'd felt like the ground had opened up beneath me and pulled me down into the abyss. It left me raw.

Kylie stopped me as I headed toward the door with a hand wrapped around my arm. "Nothing really changes," she said. "The world is as vicious and heartless as ever, and that's because the universe is vicious and heartless. It doesn't matter what form it takes, it's always the same."

"You said I changed."

"I said you *grew*. A tadpole grows into a frog, but they are still the same life form. You've grown into yourself, but you are still the same person."

"Why do you always help me? You never had to, but you always do."

Kylie tilted her head as if she'd never really considered it before. "I saw you that first day, and there was something about you that I couldn't help but find interesting. It was as if you stood out somehow, no matter how much you tried to blend in. In the years since, that hasn't changed. I think I help you because I want to see what you become. I'm fascinated by what you'll grow into, so I want to do what I can to ensure you get there."

"That's it? Just entertainment?"

She shrugged, though the fondness in her smile took away the sting. "That's the only reason most people do anything—for entertainment. Living things tend to fall to boredom easily. Life is long no matter how short it is, so novelty helps it to pass. I don't know what it is about you, but when I look at you, I know you have the potential to be interesting, and I can't wait to see what you'll end up doing."

Her words felt strange, reminding me slightly of Yazmor when he spoke and I understood the individual words but they made no sense in the way Yazmor—or Kylie—put them together.

I didn't know how to respond to it, how to figure out what she meant.

Kylie smiled wider and patted me on the shoulder. "Go on, Loch. I'll never get to see what you're capable of if you don't go do it."

Unsure what else to say, I followed the gentle pressure as she pushed me from her apartment, leaving me on her doorstep alone, wondering just how she could confuse me so much. After everything I'd gone through, all I'd been around, how was it some human woman could put me as off balanced as the devils in hell.

Well, at least I'm never bored…

Chapter Twelve

I peered through the window of the pharmacist's house, waiting to ensure no one else was coming. I didn't need collateral damage or to end up surrounded all because of a booty-call.

Wayne Killor. Kylie had given me a card with his name and address scribbled down as she'd shoved me from her place, but I knew nothing else about him. Clearly, he had connections to some less than savory people, given that he was on call with the Sand Snakes. It meant I needed to be extremely careful.

People who played with snakes tended to be cautious, since they didn't want to get bitten.

Still, I'd been here in the dark for two hours and Wayne had shown no signs of anyone else. No nice clothing, no food or drink sat out. Instead, he'd grabbed a beer and settled himself on the couch to watch some weird anime with talking animals. In fact, I wasn't sure he hadn't fallen asleep.

I went to creep closer, when a voice whispered into my ear. "Are we being Peeping Toms? Because I think we could find better subjects."

I twisted, the action causing me to topple and fall right on my ass. Silhouetted by the moon, Yazmor crouched there above me and stared down at me.

Though his face didn't hold the same humor as usual.

I glared, then moved and rubbed at my sore ass from where I'd struck the ground. "You shouldn't sneak up on people like that."

"You're watching someone through a window while you hide in the dark—are you in any position to tell people not to sneak up on others?"

"What are you even doing here?"

"Well, after you got hurt, you didn't visit me. I had to check up on you. It's easy to sense other demons on Earth."

"You heard about that?"

"Tyrus called me."

That was the last thing I'd expected for him to say. I didn't get the feeling that any of the Demon Lords interacted with each other, at least not if they could avoid it. Their people clashed, but they didn't just call each other up to gossip as far as I knew.

Maybe I was mistaken.

Now I had a weird idea that they got together for manis and pedis, complete with margaritas and fluffy robes.

Talk about an image I didn't need in my head.

Yazmor grinned, the moonlight glinting off his teeth making them seem even sharper. Sometimes, when he looked at me, I wasn't sure he was the same as me at all. The other Demon Lords all struck me as human-ish.

They were twisted, sure, changed by their time in the Chasm until they seemed like the devils I called them. Yazmor, on the other hand, didn't seem to fit in anywhere.

Which I sort of understood, that feeling of not belonging.

Yet where it bothered me, Yazmor didn't seem to even notice.

"I didn't think you were so lonely that you would spend your time creeping around outside men's houses."

"This is for work."

"Gorrin gave you a task for this? I never thought he'd order you to go peep in the windows of random people."

"Well…" I hesitated, especially after finding out that Yazmor had been chatting it up with Tyrus.

I didn't need them all ganging up on me or working together.

Yet, the lift of his eyebrow said he wouldn't accept some bullshit response.

So, instead of trying to lie, I sighed and answered honestly. "I'm looking for someone, and this guy works with the people who took that person."

Yazmor twisted his head to peer into the window. It reminded me that despite his carefree attitude, he was far smarter than anyone would suspect on first glance. "So the person you're looking for requires medication, and since this man is a pharmacist, you're hoping to use him to then locate them?" The fact that Yazmor could figure that all out on his own — including details like Wayne's profession — was terrifying.

"Since you figured it out, you should know I really don't *need* any help right now." By which I meant that

Yazmor was a problem, and I didn't need him causing *me* any problems when I was in the middle of questioning someone.

"Is that your way of telling me to leave?"

"I'm surprised you noticed."

Yazmor shrugged. "Gorrin told me that I don't understand social cues or 'read between the lines,' so I've been trying harder!" He pulled his lips into a wide smile as though proud of all his hard work.

And yet everything he did or said only made me more certain that this would go better if he stayed about a hundred miles from it. In fact, I had a feeling *everything* would go smoother if it had less Yazmor involvement.

"So, it's been nice to see you—"

"I'm not leaving." Yazmor totally ignoring my opinion while smiling *that* widely was beyond disconcerting. He peered past me and at the window. "We should get going or it will turn to morning before we get anything done." With that, Yazmor rose to his full height to stroll forward.

Which was *exactly* why I'd not wanted him with me. He was over six feet tall—did he really think Wayne just wouldn't notice him? Wayne twisted, as if he'd seen the movement and was turning to check.

I grabbed Yazmor's arm and yanked him down and to the side, hiding us behind a large tree. I shoved his back against it, using a hand on his chest to pin him in place. I leaned slightly to peer around the tree. Wayne had his back toward us again, which meant he must have decided there was nothing to see outside.

I let out a long breath, relieved to have fixed this before it all went bad.

At least, I thought that before I turned my gaze back to Yazmor and realized our position.

I had a six-foot-tall, extremely powerful and dangerous Demon Lord pinned to a tree like this was a cheesy shojo manga gender-reversed. Worse, Yazmor stared down into my eyes with such intensity that I knew this was a *huge* mistake.

And yet, I struggled to move. His heart beat against the hand I had on his chest, and somehow it locked me into the moment with him. I didn't know how to break free, how to change this sudden tension between us.

This was *Yazmor*. Unreliable, impossible to understand, always smiling Yazmor. When had *this* become weirdly sexually charged?

In fact, a part of me had no idea how I could even consider Yazmor connected to sex. The man was so strange that it was far easier to think he had zero interest in anything like that.

However, he didn't stare at me now as if we were just old buddies…

"Sorry," I whispered and pulled my hand back. Unable to tolerate the awkwardness between us, my mouth continued to ramble, and my brain completely let go of the wheel. "I guess I shouldn't be pinning devils against trees, huh?"

"Not a devil," Yazmor said, his face transforming before my eyes from the intensity of before to a more casual, familiar smile. "Though I agree, you probably shouldn't do that often. If you did this to someone else, they might get the wrong idea or not let you off the hook so easily."

His words shook me, as if he wanted to remind me that he was still a man.

Or, well, a Demon Lord…

I shook away the weird moment, then gestured for Yazmor to crouch and follow me, using my plan to distract me from whatever *that* had almost been.

Breaking into Wayne's place ended up far easier than it should have been. The man worked with a motorcycle gang and he'd gotten himself mixed up with some extremely dangerous people. He should have had *way* better locks and security in place.

Instead, he had no cameras, no security system, just a shitty deadbolt on a backdoor. I could have picked it, but Yazmor waved his hand over the lock, and it clicked open.

Well, that's useful, I guess. Not that I was happy he was with me. Sure, he'd started to crouch, as if following my lead, but his focus left a lot to be desired. No less than three times he ended up distracted by random shit. Once it had been a pretty flower by the back door, then he'd pocketed a cup from the kitchen counter because he liked the pattern, and the last time had been due to him inspecting the baseboard because, *'my place needs some spiffing up and this looks fancy.'*

We moved down the hallway, and at the end, I peered around the corner to find the back of Wayne's head as he watched the huge television mounted on the wall. It also let me see what he had on the TV more clearly. What I thought was a weird animal cartoon got even weirder as I watched from this distance.

Yep. That wolf creature is fucking that cat creature.

And these were the eyes I had to keep using, even after seeing that. I doubted bleach would prove strong enough to scrub that away. Worse, he moved slightly as he sat there, tiny twitches I was pretty sure I understood without needing any additional context.

Then the asshole added that context by letting out a low, drawn-out groan.

This is my life. I'm watching a pharmacist masturbate to furry porn.

If I ever doubted that I'd landed myself in hell, this was really all the proof I needed.

"A kitten!" Yazmor rose to his full height from behind me, seemingly having forgotten our entire sneaking idea. He rushed past me and into the living room, taking no notice of Wayne, who rose *without* tucking his junk back in place.

I didn't have time to think about anything else, though. Wayne might be a perverted criminal — but really, weren't we all? — but he could grab a weapon as easily as anyone else. After getting shot to death once, I wasn't about to second-guess just how much damage a gun could do even in untrained hands.

So I rushed him before he had the chance to do anything else. While he clearly didn't have a weapon right now — given he was entirely nude from the waist down — he could still have one hidden close by.

Wayne wasn't a large man — at least, not in height. Even I had to admit his goods weren't lacking. Or maybe it just seemed that way because he was short — proportionally, it made everything he had look far grander.

Even still, my small frame couldn't do a lot of damage. I crouched slightly and drove my shoulder into his stomach to send him off balance. He let out a startled shout, then fell backward. He missed the couch, sprawling out on the ground beside the table, and I did so, too. I ended up on top of him, which was so *not* the way I wanted to be on top of a pants-less man.

When Wayne gathered his wits, he twisted, throwing me off. I struck my shoulder on the table when he unseated me, but I ignored the pain. Pain was temporary — death was forever.

Well, sometimes…

Wayne and I both scrambled to our feet, panting hard. I didn't see Yazmor anywhere — had he left?

Perhaps it was terrible, but I was rather grateful for that. I wouldn't even be wrestling a man with his dick out if it weren't for Yazmor and his erratic behavior!

"Who are you?" Wayne asked, his gaze hard. "What do you want?"

"Just some information. This doesn't have to be hard." I dropped my gaze to his crotch at my unintended innuendo but had to be impressed he was still risen to the occasion. "Most men would be limp as cooked noodle after a surprise like this." The moaning on the television from the cat who had apparently bound the wolf creature and was now pegging him made it clear. "Look, if this is your kink, that's all you, but don't you *dare* get off on this." I waved my hands between him and me.

"You're barking up the wrong tree here," Wayne said. "I've got friends you don't want to screw with."

"The Sand Snakes? Yeah, I know — I've dealt with them already."

He snorted. "If you had, you wouldn't be here."

I recalled the pain as Clint had tortured me, the terror, and something between fear and anger rushed through me.

Wayne took my moment of distraction to charge at me. He struck me far harder than I'd hit him, and the air rushed from my lungs when we slammed against the hard floor.

"Aren't you just the bestest girl?" Yazmor's voice made me glance up to find him back in the living room, a black cat in his arms who looked far less than happy about the forced cuddles.

"Are you kidding me?" I muttered before twisting to bring my knee up. I collided with something firm and slightly wet—*gross.*

Wayne let out a sound that came across as less pain and more excitement. Was there anything he *wasn't* into? How was I supposed to fight a masochist who got off on damn near everything?

"Would you help me?" I snapped at Yazmor when Wayne rolled to the side, clutching his groin. "I just felt his dick on my leg!"

Yazmor didn't seem to even notice me as he struggled with his own battle, which in his case was trying to get a clearly uninterested cat to accept his affections.

Wayne got to his knees, one hand still grasping his bits, his face twisted in discomfort. "This is stupid. If I told you anything, I'd end up dead."

"You'll end up dead even sooner if you don't."

"What? From you or the weird cat guy? Because from where I'm standing here, neither of you seems all that tough."

"Where you are standing is pants-less and watching furry porn! Do you really get to call him weird?"

"Who is the prettiest girl? Yes, you are." Yazmor's cooing to the cat made me close my hands into fists, wishing I could slap him instead of dealing with Wayne. They were both, at this point, equally annoying.

I turned to glare at Yazmor, but once again, Wayne charged me when my focus drifted. I stumbled backward, especially because he drew his hand into a fist. He swung at me, and I raised my arm to fend off the hit.

Except, it didn't land. A crash snapped my eyes open, and I spotted Wayne across the room, slumped down on the floor, with a huge crack in the drywall.

Yazmor walked up beside me, the cat still struggling in his arms, and angry red scratches covering his cheek and hands. He didn't seem to even notice the man he had clearly just thrown across the room, as if that didn't matter compared to the cat.

And it confused me as much as anything else he did. He didn't seem to focus on me at all, distracted by a cat, and yet when I'd nearly been hurt, he'd been right there. Even when it seemed he was miles away, he was still watching out for me.

And I really had no idea how to deal with that…

* * * *

I'd never learned how to tie a person up. It just wasn't a skill I'd spent any real time practicing and no one had ever taught a *Bondage for Beginners* course for me.

I wasn't the sort of girl who wanted to bind up my sexual partners, and I'd never needed to do so outside of the bedroom, either.

Still, I was pretty sure I did it well enough to keep our perverted pharmacist in place. He struggled, now that he'd woken, but the rope I'd found in his garage held him tight.

And Yazmor sat on the couch in the living room, the cat happily resting on his lap. It seemed the cat had accepted him — *stupid, easy feline.*

I thought cats were too smart to fall for bullshit like that, but I guess there were stupid beings in every group.

"Okay, so let's talk." I faced Wayne after closing all the windows. Thankfully, it was easier to talk to him now that I'd tossed a throw blanket over his lap. This interrogation was between Wayne and I—it would not be a threesome involving Wayne Junior there.

"How the hell did you do that?" Wayne asked, his voice groggy. Then again, a lump on the back of his head said he'd hit the wall really fucking hard.

"Trade secrets," I answered before dragging a chair over, letting the legs scrape along the floor for tension. I'd been thinking about all the shitty cop movies I'd watched where they'd questioned suspects and increased the tension until they broke.

I could do that, right? How hard could it be?

I turned the chair backwards just in front of him and sat on it, trying to look comfortable, as if tying up and questioning men was an everyday occurrence for me.

He let out an unimpressed snort. "You aren't exactly the picture of threat, you know?"

"And yet you're the one tied up."

He narrowed his eyes as if he didn't care for the reminder. "If you want to ask questions, get to it. I want to not answer so we can finish this."

"You're that sure you want to stay quiet? I mean, I doubt Hopper does that much for you to earn your undying loyalty."

"He keeps me happy," Wayne said. "It's a good partnership, and he's the sort of man who only an idiot would double cross."

"That doesn't really matter."

"No? You don't think it matters what he'd do to me if he found out I was telling his secrets? Then you don't know anything about him or the Sand Snakes."

I rested my forearm on the back of the chair as I stared at Wayne. "Think about it like being in a field and seeing a sign about a dangerous bear. You turn around to leave, but a mountain lion is standing on the path. Sure, the bear might be a threat, but the mountain lion is the immediate danger. I'm the lion—Hopper is the bear. Deal with surviving me first, because if you don't, you won't live long enough for the bear to be a problem."

He didn't flinch at all, which was really fucking rude. I'd just threatened him, and done a damn good job with it I thought. He stared at me as if I weren't something to worry about, though. "You're not nearly as scary as you think. You might have snuck in here, but you both seem like bumbling idiots."

I ignored his insult as I took his phone from the table. I pressed his thumb against the screen to unlock it, then took a seat to scroll through it.

Getting him to talk wasn't my only option.

"As a professional, what would you recommend for scratches?" Yazmor asked Wayne.

I peered at him, noting his wounds from his battle with the cat looked worse. "Really? Is now the time? We don't have *anything* more important to deal with?"

Yazmor glanced past me at Wayne. "How long will an infection from a scratch take to kill a person?"

Wayne furrowed his brows, as if he couldn't believe he was actually having this conversation. *That makes two of us, buddy.* "Assuming it gets infected from the scratch, it would take days before it got bad enough to be dangerous."

Yazmor nodded then looked back at me. "Okay, then my question can wait until later. Carry on."

I rubbed at my temple as I returned my focus to the phone and away from Yazmor. I went through Wayne's contacts, but none stuck out to me. Then again, I highly doubted he saved them under names such as — *shady guy I sell drugs to*. Names like James, Kelly and Paul meant nothing to me.

I opened his email, but again, nothing stuck out to me. The idea of Hopper emailing seemed all together out of place anyway. He hit me as the sort of man who squinted at his cell phone, put calls on speaker, then yelled 'can you hear me?' constantly.

Which left me with one last option. I went to Wayne's text messages.

"Why is that cat in fox ears?" Yazmor asked.

I glanced up at the television to find the furry porn still running, and sure enough, the cat character had a pair of fox ears on. *Are they animals role playing as other animals?* "Why is that still playing? Just turn it off." I went back to scrolling through the messages.

"But...the plot..." Even though Yazmor complained, the sound of the show stopped and the screen went dark.

Mostly, I found text messages to a multitude of women — and lots of poorly lit nudes. The more I saw, the more I realized just how freaky this individual was. *And to think I wrestled with him while he was naked...*

Still, about six threads down, I opened a message from the contact *Frankie*. It only took a glance to know I'd found what I was looking for. The message wasn't entirely clear, but I'd spent enough time seeing things in code that it was easy to pick it up. The messages talked about baked goods, but the reason I could break it was because then they'd come right out to ask for what they wanted, just not by name.

No one in their right mind asked for a brownie that would treat infection after a gunshot wound. Likewise, from a few days ago, I found a text message asking for cookies that help with asthma.

Wow, talk about being bad at subtlety. It would take even the worst cop only a few minutes to figure this shit out.

I turned my gaze back to Wayne. "So, where's the drop-off place?"

He pressed his lips together and lifted an eyebrow.

"You know, acting tough is one thing, but I grew up around some of the worst of the worst. A kinky pharmacist doesn't intimidate me."

"I feel like a kinky pharmacist is something to fear," Yazmor chimed in. "They know about drugs, and they might want to do some things after those drugs take effect…"

"Can we not talk about the sexual deviancy of pharmacists right now?"

Yazmor turned his attention back to the cat in his lap as though I'd bored him.

Good, things would always go better if I didn't have to deal with him as well. Yazmor could manage to feel like yet another enemy sometimes. He was just another person fucking up my plans.

Worse, our childish back and forth seemed to make Wayne all the more certain he didn't need to answer.

I went to reply to the text. "I'm going to tell them you have a new cookie for the asthma because you got a recall on the old one."

"If you don't know the drop-off place, it won't do you any good," Wayne said.

"Which is why you're going to tell me." I pressed Send, then set the phone on my lap to wait for a reply. "Believe it or not, I don't give a fuck about the Sand Snakes or you. I'd be happy to get what I need done and leave you all the fuck alone. I'm not here to take out any of you. You can go back to your compelling cinema and forget you ever met me."

"How reassuring." Even I had to be impressed by his deadpanned delivery of that. It was a talented amount of snark.

Still, I needed his cooperation. I needed to get him to talk and tell me where he met with the Sand Snakes. I wasn't above causing a bit of pain if it meant saving Brendon and Jay, though I didn't savor the idea.

I'm damned anyway. What does it really matter?

"I think we got off on the wrong foot," I said and flashed a wide smile. "My name is Loch. I've dealt with assholes like you before — you aren't as scary as you think. The information I'm after is very simple, and this will go much easier for you if you just tell me what I need to know. As soon as you tell me, I'm out of your hair and you'll never see me again."

"Thanks, but I'll pass." He pulled his shoulders back as if to look taller — stupid, given he was bound to a chair with a throw blanket over his waist. It was hard to look tough in that position.

The phone vibrated in my lap, so I glanced down at the screen.

Two hours from now at the normal place.

Well, at least that meant Brendon was alive and they wanted him to stay that way. If they'd done something to him, they wouldn't give a damn if they had his inhaler or not.

But it also started the clock. I needed the information so I could get there in time. I rose from my chair and approached Wayne. It was one of those times I was sorry I looked the way I did. I didn't strike much fear into the hearts of my enemies.

Bringing Hale or Tyrus would have helped, because they both looked like people no one wanted to come face to face with or piss off. Instead, I had Yazmor, who looked like a young guy trying to pass himself off as old enough to get into a club. Yazmor was terrifying in the Chasm because people knew him there, they understood his power, but here?

Here he was just some weirdo obsessed with a cat. In fact, Wayne seemed to not even know exactly how he got thrown across the room. The hit to the head must have clouded his memories.

Still, even someone as small and non-threatening as me could manage to hurt someone if I wanted to.

And I sure as hell didn't mind it right now.

I wrapped my hand around the front of his throat, squeezing tightly. I wasn't all that much stronger than a human, but just enough for his eyes to widen a hair. "I don't have time to play these games with you. You're useful right now, but if you won't tell me what I need to know, I've got no reason to keep you alive."

I waited until he started to really struggle before I released him and let him pull in a deep, frantic breath. After coughing for a moment, he lifted his head to stare at me.

He had a surprising amount of determination in his eyes. Then again, he was probably into erotic asphyxiation, judging from every other thing he was into. I felt like this guy took a list of kinks as a challenge rather than a list of options.

Sure enough, a glance down showed a tent forming under his blanket.

"For fuck's sake!" I threw my hands up and turned around. "How am I supposed to torture someone who is into everything I might do! God help us, because masochists make the worst interrogation subjects." I faced Yazmor. "What am I supposed to do?"

"You want my help now?" Yazmor asked, voice full of innocence.

"Well, I'm out of options and almost out of time. I need to know where the drop-off location is so I can follow whoever shows up back to where they're from."

Yazmor blinked slowly, then tilted his head. He stared at me without a smile, as if trying to figure me out. I wasn't sure if he came up with anything or if he simply gave up, because he spread a smile across his lips and set the cat down on the couch.

"What, you think this kid could frighten me? You've got no idea the sort of people I deal with."

Yazmor took my chair and turned it around, then sat. This put him so close that his knees almost brushed Wayne's. It really made it clear how much less dangerous he appeared, even compared to the bound pharmacist. "Tell me where the drop-off location is."

"Fuck you," Wayne snapped back.

Yazmor grinned, but had it ever looked quite so threatening before? It wasn't that it lacked humor, but more that he seemed to enjoy the threat. "You're not really my type, especially after I saw what you were watching when we came in. I don't like to harm lesser beings when I don't have to, so I'll give you one last chance. Tell me what I want to know, and I'll walk out of here. Don't? Well, you'll still tell me what I want but you'll always regret trying to hold out."

A shiver ran through me at the tone of Yazmor's voice. Had I ever heard that before? It felt like a different person, but I told myself it wasn't. It was Yazmor. Silly, irreverent, annoying Yazmor.

Wayne gulped, and when he spoke again, his voice lacked the same confidence from before. Still, he seemed to want to hold his ground. "I can't."

Yazmor held his hand out, but it wasn't the hand I'd seen before, the one I was used to. Instead, his skin was a mixture of black and red tones that reminded me of flames in the darkness. He didn't just threaten Wayne with it—and it made for a damn good threat considering the knife-like claws that tipped his fingers. Instead, he drove one of his claws into the top of Wayne's thigh, plunging it in a good two inches.

Wayne screamed, making me glance around the house. We needed to keep things quiet. The last thing we wanted were cops showing up.

"You have a pretty scream," Yazmor said, his voice different, darker. "But we don't have time to enjoy it right now. Tell me what we want to know." He shifted his hand, digging his claw around, drawing more agonized sounds from Wayne.

"It's a mailbox in the lobby of the Harlton Motel. To the left of the front door there's a bunch of them for long-term guests. Number thirty-eight is the one we use. I drop the medicine there and walk away. They send the payment a day or two later." Wayne had tears streaming from his eyes as he blubbered on, clearly desperate to say anything if it meant stopping Yazmor.

And Yazmor, despite having his claw buried in Wayne's thigh, didn't look bothered at all. In fact, he had the same amused grin as when he'd played with the cat.

Which reminded me that the man was truly a Demon Lord.

"Is that enough?" Yazmor asked me.

I nodded, not trusting my voice.

"Wonderful." Yazmor ripped his claw from Wayne's leg like it was nothing. "It was lovely doing business with you. I suggest you forget you ever saw either of us or I'll have to plan on a reunion."

Wayne said nothing back but trembled, a sure sign that he understood the threat and would do as Yazmor said. Then again, I doubted anyone — even someone as freaky as Wayne — wanted a repeat visit from a man who had just shish-kabobbed his leg.

Yazmor sliced the claw down over the rope, proving just how sharp it was. Even freed, Wayne didn't dare move. Not that Yazmor seemed to care — he turned and headed toward the front door.

I followed, keeping Wayne's phone with me in case I needed it and to prevent him from betraying us after we left. Yazmor said nothing as we walked, and I fell into step beside him. The darkness of the night felt more intimidating than it had before and I suddenly recalled shoving Yazmor against that tree earlier.

Would I do that again now? After seeing what he'd done, would I so casually touch him?

We paused in front of the car I was using, and the silence between us felt strange. Yazmor was *never* quiet. It was tense and full of things neither of us seemed to want to say.

He held out his hand — the one he hadn't used to stab Wayne — and an inhaler appeared in it. Those Demon Lord powers sure were useful. "There is no telling if the person will return to the individual you're looking for unless the medicine is at the drop."

"And this won't hurt the person, right?"

"Not a chance. It is a general rescue inhaler. If I wanted to kill asthmatic people, I'd just make them cuddle with kittens and wait for the fun."

I cracked a smile, the joke weak but reminding me of the man I'd thought he was. "You like cats, huh?"

"They don't trust easily — they make you earn it. I like that in a person. Dogs are too simple, too boring. I like cats, hyenas, sharks and owls. They make a person work for affection, and that keeps me interested."

"And interesting is what matters?"

"When you live as long as I have? Yeah. Also, that inhaler has a tracker inside already connected to your cell phone. You'll be able to follow it no matter where they take it." He paused, then stared off into the sky. "You should remember what you just saw."

"What?"

He didn't look back at me right away, as if he didn't want to see me while he spoke. "What you saw me do? That's me. You've always seen me in a different way, have let your guard down too much around me, but I'm not safe. You should know that."

"You've never hurt me," I said.

That made him bring his gaze back to me, and his violet eyes had never looked so intense before. They seemed even less natural than usual, more unhinged. "No, I haven't, but you should know it's possible."

"You're not like that."

He set a hand on the roof of my car, boxing me in, making me crane my neck to look up and into his eyes. "I am. I'm not like anything you've ever dealt with, like nothing else around. You have no idea what I'm capable of."

The air around us crackled, as if electrified, and it somehow grew even darker. It seemed as if he leached the light from the very air. Sounds shorted out as well, and it almost felt like when I transported back to the Chasm, that shifting of reality around me.

What the fuck are you?

The question had never occurred to me before, but it did now, especially when I pulled my gaze from his and it landed on the hand that had driven that clawed point into Wayne. He still had blood covering the hand, even though the actual form was back to good old-fashioned, five-fingered human.

"Are you trying to scare me?" I asked.

"I don't need to try, do I?" The sounds that surrounded us increased, and it almost seemed like the world melted, a deep, instinctual fear rising inside me.

Which was hilarious since I hadn't been afraid of much in the Chasm. I'd known the dangers, but because I'd always had to tip-toe around people who might kill me, they didn't really faze me.

Yet now, when confronted with the glow of Yazmor's unnatural eyes, the blood covering his hand, the way he twisted the world around us to something sinister, I couldn't stop it.

"Why are you doing this?" I asked, ignoring the quaver in my voice.

"I want you to understand." He brought his hand up, the one with blood on it, and cupped my cheek with it. "You deserve to know exactly what I really am."

"I've been around you for five years. I'm not afraid of you."

"No?" He tilted his head as his lips curled into a smile that made me question my own feelings. It seemed as if his mouth was too wide, his teeth sharp even when they shouldn't have been. A few strands of his violet hair had fallen forward, but his bright eyes shone through the gaps. That look on his face felt like a warning, telling me to watch my step very carefully.

Still, I shook my head. The fact that I couldn't say it out loud really drove home his point, didn't it?

He leaned closer until his breath spilled across my face, warm and threatening. "Never forget what I am, Loch." As soon as he spoke, the world went silent around me.

That strange noise, the way it had gotten darker, even Yazmor himself had all disappeared. When I brought my hand to my cheek, to where my skin chilled after losing his touch, I found wetness.

I pulled my hand away and stared at my sticky, red stained fingers, from where Yazmor had touched me with Wayne's blood still on his skin.

I took a deep breath there, in the darkness, alone with nothing but Wayne's blood and the memory of Yazmor's warning.

* * * *

I peered over the edge of the book in my hands to keep an eye on the mailbox. The motel was beyond gross. Just walking into the lobby made me worried I'd contracted some weird STI that even antibiotics couldn't tame. I'd never stay here, at least not willingly.

A roach scurried across the floor, disappearing beneath the door to the office. *I don't think anyone stays here willingly…*

I'd pulled my hair back into a tight bun, then covered it with a beanie to hide the green. I had no idea if Clint or one of the others who had been at the bar might be the one to do the pickup, so I didn't want to risk getting spotted.

I wasn't exactly well liked at the moment when it came to the Sand Snakes. Best to keep things low-key.

I glanced at my watch. Ten minutes until the time they'd told me.

"Hey, sweetheart, how much?"

I turned my gaze to the man standing beside me, his salacious grin telling me exactly what he meant by 'how much?' It wasn't the first guy to try it.

"Sorry, waiting for someone." I brought my gaze back to my book in the universal, 'I'm reading and ignoring you,' sign.

"Come on—I can pay you better than him. You look like the sort of wild girl who would make that worth it. I mean," he tilted his head slightly, as if trying to peer beneath my cap. "Green hair *screams* Daddy issues."

I dropped my book into my lap to give him my full attention. "Let me make this clear to you. I wouldn't let you get your shriveled dick anywhere near me, no matter how many pennies you tried to roll for it—in fact, I'd rather fuck the rolled pennies. I'm meeting someone else, and the sort of man who can keep a girl like me coming back is probably not the kind you want to play with."

The man's eyes widened, and something between fear and anger passed through them. It was easy to identify his line of thought, though. He was furious I'd insulted him and his precious dick, but also noted that the confidence I spoke with probably meant I wasn't lying.

He ended up muttering insults under his breath before taking off, leaving me there in peace. I lifted my book again, snickering as I saw the cover.

Pegging for Fun and Profit was not exactly a book most people would have, and I only did because Yazmor thought it would be a hilarious gift on the first anniversary of my death. Or maybe it was a suggestion from him that I didn't really want to think about?

Still, it usually kept people from bothering me when they spotted it. That meant that man had either not seen it or *had* seen it and was into it. I wasn't sure which was worse.

The door creaked as it opened, but I kept my gaze seemingly pinned to the book while peering over the top. The man who walked in wore a leather vest over his long-sleeved shirt, and the vest had the same image as the ones from that bar. It meant he had to be the one I was looking for.

Sure enough, he peered around the lobby then went right to the mailbox. He used a key to open it, then took out the padded envelope I'd put the inhaler in. He stuck it into his pocket and left.

I rose from my spot and followed him, hanging back as I grabbed my phone to watch the little red dot as it moved through the map on my screen. I could have waited until it stopped, but a part of me didn't trust Yazmor's tech skills enough to want to lose sight of him for good.

Instead, I remained over a block away, losing sight of him from time to time as that red dot followed the sidewalks. It meant he wouldn't notice me, because no one in their right mind would tail someone from so far away.

Finally, he paused in front of an expensive-looking townhouse in an older area of the city, the sort of place where people had owned the houses for generations but rarely had enough money to do the proper maintenance now. It meant while they were nice, they weren't well-kept. He took one more look around, and I shifted behind a tree on the sidewalk before he walked into the townhouse.

After a moment, I rose from my hiding spot and walked by the door he'd gone into, trying to come across as casual as I studied the place. It was three stories from what I could see, and had a door on the front to get in. Lights shone from inside, and shadows passed by windows—the drapes closed but thin enough for silhouettes to bleed through. Because the buildings were townhouses, they were pressed up against each other, which meant there was no fence to jump to get to a backyard.

I crossed to the other side of the street to make me less obvious, then studied the place. On the top floor, a large shadow moved into one of the rooms. A smaller shadow moved as well. Was that where Brendon was?

It would make sense, because they'd want him to stay in a room that was harder to get to and harder to escape from. I also doubted they'd keep other kids around, which made that my best bet.

I gave myself a moment to consider how best to handle this. What I didn't want was a fight. My run-in with Clint had taught me that I didn't need to do that bullshit again, especially with a kid in tow.

Which meant I had to do this as quietly as possible. Townhouses sucked because I couldn't get into the backyard, but they had the advantage of being in the city, which meant a person couldn't exactly set up a guard with a gun outside without attracting unwanted attention.

My gaze moved over the building as I formed the best plan I could. The third floor wouldn't be easy to get to. Climbing up was out of the question, which meant I needed to get inside and past the guards.

Despite the dagger at my wrist, I really *didn't* want to play up close and personal with the muscle charged with guarding a hostage as important as Brendon. They were in a shoot-first-and-ask-questions-never situation. Just as I ground my teeth in frustration, a car pulled over in front of the house. The driver got out, muttering quietly to himself as he got things from the trunk. "Every fucking night and they don't tip worth shit."

He carried what seemed to be a few pizza boxes and two bags of groceries toward the front door, giving me my way in.

Now I just had to set up the final details. Tomorrow night, I'd make my move. Brendon would be safe and this would all be over.

At least, that was the plan.

Chapter Thirteen

As it turned out, drugging people made time pass strangely. I knew, logically, it hadn't taken that long from the time the delivery guy brought their food to when the sleeping pills mixed into the alcohol would take effect, but it sure as fuck *felt* like forever.

I would have had it put into the pizza, but I couldn't ensure they wouldn't feed that to Brendon. Instead, I'd slipped the delivery guy enough money for him to exchange the beer they'd ordered for that with the drugs. The shady asshole I'd gotten the alcohol from had said it would work fast, and that within thirty minutes of drinking even a quarter of it, a two-hundred-pound man would be snoring for a couple hours. Maybe I should have felt bad—there was always a risk—but these guys felt like kidnapping a kid was an a-okay move.

They deserved whatever they got.

The shadows that passed the windows lessened, and within an hour, they stopped entirely. Was that it? Did it mean the drugs had worked? When I hadn't seen any movement in ten minutes, when no guard stepped outside for a check as they normally did every fifteen minutes, I figured I had no good reason to wait anymore.

I curled my fingers into the soil in my pockets, reassuring myself that I had an out if it all went badly. *Guess this is it…*

Each time my foot hit the ground, despite how carefully I moved, felt like a gunshot instead of a quiet step. Even still, I moved across the street from my spot, rubbing at my ass because sitting on a hard stoop for hours will make a person do that.

The door was locked—no surprise there. I slid the lockpicks from my pocket in and popped it open in just a few seconds. The lock clicked, then I twisted the handle and pushed the door open.

No sounds echoed around the house, nothing that showed signs of life. It had the silence of a house the morning after a rager, when everyone was hungover and passed out. *Perfect.* I moved farther into the house, crouching slightly as I walked. In the living room I found three men, all slumped over and drooling with open bottles on the table.

Talk about heavy drinkers…

Still, that worked fine for me. The quicker they went down, the better. Since I heard nothing else in the house, I had to assume these three were it in terms of guards.

I went up the stairs, keeping my steps light and quiet just in case. By the time I reached the third floor, I realized how little exercise I'd gotten since dying, which was odd. I would have thought hell would have a *lot* more stairs to climb and involve more running from things.

On the top floor, I peered around to get my bearings. Outside, the kid had been in the far-left room, which meant... I twisted around, then nodded at the door. A slide lock sat on the doorframe on the outside, and I undid it with a flick before pushing the door open.

Inside, a boy sat on the bed, one who looked exactly like the pictures I'd seen in Gunnar's book. Well, other than the fear on his young face. He had a plate with pizza set on the bed and a handheld gaming system in his hands.

Which were great ideas for keeping a young boy quiet and out of trouble, all things considered.

"I'm a friend," I said, keeping my voice soft. "I know your sister and your dad." I stepped into the room and held my hand out.

He shrank away from me on the bed.

Then again, I couldn't blame him. He didn't know a damn thing about me. For all he knew, I was even worse than the men who had taken him.

So I took a deep breath and tried to keep my expression kind. "Your sister, Jay, asked me to help find you. I drugged the men downstairs to get you out of here, but we have to hurry up before they wake."

Brendon furrowed his eyebrows for a moment, then got to his feet. He probably figured getting out of here was worth the risk. I ignored the way his legs shook — he was trying to be tough, and I wouldn't take that from him. I held my hand out and waited for him to take it. His was so small in my hold, a reminder that I didn't have a lot of experience with kids.

I tended to avoid children — they always seemed dangerous. They felt like a huge wound that was just asking the world to poke at it. This mess with Charles proved it.

Charles ran a powerful and vicious crime family. He was respected or feared by dangerous people, and yet all it had taken was one kid to bring his empire tumbling down.

Still, I didn't want anything to happen to them, which was why I clutched Brendon's hand as I led him down the stairs. We moved quickly—I didn't trust shady drug-experts too far—toward the door. We passed the large dining room table that had the pizza box open on it, some of the slices missing.

"What the fuck?" The startled male voice yanked my gaze up to find a man, his eyes wide, in the doorway to the basement.

He wasn't one of the three passed out on the couch, which meant I'd missed at least one person.

I pushed Brendon further behind me. I wasn't a great shield, but even my small body could hide a kid his size. The man before us already saw him, but I didn't want the kid to be a target.

"Why are you still awake?" I asked. Maybe he was on enough other drugs that they'd countered the sleeping drugs? Who would have thought being a human chemical cocktail would actually help him?

He peered past me, to the men unconscious on the couch, then to the food and drink on the table. The way understanding came to his features said he wasn't as stupid as I would have guessed at first. "I didn't eat or drink any of that because I'm gluten free."

I let out a long groan. "Of course you are. I swear, I didn't think gluten-free people could get any more annoying than they were but look at this—you managed it. For fuck's sake."

He narrowed his eyes, but thankfully, he didn't go for the gun at his hip. I doubted he gave a damn about me, but he probably couldn't risk hitting Brendon. He stood at the basement doorway, which placed him between the front door and us.

We needed to get past him, but at his size and with his weapon, a fight wasn't what I wanted to try for. The better option was to go for a distraction.

So I reached to my side, curled my fingers around what I found, and flung it at him.

He flinched, but his expression held more confusion than anger when he realized what I'd done. "Why did you throw pizza at me?"

"Because it has gluten in it!"

"Are you an idiot?"

I'd asked myself that before, and it probably wasn't a great thing when I couldn't really answer that confidently.

"That's not how it works," he added on as if so embarrassed for me that he had to set me straight.

I used his confusion to my advantage, though, and threw myself toward him. Apparently, a possibly stupid woman rushing someone can work to throw them off balance, because he stumbled a step backward and reached for his gun.

It was too late, however. I slammed into him, then caught the doorframe to keep myself from following as he sailed backward, into the basement, tripping on the steps.

The crash from him as he went down the stairs said he hadn't landed quite yet, but I didn't have time to wait and see how it worked out. Instead, I took Brendon's hand and bolted, all but dragging the kid behind me.

I headed west from the house, toward where I'd stashed the vehicle about two blocks away. I hadn't left it too close in case anyone caught sight of it. However, when I turned the corner, a deep rumble made me clutch Brendon's hand tighter and duck down a dark alleyway that gave access to the backyards for some of the houses. As soon as we got off the main sidewalk, a large motorcycle passed by, slow enough to show the person wasn't just out joy riding.

The man I had knocked down the stairs must have managed to call in reinforcements, and they weren't going to play nice when they found us. I crouched, pulling Brendon along with me, keeping to the shadows.

The glow of a headlight lit up the street as we went to exit the alley, and I yanked Brendon behind a trashcan to avoid getting spotted as the motorcycle went down the road, not noticing our hiding spot. Or maybe they were just creating a perimeter before tightening the noose.

Each time I tried to move us, to get out of the area, another passing motorcycle forced us to hide again, closing in on us.

We were trapped.

I could get out of here, could get back to the Chasm, but that didn't help since I couldn't take Brendon with me like that. Only a Demon Lord had the power to do that, which left me shit outta luck.

I was out of options, so I grabbed my phone and dialed the number for the only person I could think of who might actually be able to do something.

Of course, calling a devil when I was already in trouble wasn't a great idea, and might just land me in a worse off position. This felt like the saying of, 'out of the pan and into the hellfire.'

And yet there I went, dialing the number.

After a quick, quiet conversation, within three minutes, the roar of a motorcycle had me pulling Brendon against me, terrified that this was it, that I'd failed.

The large black motorcycle slowed right in front of us, and I let out a shaky breath when I met Hale's familiar blue eyes.

Never figured a devil would be my savior.

Still, never look a gift horse in the mouth, so I went with my unlikely hero.

I clung to Hale with one arm, the other around Brendon who we sandwiched between us on the bike. Hale had asked no questions, simply nodded for us to get on then handed us both helmets.

Not that he wore one.

Then again, he was a Demon Lord. A little bike accident on Earth wasn't about to take him out, but it could do a lot of damage to Brendon.

We'd gotten noticed on the way, but the chase hadn't lasted long. As it turned out, on top of his other skills, Hale was a terrifying and amazing rider. He took the turns faster than anyone else was willing to try, and it took only minutes of him opening it up to lose anyone who tried to follow.

I had no idea where Hale was headed, but I had no specific ideas. I needed to get Brendon back to the Kannors, but that sort of handover had to be done right. There had already been one mole — I couldn't risk there being another.

Worse, while I'd had a motel rented and ready for us, I couldn't go there now. The plan had been to get

Brendon out without anyone seeing me, but given that hadn't worked out as planned, people would be looking for both Brendon and me. We needed to keep our heads down and out of sight.

The bike slowed, and Hale pulled it off the road. At first, I thought we were in the middle of nowhere, but then I spotted a shadowed building just off the road. The bike shuddered as it made its way over a poorly maintained gravel driveway.

The building was large, like an old school or church, but the sign it used to have had faded so much that I couldn't read it.

Hale pulled the bike up to the front, then turned the engine off. He put down the kickstand and got off. When he turned toward us, I tightened my arm around Brendon.

I didn't trust Hale much with myself, so I sure as fuck wouldn't be trusting him with a child. He looked like a poster boy for the sort of person mothers tell their children to avoid.

His gaze settled on where I clutched Brendon, and he pressed his lips together and shook his head. However, where he normally would have said some shit to me, he didn't. Instead, he reached out and undid Brendon's helmet, then pulled it off. I did the same, removing mine so I could hear.

"What's your name, kid?"

"Brendon."

"I'm Hale. How'd you like the ride?"

Brendon swallowed hard and I could tell what he wanted to say. "It was fine," he lied. It reminded me of what Gunnar had said about the kid being too timid.

Hale let out a soft laugh. "Really? First time I got on the back of one of these I pissed myself. Fucking scary going that fast."

His words had me opening my eyes wide as they caught me entirely off guard. Hale was the epitome of a tough guy, and yet he was admitting to some kid that he'd pissed his pants once?

Yet, Brendon offered a small smile in return, as if Hale's words had gotten past his defenses. "It was really fast," he admitted.

"Next time, I'll put you on one with a proper back seat—back rest and all—or fuck, we'll get one of the smaller dirt bikes and teach you to ride yourself."

"We are not putting him on a dirt bike," I blurted out.

Hale glanced my way, a smirk on his lips, then looked back at Brendon with a conspiratorial wink. "Women don't like motorcycles. Lesson for life, kid— women worry too much."

"Then can we not go?"

"Nah, we'll go."

"So we just ignore what she says because she's a woman?" Brendon asked as if he'd heard that sort of thing before but didn't fully accept it.

I opened my mouth, ready to tell Hale to shut the fuck up, when he spoke over me. "Fuck, no. Only an idiot ignores a woman, especially one with a temper like this one." Hale gestured my way as he reached out and helped Brendon off the bike, the kid not the least bit afraid of him. "Women worry too much, but men don't worry enough. It's about finding that balance and finding a woman who's worth listening to." He looked my way for a moment and offered a wink before lifting

Brendon and setting him up on his shoulders like it was nothing.

And Brendon's face lit up, as if this one thing had managed to wipe away the horrors of the past weeks for him.

It left me to follow, staring at Hale's wide back and Brendon's small form, more confused than I'd been when I'd gotten to the Chasm.

This was not how I'd expected things to go.

* * * *

"Sleep, kid." Hale pulled the blanket over Brendon's shoulders, tucking him into the bed in one of the rooms.

We had tried to feed him, but given the hour and the excitement, he'd been all but falling asleep standing up.

Even stranger, Brendon hadn't clung to me. No—he had taken to Hale so much that he'd been all but glued to the Demon Lord's side. And where I had thought it would annoy Hale, he'd seemed to enjoy the interaction.

"You'll be here?" Brendon asked, his voice soft and worried.

"Yeah, kid, I'll be here. No one'll fuck with you tonight—trust me. So close your eyes and get some sleep. Tomorrow will be a hell of a lot easier if you ain't tired." Hale ran his hand over Brendon's head once, then checked the lock on the window before taking a step backward.

I pressed a kiss to Brendon's hair then left him as well, closing the door behind Hale and me so we didn't wake him with the conversation I was sure Hale wanted to have.

Except, Hale didn't say anything at first. He turned away from me and walked down the hallway, toward the huge kitchen we'd been in before. The fridge had food and alcohol in it—telling me he used this place often enough to keep it stocked—and he seemed comfortable here. He reached into the fridge and grabbed a beer, knocking the top off the bottle on the side of the counter.

"What is this place?" I asked.

He turned toward me and leaned his back against the counter. "It's my place. I don't bring people here usually."

"Well, thanks for making an exception."

He snorted softly and took a big gulp of the beer before responding. "So who's the kid?"

Which made it time to put my cards on the table, right? I sighed and leaned against the counter across from him. "His name is Brendon Kannor."

"Fuck," Hale muttered under his breath. It wasn't with surprise, as if he'd known he wouldn't like my answer, but it still ended up worse than he'd thought. "Why are you twisted up with that bullshit?"

"His sister wanted to trade her soul for his safety."

"So? Sounds like a pretty good deal."

"I couldn't do it." I shifted back and sat on top of the counter. "His sister is still a teenager. She has so much life ahead of her. I didn't want to see her do this, to regret it. It'd be different if she wanted fame or money or something stupid—in that case, it'd be her own fault. The only thing she wanted was her brother to be safe, though…"

Hale rubbed the bridge of his nose. "So Gorrin ordered you to make this deal and you decided to try this bullshit yourself instead? And now you fucking with the Sand Snakes makes sense." He shook his head then took another few big swallows of the beer. Once he finished, he met my gaze head-on. "You're an idiot, Loch. You try to go up against Gorrin? Do you have *any* idea what the fucker does to people who try to betray him?"

"I couldn't just do what he said. I remember waking up in the Chasm, and I've spent every day since regretting my choice."

"Your life ain't so bad, you know," Hale said. "There are people a lot worse off than you. Gorrin's an asshole, sure, but he's miles better than some of the folks farther down the line. You ended up a Demon, too, which set you up pretty well. And now you're risking that all for what? For a fucking teenage girl?"

I dropped my gaze to my hands, not thrilled with having to be honest about things I'd worked at ignoring for so long. "I hate that I gave up my entire afterlife for someone else, someone who never gave a damn about me. When I looked at that girl, I saw myself. I saw me when I didn't think I had any choices, and I know how that feels. It was so easy to think trading my soul away was worth it back then, but now? Now that I've experienced what it feels like to lose my free will? To be at the mercy of another person? I can't just sit here and watch someone else go through it when I can do something."

Hale came closer, his expression unreadable. His beer hung between his fingers, and he set his other hand on my cheek. "You're too fucking sweet, you know that? This all started not because you sold your soul but because you worried too much about other people and not nearly enough about yourself. You're making the same fucking mistakes again." He leaned in and brushed his lips against mine, igniting a fire inside me as my body remembered the last time he'd touched me like this, when I'd slept with him.

It had been a mistake but suddenly one I wouldn't mind making again. I traced his bottom lip with my tongue then bit down softly, trying to explain without words how I felt.

Trapped. Frustrated. Worried. I wanted him to take that all from me.

Except, he groaned before pulling back. "Kid is sleeping in a place he doesn't know. I fucking guarantee he wakes up, and I don't much want to have to explain to him the birds and the bees when he walks in on us — especially because you ain't the type to keep quiet and I ain't the type to let you." He smirked, and it melted me.

"I didn't think you'd be so good with kids," I admitted to hide the blush that no doubt covered my cheeks from him being the responsible one.

Hale let out a soft laugh. "Yeah, guess I don't much look like someone who'd deal well with kids."

"But you are. Brendon was smitten."

Hale pulled away from me and reached back into the fridge for a second beer. He opened it as he had the first, then handed it off to me. He must have decided not to be mad at me anymore. "I've had a lot of practice," he said before nodding for me to follow him.

I hopped off the counter and took a drink of the ice-cold beer.

Hale walked through the place, allowing me to get a look at more of it. I wasn't sure what the building was, but it wasn't a school or church as I'd first thought. The front doors opened to a reception area, then beyond that were a number of larger rooms — most empty. The kitchen made it clear the place had cooked for many people, and there were rows of doors where he'd settled Brendon in. "I was raised here," he said.

That made me frown, but the pieces fell together slowly. "This is a group home?"

He nodded, then stopped in front of one of the doors. It looked just like the one where we'd placed Brendon, but Hale hesitated here. After one more drink, he opened the door and gestured for me to enter.

I walked in, finding the layout similar to the room where Brendon slept. They all had two beds, two desks, two closets, set up almost like a dorm room. I tried to picture Hale as a child living here, but I struggled to do so. He was bigger than life, scary as fuck, and thinking of him as some frightened, lonely child just didn't make any sense.

Still, Hale went on, saving me from having to figure out what to say. "I've been a Demon Lord a lot less time than the others."

"I figured that with your whole style."

He snorted and crossed his arms but didn't come inside the room. "I lived in this group home for as long as I can remember. Records say I came here at three, but fuck, I don't remember that far back."

"You never got adopted?"

"People who adopt want cute babies without baggage. I'm a lot of things, but that ain't even close. Don't know exactly what I went through before getting dropped off at a fire department, but I couldn't talk, was terrified of everything—damned near feral, really. Guess that wasn't in high demand as far as kids went, and my attitude only got worse as I got older."

Which meant he'd spent his entire life here, without a family, without parents that loved him.

"Don't look at me like that," he snapped.

I took a step backward at the harshness of his tone.

He softened his voice as he went on. "Don't look at me with that pity. I was luckier than a lot of kids. This place was a hell of a lot better than wherever the fuck I came from. I probably wouldn't even be alive if they hadn't dropped me off at that station. This place might not look like much, but it was home."

"Why is it empty?"

"Closed down a few years after I aged out. I did what I could to help out here, but there just wasn't enough money to keep it afloat. When it shut down, I bought the place. Lot of memories."

"So you're used to being around kids because of growing up here?"

He gestured at one of the beds, which I had to guess was his way of telling me which had been his. "Places like this don't have nearly enough supervision. It usually falls to the older kids to watch after the younger. We made our own family, took care of our own. I remember how scary it was here at first, how alone a person would feel. Guess I never wanted anyone else to feel that way, so I'd always try to look after the new kids. I still love kids, but as I got older, I looked more and more like the sort of person kids shouldn't be around." His self-deprecating laugh held no real humor.

Then again, he *did* look scary. Everything about his appearance seemed intended to keep people away, between the tattoos, the piercings, the leather jacket, the motorcycle. "Why do you dress like that if you don't like that people are afraid of you?"

He shrugged and leaned his shoulder against the doorframe. "This is how I looked when I died. I'm stuck now."

"But why did you go that way?"

"Because it's what people saw when they looked at me anyway. They heard the way I talk, they saw me on my bike and they got scared anyway. Why fucking not let them see that up front and get over it? I'd rather they figure that shit out from the start instead of letting them get close then dealing with them turning on me."

I touched the tattoo on my cheek, the wings I'd had put there on my nineteenth birthday.

His gaze followed the movement, softening as if he understood. "You said before you did that just because, but I bet there's more to it than that. They're your only tattoos—I know because I studied your body pretty fucking thoroughly." One side of his mouth lifted into a lopsided smirk, but he kept speaking instead of focusing on that. "So why'd you decide to get them on your face?"

"I felt like I was always doing what other people wanted me to. I was stuck reacting to everyone else instead of acting. I had to tiptoe around a world where I had no power, no real worth, no importance, no control over my own life. So I got drunk on my nineteenth birthday and decided I was going to do something for me, something only for me because I wanted to, because I own myself."

"So you got a tattoo on your face?" Hale made a soft sound as if it made no sense. "I'm sure that showed 'em."

"Maybe, maybe not, but I felt better. I did what I wanted no matter what anyone else thought."

"And why pick what you did? You could have gotten anything."

"You grew up here—I'm going to guess you know exactly what it feels like to be torn between what you have to do and what you want to do, between your better nature and your worse. These were to show that, to remind myself that I have a good and a bad side, that I'm not just one or the other and that's okay."

He peered at my cheek, his eyes locked in as if deep in thought. After a moment, he smiled and shook his head. "It's weirdly fitting, ain't it? I mean, you get a tattoo with a devil wing on your cheek and you end up a demon."

I laughed softly at that fact. It was fair, all things considered. Who would have figured that these tattoos that people had hated for so long would end up fitting the bill so well?

"So, what now?" Hale asked. "You did what you came to do, so what's the plan now? How are you going to finish this?"

"I've got to get Brendon to his dad, where he'll be safe, but I need to do that carefully. He's still in danger until he's back there."

"And Gorrin?"

"Well, he won't know I'm involved. To him, someone saved Brendon and that made the deal useless to Jay. I just have to get Brendon to someone close to Charles and work on my surprise face."

"And you think you can drag a kid around with you and no one will notice?"

"Well no…" I guess I hadn't thought that far ahead. I couldn't exactly take Brendon with me as I figured out who to hand him off to.

"Just ask."

"Ask what?"

He lifted one eyebrow, the action causing the ring there to catch the light. "You asked me for help once before. Why not just fucking ask me?"

His words surprised me so much they didn't fully hit me at first. "Wait, so you're telling me you want to babysit Brendon for me?"

"*Want* isn't the right word. Ain't like I'm just begging to be saddled with a kid right now. It just makes sense. I already know about him, so you don't have to worry about telling someone else what bullshit you've gotten yourself tied up with. He likes me so he won't mind staying with me and not much can threaten him with me around."

I opened my mouth to tell him *fuck that* until no good reason against it came to me. Sure, Hale was shady and scary-looking and more than a little dangerous, but it seemed he had a soft spot when it came to kids. I needed someone to stay with him, and it wasn't like Hale was going to out me to Gorrin—they hated each other. I couldn't picture a better guard for Brendon, and having him with Hale would give me the chance to focus on what I needed to do.

So I pressed my lips together then nodded. "Okay. I'll go and talk to Gunnar, set up a hand-off, then contact you." I turned to leave the room, but Hale didn't move, didn't give me enough space to squeeze by.

It forced me to lift my gaze to his shockingly blue eyes. They drew me in, reminded me of how it had felt to be tangled together with him in bed, how it felt to see him when he'd shown up to save me when he hadn't needed to, and here he was again.

It made me question myself. I'd been so sure that the people around me were dangerous, that they couldn't be trusted, and yet they kept saving my ass.

Hale had done so, even offering to help. Yazmor had given me advice and helped me with the pharmacist. Tyrus had literally saved my life by keeping me safe when I'd been vulnerable and nursed me back to health.

Even Gorrin had healed me when he hadn't needed to.

It made me wonder just what the hell I was thinking. Hadn't I learned my lesson before about why trusting others was a bad idea? I'd died and lost my soul over putting my faith in the wrong person.

"What's with that look?" Hale asked as he caught my chin.

"I was thinking about how I know better than to trust people, and what am I doing now? Putting my trust in devils."

"Not a devil," he whispered. "And if you found trusting humans didn't work, why not try with demons?" He leaned in and took my lips in a kiss that was shockingly gentle. Just like before though, he broke it off well before I was done. "Go on, Loch, or I'm going to forget all the reasons I can't have you right now."

"Aren't you going to tell me to be careful?"

"Why would I do that? It's you we're talking about here."

I frowned. "So you're saying you trust me? That you think I can handle this?"

"Not even close. I'm saying that you're a fucking disaster and telling you to be careful is like telling a bull in a china shop to be careful — pointless. So all I'll say is to watch your ass and make sure you come back." He ran his thumb along my jawline once more before letting me go.

Just like that, he made it hard to focus on the task at hand, because he threw all my thoughts into disarray.

And he wanted to try and say *I* was the troublemaker…

Chapter Fourteen

Seeing Gunnar felt like looking at a huge meal after I was stuffed full. By all accounts, he was a catch — at least for anyone who didn't know him well. He was handsome, he had power, position and money. He was a man with a future that anyone would be happy to attach themselves to.

Yet, where I used to get butterflies from him, I felt nothing but a sinking pit in my stomach now.

Why was that? Probably because I knew who he really was, how little he actually cared about me, at least. Plus, compared to the others I'd spent time with over the past five years, Gunnar was as tough as a fucking puppy dog.

Still, that didn't stop a slight nostalgia when I saw him, as if a spark of the woman I used to be was still there, still wanted him.

Or maybe I wanted to rewrite the past. I wanted to make it so he actually cared about me the way I had for him, as if that would make his lies into the truth.

The world didn't work like that but fuck if I wasn't still drawn by the idea.

He narrowed his eyes when I walked into his place without asking. We were long past manners. "You sure fall off the face of the Earth," he said.

"I've been busy."

He looked closely at me, as if trying to figure something out. "I heard a couple of the Sand Snakes ended up dead."

"And? Didn't think you'd care much about them."

"I don't, but anything that poses a threat to them might just pose one to us. Remember when I told you they'd picked up a spy? Well, rumor has it that the dead men were part of that little event. No one heard from the men who had grabbed her, so Hopper sent a couple guys to their safe house—well, what was left of it."

"What do you mean?" Finally, his words interested me. I'd gotten out of there but I sure as fuck hadn't killed anyone.

"No one seems to know exactly. Heard a rumor from one of the guys who went to check it out when they hadn't heard a word. Seems like the whole damned cabin was torn down like a fucking tornado went through. Had a dozen men stationed there but they were all ripped apart. The guy who talked about it was far from new, but the fucker about trembled as he drank and said what he'd found."

I stared at Gunnar, trying to come to terms with that. What could have happened?

Tyrus? No—I hadn't told him who had attacked me, and he'd been there each time I'd woken up. Yazmor? He knew something had happened, but I didn't think he'd do something like *that* even if he knew who had done it.

"You look like you know something about that," Gunnar said.

Which snapped me out of my moment of thought. I quickly shook my head. "No, nothing. Just seems like an ugly way to go." I swallowed hard to try and hide my reaction, to make it seem as if I were just startled by the level of violence rather than by the question of who could have done it and how I might be connected.

"So why are you here?"

"I need to set up a time to see Charles."

"Why?"

"Does it matter?"

He crossed his arms, not giving in at all. "Yeah, it matters. Things are tense for him right now so he's not taking any meetings until they're vetted first. That means if you want to talk to him, you have to go through me, first."

I sighed, then stuck my hands into my pockets and faced him. "I found Brendon."

Gunnar's eyes widened, telling me he sure as fuck hadn't expected *that*. Seemed his information didn't get him as far as he thought. "You fucking with me?"

"Nope. I've got him."

"Where is he?"

"Safe." I shut up with that. I sure as fuck didn't trust Gunnar enough to tell him where I'd stashed Brendon. I might have to rely on him at some point, but I wouldn't do that until I had no other options.

"*Where*?" he asked, his voice dropping down as if to threaten me.

I didn't flinch, though. I met his gaze head-on. "Clearly, five years has been enough time for you to forget that I don't intimidate easily. You didn't scare me five years ago and you sure as fuck don't scare me now.

You can take that 'do as I say' tone and shove it up your ass for all the good it'll do you."

He made a frustrated sound then slammed the door shut.

I didn't mind. Let him bluster all he wanted.

"You are in *way* over your head, Loch. Do you have any idea how dangerous these people are? How much trouble you'll be in if you're caught with that kid?"

I thought back to what I'd suffered at Clint's hands, unable to suppress a shudder at the memory. "I know how dangerous it is, but I still managed what you apparently couldn't. Maybe that should tell you that I don't need your advice—I just need you to set up a meeting so I can figure out how to get Brendon to Charles."

Gunnar kept his back to the door. Maybe it was my imagination, maybe it was a result of what I'd gone through, but it felt as if he were guarding the door to keep me there.

Which put me on edge.

"Why not just bring Brendon to me? It'll be the safest, quickest route."

I shook my head. "I don't think so. I'd feel better dealing with Charles directly."

"What, you don't trust me?"

"Need we go back over how that you called me 'a convenient hole?' You haven't shown yourself to be all that trustworthy."

He snorted but didn't move from his place at the door. "What, you wanted me to break down and cry? I'd just been attacked too—revenge was more important than anything else."

"I saw you. You sold your soul and only cared about power."

"Because I needed that power to keep me safe and to avenge you!"

"You never gave a fuck about me!"

"What, you think that just because I didn't fall apart afterward I didn't care? You and I know better than that—we grew up in this world, we know exactly how dangerous it is. If you don't keep moving forward, keep after what you want, keep your guard up, it'll eat you alive. So you really going to fucking hold it against me that I didn't cry enough about you?" His words were oddly honest, as if he'd thought this through. "And you sold yours to save your own skin, so maybe don't try to balance up on that pedestal."

And that snapped my hold on my temper. "I sold my soul for *you*, you fucking asshole!"

He paused, even his breathing seeming to stop at my words.

I regretted admitting it the moment I'd uttered that, but I couldn't take it back now. I'd jumped into a raging river—I couldn't fight the current so I might as well try to swim with it. "I didn't ask for my own life—I traded my soul for your life. I gave up my soul to save *you*."

Deep lines sat between his eyebrows as if he tried to make sense of my words. "Then how are you here?"

"You've sold your soul—are you telling me they didn't give you a pamphlet for the damned? I died and I went to the afterlife and I've been there for five years now at the beck and call of a Demon Lord, and all for a guy who never really gave a fuck about me. You laughing now?"

He stared hard at me as if he could make it make sense that way. "But you look exactly the same. You couldn't have died—"

"Don't pretend to know how the world works," I snapped and lifted my sweater to show off the mangled skin at my stomach. "This killed me. I could have saved my own life and gotten more years, but I chose to save you, instead. And now I'm back here, trying to save someone else at the risk of my own wellbeing. Seems like I haven't learned a damn thing in the last five years, but that isn't true. I did learn a few things, like how trusting you is stupid."

Gunnar opened and closed his mouth again a few times. Judging from the look on his face, this was the last thing he'd expected to hear. He turned his head away, breaking eye contact.

Was that shame?

No, it couldn't be. That didn't make a damn bit of sense to me. Gunnar hadn't been embarrassed by a thing he'd done ever—I doubted he'd start with me.

"You're not kidding, are you?"

I shook my head, hating myself for saying it out loud. I didn't want him to see that pain, to know how stupid I'd been. Too many people knew it already—I didn't need to add to that embarrassment, especially from him.

He let out a long sigh, then shook his head. "I always knew you were too fucking soft."

"Yeah, well, you benefited from it, so you don't get to complain about it now. Besides, I didn't say it so we could talk about it or for you to say thank you."

"Why did you tell me, then?"

"Because you want to stare at me and tell me to trust you, to say I don't understand, that I would do the same thing, but that isn't true. I've made a lot of mistakes, and I wouldn't ever say I was a good person, but don't try and tell me that I don't understand how you feel, that I would have done what you did. That's not true, clearly."

He took a step toward me, but I moved backward. Something in his expression put me on edge—I didn't want him near me, didn't want him looking at me with anything from our past.

Because no matter what, I wouldn't go back there. It had been comfortable, but I knew now that I hadn't loved him either. Love required two people who knew each other, who cared for each other, and I'd been in it alone.

There was no way I could have loved him.

"I'm not here to rehash our history," I said. "That's a long fucking time over. I'm here to set up a meeting to hand Brendon over to Charles—that's it."

Gunnar pressed his lips together into a tight line, as if unhappy with my statement. *Too fucking bad.*

Eventually, he nodded. "Fine. Let me call Charles." With that, he walked out of the room.

Standing alone in his apartment felt somehow even stranger than being there with him. I didn't have his oppressive gaze on me, but at the same time, it forced me to think about the years that had passed. I'd lived in the Chasm, had survived there with my own problems, but Gunnar had had his own life during that time.

He'd kept going, found other people, spent those years believing me dead.

I could have checked up on him, but I hadn't wanted to. After realizing how stupid I'd been for his sake, actually seeing him had felt like tearing open the stitches on a never-healed wound.

Having come face to face with him, however, I couldn't just stick my head in the sand anymore. I pictured him eating meals and bringing women over and falling asleep here night after night. He'd had an entire life here that I wasn't a part of. So much of our lives had been intertwined together until they'd split five years ago, but I hadn't spent much time thinking about the fact that he'd still lived.

I didn't have to fall any farther down that rabbit hole, because Gunnar walked back in and he slid his phone into his pocket. "Handled."

"What exactly does 'handled' mean?"

"I talked to Charles, and we came up with a plan."

"I'm not just handing Brendon over to you without talking to him myself," I repeated.

"That's fine—you keep him for now."

That was about the last thing I expected... "Wait, really?"

Gunnar nodded and crossed his arms. "The threat to all the Kannors isn't over. It wasn't like you got Brendon while also taking out Hopper or decimating the Sand Snakes. They'll rattle their tail and come right back at us if they get the chance."

"Which means you have some twisted plan, right?"

"You sure do love to put me down, huh? But yeah, I do have a plan. We keep the hand-over as is."

"But there's no Brendon for them to hand over..."

"You were never great at the details, were you? The Sand Snakes don't know that we know about Brendon. If we move forward as if we don't know you have Brendon, they'll still show up to the meeting. Fuck knows the whole thing was nothing more than getting a shot at Charles—so we'll give them that."

I frowned. "That seems counter-productive..."

"You don't get it. Before, I wanted to set up men to lay a trap, but because of the risk to Brendon, Charles wouldn't give me permission. Now I can set up that ambush. When the Sand Snakes show up expecting an easy target, we pretend we don't know anything has happened with Brendon, go ahead with the hand-off as planned, and remove the threat."

"And you're fine with me keeping Brendon for that time?"

"I don't like it, but you being so far outside of the box means that no one'll know shit. If we try to get Brendon back first, well, you've seen the trouble a mole can cause. Better he stays out of sight until it's over. I need proof of life, though. Send me a picture of Brendon holding a note with the number eighteen written on it to prove you've really got him."

"You don't trust me? I'm so offended." I rolled my eyes at *him* being suspicious. Then again, since Gunnar would fuck over anyone, no doubt he expected the same from others. His request was reasonable, though—it was fair to want proof that I actually had Brendon.

I pulled my phone out and shot a text off to Hale requesting the photo. A few moments later, the chime of an incoming text signaled that he'd done it. Sure enough, I opened the attachment and couldn't stop a bark of laughter.

There sat a smiling Brendon with both middle fingers up and a one and eight written on the backs of his hands. *Thanks, Hale, I see you're a great influence on the kid...*

Still, it was what I needed. I saved the photo to my phone then opened it so Gunnar wouldn't see who the text had come from then turned the screen toward him.

Gunnar lifted one eyebrow then shook his head. "I guess that works. Just so you know, since you wanted to go this route, if anything happens to Brendon from this point on, that falls on your head. Any scratch that happens, you'll pay the price for. Hope you picked yourself a good babysitter."

I thought back to the Demon Lord currently watching Brendon.

I nodded. "Fair enough. Trust me, hell would freeze over before anything could get to that kid right now."

He snorted softly. "Quite the turn of phrase, huh?"

I moved past him, ready to be done with this all, to finally have something work out in my favor.

Except, as I went to leave, he wrapped his hand around my arm. It pulled me to a stop and forced me to look into his far too familiar eyes. Worse, when I saw them, it wasn't all negative emotions that hit me.

Things hadn't always been bad with him. Maybe it hadn't been what I'd thought or wanted, but we'd shared so much of our lives together, knew one another so well, it was hard not to fall back into that familiar comfort. It was like eating fast food—I knew it wasn't good for me, knew I'd regret it later, but fuck if I didn't still give in.

"You know, you're the only person who would ever throw their soul away for me," Gunnar said.

"Well, at least you had one—more than I had."

He leaned down, as if to kiss me, but I turned my head. His lips fell to my cheek, and his chuckle said my refusal amused him.

But if he kissed me, if I let myself fall down that tunnel into our past, I had no idea how I could ever dig myself out again.

"I'll see you later, Loch," he said. "No matter how this all turns out, seems like we're both headed for the same hell, so one way or another, I'll see you."

"Not hell," I muttered under my breath, an echo of what I heard so often in the Chasm.

What did the name matter, though? I was pretty sure if I had to spend eternity with the man who had broken my heart, it might as well be called hell.

Chapter Fifteen

Walking into the bar Tyrus owned felt somehow more intimidating than it had five years ago when I'd come with Yazmor my first time. That was weird, given the fact that I was no surer he didn't want to kill me — he'd had the chance, after all — but the pressure of the situation felt ten times as large.

In fact, I froze when I walked into the main bar area to find the devil himself seated at his normal booth in the middle of a tense conversation with a damned.

Then again, *all* his conversations were tense. In all my time around him, I'd yet to see him have what I would consider a nice friendly chat.

Nope — he seemed moments from violence at all times.

It meant it didn't shock me to find him in that state, but I also wasn't sure how to address him. Each time I thought about how I'd done it in the past, I went back to that room, to when he'd taken care of me. I struggled to think that man was the same one who stared so coldly at the damned across from him, the man I knew would have no issues killing someone in the middle of this crowded bar, then move on to his next meeting like nothing had happened.

How could they be the same person?

"You're looking better."

I twisted to find the bartender, Koya, smiling at me, the kindness as odd from him as it ever was. Kindness in the Chasm didn't typically last long, which was probably why I struggled to understand or accept it. Still, no doubt he was part of the reason I came here.

"Well, anyone would look better than I did then," I admitted.

Koya laughed softly before pouring a drink and pushing it across the bar to me. "That's true. I wasn't sure you were going to survive. It's weird to think you're the same girl who slunk in here that first day afraid of her own shadow, huh? Seems you're a lot tougher than people thought."

I went back in my head at that statement, over the past five years.

No, further back than that, all the way back to my childhood. Everyone had counted me out over and over again. They saw a young girl trying to survive a difficult world and had underestimated me because of it.

But here I was, having gone up against Gorrin, a Demon Lord, and succeeded. I'd pitted myself against the Sand Snakes, against criminals and killers, and I'd come out on top. People had tried to kill me, to put me down, but at the end of it I was still standing.

Sure, I hadn't done it all alone, but I'd been the one to take the risk, to go for it, to even believe it possible.

Maybe I was tougher than even I thought.

"Thanks," I said, meaning so much more than just the drink as I took it. The liquor was sweet, the sort of drink that could knock a person on their ass before they even realized it. Then again, Koya was a phenomenal bartender who always knew just what a person was after.

"I think the boss is wanting to talk to you." Koya gestured behind me.

When I turned, I found Tyrus in his booth, alone, staring at me with his eyebrow lifted.

Of course the pompous man would expect me to come trotting over with just a cocked eyebrow like some king.

And my stupid ass went right along with the unspoken demand, giving a smile to Koya before heading over and taking a seat across from Tyrus.

"You look as though you've healed well," he said.

"Yep." I held my hands out as if that proved it. "Can't keep me down for long."

He didn't acknowledge my statement, but I could almost see in his eyes as he recalled how I'd looked when I'd shown up, how banged up I'd been. I shuddered when the same memory hit me.

Sure, I lived in the Chasm, and here torture and pain were sort of par for the course. I'd managed to avoid most of that mess, probably because I was so close to the top when it came to the Demon Lords — and fuck knew their protection kept me safe — but actually experiencing something like that hit me hard.

"Loch?" Tyrus' voice was soft, taking me back to that room, to when he'd nursed me back to health. It was a tone most people probably never heard from him.

I tipped my glass back and let the alcohol numb the ugly memories from the attack. I finished off the drink, then slammed the glass down on the table as if that would end my unwanted trip down memory lane. When I met his gaze, he nodded after a moment, as if he saw that I'd pulled myself together.

"I'm glad you came back," he said.

"I always come here. It's the only decent bar in the Chasm." At his expression, I added, "Well, it's one of the places where I'm less likely to be stabbed as I drink, at least."

"You wouldn't get stabbed here."

"No? Why not? Last I checked, lots of people still get killed here."

"Only people whose deaths I don't care about." He stopped there, as if he felt he'd said enough.

Which he sort of had... Reading between those lines wasn't all that difficult even if it didn't make much sense. His words meant that he cared if I died.

I knew that, in a way, given how he'd taken care of and protected me. Still, hearing him say it made it real in a way I wasn't sure how to deal with.

"Why?" I asked.

"Why what?"

I didn't look away, wanting to read his expression as he answered — if he answered. "Why do you care if I get stabbed? Why did you take care of me when I showed up here?"

"Ah, that." He shifted in his seat, a strange thing to witness because it almost made him look nervous, something I never would have associated with Tyrus. He was steady as they came.

I remained silent, giving him a chance to work through whatever was in his own head. From what I knew of Tyrus, no doubt his brain was a twisted, fucked up place.

After a moment, he slid from the booth and stood. I sighed, figuring that was his answer, that he didn't intend to give me the truth. Not a shocker, since men — especially ones who wielded power the way he did — didn't tend to like to bare their souls.

Except, he paused and turned back toward me. "Are you not coming?"

"Where?"

"This isn't a discussion to have in public. If you want to talk, we should do so where our conversation will remain just between us."

His words made me peer around to realize more than a few sets of eyes were on us. They were casual, sure, and they darted away as soon as I looked at them, but there was no doubt that we had an audience.

So I rose and followed Tyrus, walking to his side and a step behind. We went through the backdoor in the bar, to the private elevator that went up to his quarters. I'd taken it to leave before, but I didn't recall riding it up with him the first time.

"Was the elevator always this small?" I asked when I couldn't stand the silence and the tension another moment.

Tyrus offered me a sidelong glance, looking every bit as in control as always. It was frustrating how easily he did that, how he could seem to handle any situation without nerves or discomfort. It seemed I wasn't as adept at that just yet.

Or, well, ever, I guess. I doubted I'd manage that stoic exterior. I was far too high strung.

"The elevator is the same size it has always been."

"Oh." I shuffled my feet against the ground. "Guess it just seems smaller…"

"Relax."

"I am. Super relaxed. No stress or issues over here." I let out a thin laugh intended to prove my point that only managed to make me sound even more unsettled.

He sighed as if I were a lot to handle. "I find it frustrating that you still behave like this around me."

"Like what?"

"Like I am a Demon Lord." The elevator doors opened, leading us to the familiar sight of his living room. It was strange to think I'd stayed here so recently, that I'd been here with Tyrus.

Then his words hit me. "Um, but you *are* a Demon Lord."

"You are a demon, but you are more than that, are you not? I hold the position of Demon Lord, but that is just a title. I am still a man."

"Devil."

"Not a devil," he muttered. "If I wanted to cause you harm, don't you think I would have already? I have had both the power and the opportunity to have done so had that been my plan. Because I haven't, I wish you would relax around me more, that you would not guard yourself so heavily from me." He went to his kitchen, the sight odd. Tyrus struck me as the type to be waited on hand and foot, so him even existing in a domestic setting was weird as fuck. He opened his fridge and took out a glass bottle of water, then handed it over to me. "Drink. Koya tends to make his sweet drinks stronger than people realize."

"Fine, but I'm only drinking because I want to, not because you told me to." I flipped the metal clasp that held the lid on, then took a drink.

Tyrus shook his head, though he didn't look all that annoyed. Instead, he seemed oddly charmed by my defiance. Then again, how many people talked back to him?

"Are you truly all right after what happened?"

He didn't need to spell that out—I knew what he meant. I ran my thumb along the edge of the bottle as I answered. "Yeah, I'm okay. I healed up perfectly. Gorrin helped speed it along and even the bruising's gone now."

"I am not talking about your physical health."

"Oh." I froze after saying that one word, as if it made my point. I just got stuck after it, unsure what else to say.

He gestured at the couch, then took a seat on it, leaving enough room for me beside him.

And I never figured I'd sit next to Tyrus like this, all casual and shit. It felt strange, like we were both outside of the roles we'd always held.

Still, I found myself doing as he'd asked and taking a seat beside him. I clutched the water bottle in my hands as if I could focus on that and not my nerves.

"You asked why I helped you—I suspect you will not find the answer all that satisfying."

"Tell me anyway."

He nodded, then turned slightly to face me even though I kept my gaze purposely down and away from him. "I couldn't not help you. I've seen many come to the Chasm and many leave and you are the first I didn't want to see gone. The Chasm would be a poorer place for losing you, but I care little about that. *I* would miss you."

"But you don't even talk to me," I pointed out. It wasn't like we were besties, like we spent much time together chatting it up and hanging out.

"I do. Perhaps not much—you always have your guard up around me—but what little interaction we have soothes a part of me I didn't think could be soothed, not anymore. So when I saw you there, bloodied and broken and so close to gone, my anger surprised me. Not much angers me anymore, not much touches me. I have seen too much, done too much for things to bother me, but seeing you in that state..." He trailed off, frowning as if unsure how to continue. "The fact that you came to me also unsettled me. You could have gone anywhere, but you came here, to me."

He was being honest, so I figured I owed the same. I twisted to mirror his position and looked into his eyes. They were so dark that without bright lights, they appeared almost black. "I honestly didn't think about it," I admitted. "I managed to escape the people who had me, and I stumbled outside, sank my fingers into the soil, and I didn't have time to consider where to go."

"But you came to me. You know that means something, that some part of you trusts me and knew you would be safe here."

"What does that mean?"

He reached out slowly, as if giving me the chance to turn him down, before he set his hand on my cheek. His palm was warm and large and rough. It was also covered in blood, at least metaphorically. No matter how nice he tried to act to me right now, I knew what he was. I knew the horrible things he had done, that he continued to do.

Tyrus ran his portion of the Chasm through vicious business. He treated it like a mafia, and he was ruthless in his interactions. He had no issues with drugs, prostitution, violence or anything else so long as it gained power for him.

And yet, even knowing that, I couldn't push him away. I recalled how gently he'd cared for me, how so many times in the bar he'd stepped in on my behalf, the way I would look at him occasionally and find those dark eyes locked on me.

His touch was a question, as if offering me something if I wanted it, one he left me to answer.

And I knew my answer. I set the water bottle down on the table, then slung my leg over his lap and kissed him with the sort of passion a person only had when they knew they were doing something extremely stupid.

Tyrus went entirely still for a moment as I slipped my tongue past his warm, soft lips. Had it really startled him that much?

That moment of uncertainty passed quickly, however, and a breath later, Tyrus slid a hand behind my neck to pull me tighter against him. His groan was deep and hungry, which was just fine with me. I didn't want him passive — that wouldn't be the devil I knew.

I dragged my hand down his chest, breaking the kiss so I could sit back and look. "Touching you feels like messing with a piece of art," I admitted. "You're always so perfectly put together."

"I'm not nearly as put together as you think." He ran one of his large hands up the outside of my thigh, his touch aggressive, as if afraid I'd disappear if he didn't get his fill right away. "You make me feel out of control," he whispered, then used his grip on my waist to pull me down and grind me against his erection.

His words made me almost laugh. I made *him* feel out of control? Here he was, driving me wild, and he believed this was all me?

I undid the buttons of his jacket, then pulled off his tie and worked free the buttons of his shirt. It left him with his chest bare, but the sight made me go still.

I'd never seen him undressed before, and the scars that covered him silenced all my thoughts. My next touch of him was painfully gentle as I traced the first mark, a large bullet wound on his chest. Another four sat on his chest and stomach, then, at his throat, where his tie normally covered, was a thick scar. I traced that one, surprised by how much seeing it hurt me.

Tyrus caught my hand in his, looking up and into my eyes. "Every demon here wears the scars that killed us."

His words reminded me of Hale, of my own scars, of the fact that we had all suffered and died and held on to those painful memories.

"What happened?"

"I didn't become what I am here out of nowhere. I lived this sort of life already, on Earth, and this is the price I paid for it."

"But why?"

He sighed, then guided my hand over the marks. First, he traced the bullet wounds, one at a time as he spoke. "I headed a crime syndicate, but I trusted the wrong person. My youngest son decided he didn't want to play second fiddle anymore, so he gathered supporters and at a family dinner, he made his move. He murdered my wife and his siblings to clear the way for him to take over. The others died from the bullet wounds, but I was tougher." He moved my fingertips to follow the line at his throat. "He slit my throat himself — the only moment of pride I have for that child. At least he did that with his own hands instead of leaving the task to others like a coward."

"Your own son?" I struggled to believe it. Maybe it was because despite my fucked-up upbringing, I knew my mother had loved me. I couldn't fathom a child willing to do such horrendous things, especially just for power.

He nodded, though he continued to stroke my fingers over the scar at his throat as if it soothed him. "His name was Elliot. I don't know if it makes me feel better or not, but he couldn't manage to do the job he wanted so badly. He only lasted a year before someone else took over, ending our line for good."

"When was that?"

"Eighteen-ninety."

That made me pull back slightly. "Fuck, you're old…"

He made a soft sound that was similar to a laugh. "I think this is what draws me to you. You do not play a game — at least not well. You say things no one else would dare — not even Koya, and he dares more than most when it comes to me."

"Sorry," I said, even if I didn't feel that bad about it. "It's still a bit of a mind fuck when I remember that time passes here, but people don't age."

"Most people struggle with that at first, but eventually, you get used to it."

I peered at the mark at his throat, where I touched him now even without his urging. This was the wound that ended his life, that sent him here, to the Chasm.

It made me want to know more about the history of the Chasm, the people in it. Each damned and each demon had a story, a life, a reason they sold their soul and a death that had landed them here.

It was easy to look at the twisted creatures that lived here, the horrible things they did, and write them all off. The reality was that they'd all been human before. They'd been just like me.

Tyrus was yet another example of this. He did things that chilled me to the core, was feared and respected through the Chasm, yet he carried the pain of his own death with him, the betrayal and loss of his family.

"Are any of your family here?" I asked.

"Thankfully, no. It's the only thing I can be truly grateful for. Even Elliot didn't sell his soul to make his move, so they all ended up in the Plains." His gaze took on a faraway quality, as if he'd sunk back into his own past. "I want them to be happy — even Elliot. I'm here because of the choices I made, the life I lived, the fact that my power and family meant more to me than my own eternity, and I am thankful that I could keep them from making that same choice."

"Do you miss them?"

"Of course," he admitted. "My wife was sweet and kind and she thought the world of me. My oldest son was tough and reliable — he would have made a wonderful boss someday. My daughter was a troublemaker, always sneaking out and doing what she wanted no matter what anyone said. She was supposed to marry the son of another family, but she refused no matter how others pushed."

His words had me tilting my head. "That story you told me…"

Tyrus nodded, the expression on his face softer than I was used to. Was he remembering her? "Yes, it was about her. I had tried to tell her stories that had normal, well-behaved women, but she never cared for those. If she had lived at a different time, she might have been better suited than her brother to take over, in fact." He shook his head, and when he spoke again, it was with the same tone as before, as if he had tried to get himself back on track. "Elliot was driven, always wanting to prove himself, but he wasn't evil. I don't know what pushed him, in the end, to what he did, but I recall him as a young man, when he wanted nothing more than to show me something he was proud of, for me to praise him."

I stared at Tyrus as he bared so much of his past to me. The lust from earlier had dissipated, but something else grew in that moment between us. I wasn't just looking at one of the feared Demon Lords of the Chasm—I saw him as a man, as someone who carried pain and doubts and a past.

I leaned in and pressed my forehead to his, wishing I knew the right words to take some of that pain away, to carry it for him. Anything I tried would have been an insult, no doubt, because I really had no idea how he felt, had never been where he had.

He slid his arms around me and pulled me tight against him in what sure as fuck felt like a hug.

And when I'd arrived here five years ago, I never would have expected to cuddle up with a Demon Lord…

Chapter Sixteen

Fuck. I knew I was in trouble the moment that screaming pain in my head started, the one that called me to Gorrin's side and refused to be ignored.

I'd felt it before, but never *this* bad. It had never made my brain feel as if it melted inside my skull, made me stumble and grab for the wall to keep myself upright.

However, it seemed Gorrin wasn't fucking around, and that was a *very* bad sign for me. Had he figured out what I'd done? The only good thing was that I wasn't far away from him. If he'd pulled this shit while I'd been on Earth, I could only imagine my struggle to transport back.

Instead, I was already back at his property, in my own room, cuddled up with Whalebert as I rested. With nothing to do until the hand-off, I'd been forced to pass the time, and after my meeting with Tyrus, I had figured something relaxing was the best choice.

Not that relaxing was anywhere on my mind when Gorrin decided to make my skull feel as if it were splitting in half.

I opened the door and stumbled down the long hallway, my vision blurry as that demand echoed through my head, like a focal point I couldn't move away from.

I tripped when I reached the door to his quarters, falling through it and to the hard floor. However, as soon as I entered the room, that crushing pain disappeared as if it had never been there at all.

Well, the pounding of my heart and throbbing of my head said it had been real, as did the way sweat covered my forehead. I panted hard, not pushing myself upright, unsure if I even had the strength to do so. What would the point be anyway? If Gorrin wanted to wipe me off the face of the Chasm, there wasn't a damned thing I could do to stop him.

"Do you have any idea how long I have been a Demon Lord here?"

I didn't bother to try and answer—I doubted he wanted one even if I could. Besides, the only answer he'd get from me would be, 'a long-ass time, Gramps,' which would likely only worsen my already piss-poor situation.

"In all those years, those millennia, I have never met a creature as stubborn and foolish as you."

"My mom always said I was special," I whispered before forcing myself up to at least sit. The moment I saw Gorrin's face, I wished I hadn't.

He was always so cool and collected, but not right now. His expression, normally impossible to read, was bathed in anger.

I guess that answers whether or not he knows about what I did. I could think of nothing else I'd done to earn this sort of reaction from him.

"Do you have a death wish?" He crouched in front of me as if he wanted to study my face up close.

"Already dead, in case you forgot." I lifted my shirt to show off the scar from the bullets that started it all.

"And yet you still push yourself toward another untimely end, one that will expel you from the afterlife entirely. You needed only to follow my very simple directions, but instead, you move behind my back, you lie to me, you spit in my face for all I've done for you."

"No idea what you're talking about." I didn't look away as I said it — even if we both knew the truth, I sure as fuck wouldn't admit it. It felt like when a kid knew their parent was pissed but wasn't sure why exactly. The last thing I'd do was start offering up things he might not be aware of yet.

Besides, the hand-off was tomorrow. No matter how angry Gorrin was, I only had to make it to tomorrow night, and I'd have accomplished what I'd been after.

He caught my chin, forcing my eyes to lock with his. "Do not play games with me. You once told me you were called salmon, but let me assure you that you are a very little fish in a very large pond. You are in so far over your head you do not even understand the world around you."

I shook my head, or tried to at least, given his tight grip on my chin. "Whatever you want me to say, I won't."

"You think I don't have the power to force your compliance? You believe you are any match for me?"

"No — I know I'm no match for you."

"So why do you persist in defying me?"

"Because I still have to live with myself," I snapped. "No matter what you do to me, I still have to wake up each day and face myself. I have to be able to accept my own choices. I already know what regret feels like and you can fuck right off if you think I'll do anything to saddle myself with any more guilt."

He moved his grip from my chin to my arm, then pulled me to my feet roughly. "Guilt matters little in this world. Everyone harbors some amount of guilt if they exist because we are all forced into premade roles, into rules created by a madman that can't be changed. I have tried to teach you this lesson time and time again, have tried to give you the space and time to learn on your own, have done all I can to lead you to the truth, but still you resist. Still you ignore my words and my advice and the reality in which you live, in favor of what? For a fantasy where you can be a hero? For a lie where you can change things? Things do not change, little fish, they merely crush those who do not find their place in the world."

"So let it crush me!" I yanked away from him. "If that's what it takes, I'll accept it—happily. The only thing I won't do is betray myself, betray what I think is right. I sold my soul because I thought it was the right thing to do, and while I regret the fuck out of that, at least I did something."

"You will make the deal with Jay."

"I don't think she'll want one anymore." I lifted my chin, refusing to be intimidated by him. "And if she doesn't, we can't force one on her."

He narrowed his eyes until they were nothing but slits of golden light. "And you believe that you've won because of that?"

"I think that if the Sand Snakes don't have her brother, she has no reason to make a deal for his safety."

He reached out, wrapped his hand around my throat, then used the grip to pull me closer. Even still, he didn't tighten his hand, didn't obstruct my breathing, leading me to suspect the move was a threat rather than to hurt me.

It still worked as one hell of a threat though, and when I gulped, my throat moved against his palm.

"This world *will* end you," he all but whispered, his voice low and his face so close I could have kissed him without moving. "Stop fighting the inevitable, *please.* This world requires power to survive, and the only way to gain power is to gather souls, to make deals and bind them to you. That increases your standing and your safety, but even in five years, you have yet to make a single deal."

"If that's what it takes to survive this world, maybe I don't belong in it. If I have to condemn others to an eternity of servitude, I don't think my survival is worth that."

"It is worth it to me," he said, his voice impossibly small and sounding nothing like the uncaring man I'd come to know. His expression remained angry, but his voice gave away something deeper and far more complex. "I do not wish to see you crushed beneath the others in the Chasm, and I can only do so much to protect you. No matter how powerful I am, I can't expect to protect you from everything forever. Please, trust me. Believe that if anyone here understands this world, it is me. Do as I ask because I am doing it all for *you.*"

He almost sounded as if he begged me, something I never thought I'd hear from him. Even still, his words drifted past me, not the least bit tempting.

Sure, after spending time on Earth, after feeling like myself for the first time in five years, I didn't want to just lie down and die. My time with so many others, when I got to work hard, when I got to try to achieve something, made me want a future now.

I didn't want it enough to throw away my own principles, though.

"I can't," I told him. "It doesn't matter how much you push or what you try to tell me, I can't change—I won't. If survival requires me to become someone I hate, I can't do that."

"Even if the other option is another death? A final one?"

I nodded—it didn't even require any thought. "When I saw Jay, I saw myself. I saw a young girl in a hard spot who just needs some help. I can't use that to damn her for eternity. I was that girl, and I wish someone had been around to actually help me back then instead of taking advantage of it. So, no, I can't go back on that, not even to save myself."

Gorrin pressed his lips together into a tight line, one that screamed frustration. Then again, we stood there at an impasse. He wanted me to go down one path and I refused. There was no middle ground, no way to reach a common point where we both could be happy.

"If you will not save yourself, *I* will save you. I will drag you into this new world kicking and screaming if I must. I will shove you into your place in this world and ensure you survive it no matter how you feel about it." He used his grip on my arm to pull me toward the door that led to his room, then shove me through it.

He used enough force that I tripped and fell to the floor. "You will remain here. You'll find I've made it so no communication can leave my quarters and you will be unable to transport—no matter how much sand you have in your pocket."

"What are you going to do?" I asked as I turned to look him in the face.

"Whatever it takes. Hate me if you want, but I will not lose you because of your own foolishness. Stay put while I resolve this." His words were clearly an order, especially because when I rushed toward the door, that same agony in my head hit me, a warning against disobeying what Gorrin had ordered.

He slammed the door shut, leaving me trapped, but that was fine. Everything was set up already.

I didn't care what happened to me—I'd saved Brendon and Jay and there wasn't a damn thing Gorrin could do to stop it.

* * * *

"Not even a sex toy, huh?" I dug through the nightstand beside Gorrin's bed, pulling all the items out and tossing them across the comforter.

For a bachelor living alone for thousands of years, I would have figured he'd have at least a few sex toys. Nights were long and lonely in the Chasm—especially because it was always nighttime here. I would have figured he just indulged with randoms, like Tyrus and Hale did, but I'd never witnessed anything like that from Gorrin.

He'd been a Demon a long time, so perhaps he didn't have those urges anymore, or maybe his hand worked well enough for him.

"Maybe he's so old that he can't get it up anymore." I laughed at my own stupid joke.

"He doesn't actually age, so if his penis doesn't work right, it's a pre-existing condition."

I smirked as I turned my head to find Yazmor in the room. The last time I'd seen him had been tense, to say the least, but all of that drifted away. The blood he'd left on my face, that terrifying shifting of the world around us, none of it seemed real anymore.

Or maybe I was just so bored and lonely from being locked in a room alone that I was thankful for any company—even his.

"What are you doing here?" I asked as I flipped open a small journal I found in the nightstand.

"I heard you were grounded and, if I know you at all, I was certain you were causing problems. I couldn't miss out on that kind of fun."

"Me? Problems?" I waved him off before flipping to another page. "I'm just here searching through all of Gorrin's private things. He doesn't have any sex toys. That's weird, right?"

"I don't have any either."

"Yeah, but that's *you*. I'd be more shocked if you had something like that."

Yazmor tilted his head as if deciding whether or not to be insulted by my words. After a moment, he seemed to come to a decision because he sat on the bed beside me. "Do you still not consider me a man?"

I lifted my eyebrow, then dragged my gaze down his body. He wore a loud and rather ugly printed, button-up shirt and a pair of board shorts. He reminded me of a surfer, like he could show up on the beach looking like that and fit in. All he was missing was a puka shell necklace. "I know you're male," I said. "The lack of tits gave you away. You also included yourself in the naked artwork in that book you gave me, so I've seen that you have all the right parts."

"You may understand that I'm male in form, but I don't think you truly accept what that means. You act nervous around other men in a way you don't around me."

"You're different."

He nodded, as though that were a given, but didn't continue the line of thought any further. Instead, he gestured at the journal. "Anything good?"

"Maybe, but since he wrote it in some old, dead language, I can't read it." I handed it over to Yazmor.

He glanced at the writing, then chuckled. "This is a language few could read."

"Can you?"

"Some. I mostly know the curses and insults, but I've got a passing understanding of the rest." He pointed at a few lines. "This is talking about you."

"Me?" I grabbed the journal back before remembering that I couldn't read it, which meant the scribbles meant nothing to me. "What does it say?"

Yazmor widened his grin, looking like mischief made flesh. "I can't tell you that. I'm pretty sure it is something he wouldn't want you to know."

"That's just mean. You can't even give me a hint?"

Yazmor lifted his hand and stroked his thumb across my bottom lip in a touch that made my stomach do somersaults. "He's fascinated with your lips. Even I might blush if I went into details about the specifics."

And there went my cheeks, no doubt. Something about imagining Gorrin—the picture of a man who didn't give a fuck about women—fantasizing filthy things about my mouth made me wish he wasn't such an asshole.

Then again, would I even want him if he wasn't? Maybe that was all part of his charm.

"He also truly does care."

At that, I jerked my gaze back to Yazmor's, unsure I'd heard him right.

"I probably shouldn't say that, right? I should pit you against him because him being distracted by your fights only helps me in every way."

"You never seem to be at the throats of the other Demon Lords, so I didn't think you'd care about ways to get one over on them."

"I don't care. This whole rivalry they have has never interested me, which is why I don't fight with them. Still, if the prize were great enough, it might be worth wading into that fray." His gaze was heavy on me as he said that, his smiling disappearing as if he were being serious.

A part of me wanted to ask him what he meant by that, but something kept me silent. The reason? Because the way he stared answered it.

He was saying he wouldn't go up against Gorrin for power or position, but he would for me.

Which I again struggled to understand.

"Why now?" I asked. "I've been in the Chasm for five years and no one has made a real move on me—well, Hale tried to get in my pants before, but that's normal. Now, in the last two weeks, I swear every one of you Demon Lords seem to be trying to get a piece and I don't understand why. What am I? Catnip for demons? A chew toy you all want to claim for yourself?"

"Maybe you weren't ready before."

"I don't think I'm ready to deal with this now or ever."

Yazmor shook his head as he went through the items on the bed, picking them up and discarding them just as quickly. "You were waiting when you first came here. You weren't a part of this world, resistant to joining it, just decoration really. You've changed recently."

"I really haven't."

"You say that because people don't see themselves clearly. From the outside, I can say, you've grown. You've stopped hiding, stopped allowing things to simply pass by you. You were backed into a corner and chose to move — finally."

"So what? You all were just waiting like fucking vultures?"

"Did you know vultures perform a mating ritual where they hop in circles with several others?"

I dug the heels of my hands against my eyes at his absurdity. "I guess I should know that I always get trivia from you."

"I like trivia because it is made up of facts," Yazmor said. "Facts are simple. They never change. They allow people to understand the world around them, which is nice for those of us who have seen it change so many times. If I know enough trivia, I feel like I understand this world, as if it were solid and I could make a place for myself in it."

His tone came out strangely forlorn for him. I could have taken his hand, could have told him that people made their own place in the world, but I doubted he'd take any of that seriously, so instead, I went with something that felt more in line with his personality.

I opened the journal again and handed it over. "You want facts? Well, Gorrin was dumb enough to lock me in here unsupervised with all his stuff, so let's uncover his embarrassing secrets. I want drunken one-night stands and premature ejaculation stories."

Yazmor stared at the journal for a moment, then offered me a smile that held more softness and a tad bit less craziness than usual. He took the book, then started scanning the writing.

I scooted closer, leaning against his arm, letting myself pretend for a moment that we were just two normal people instead of whatever we were.

I'd earned a moment to pretend whatever the fuck I wanted before Gorrin came back and everything changed.

* * * *

I woke hours later, after Yazmor had left, when someone slammed the door open.

Sure enough, I found the scowling face of the very man who had trapped me here. Gorrin stood in the doorway, his gaze moving over the room.

Which I had *destroyed* by going through everything I could find. I'd torn apart every shelf, every drawer—*nothing* had been safe from my snooping.

And probably out of annoyance, I'd left the evidence all over, as if to ask him, '*What the fuck are you doing to do about it?*'

"You are impossible," Gorrin muttered before looking straight at me, as if my little act of rebellion didn't matter. "Come."

A warning in my head happened, one that said I'd better obey. I followed Gorrin, unwilling to endure the pain of disobeying something so trivial. We didn't go far, though. Instead, we stopped in his office space, alone there.

Maybe he'd grown tired of this, or me, of all of it. Hell, for all I knew, he planned on killing me now.

I glanced at my watch. An hour before the hand-off time, when the Kannors would spring their trap, when they'd remove the enemy so Brendon could return home safely. Whatever Gorrin wanted to do at that point was fine.

Or, not fine, but at least I'd done what I needed to. I'd done one good fucking thing in my life, something I could point at and be proud of. Anything Gorrin wanted to do was a small price to pay.

I wanted to talk, to fill the uncomfortable silence with pointless chatter as usual, but something about the harsh set of Gorrin's lips told me I'd just make it worse. And, sure, making things worse was normally my go-to move, but I had a feeling now might be more trouble than I wanted.

When the quiet finally got to me, when I opened my mouth with zero idea what I'd actually say, the door to the hallway opened and everything ground to a stop.

Walking in were the last two people I would have expected, the last two I wanted to see.

"Hello, Loch," Gunnar said, his hand wrapped around Jay's arm as he pulled her along with him.

Looks like I didn't need to do shit to make things worse — they were headed for a clusterfuck all on their own.

Chapter Seventeen

"Jay!" I rushed forward, wanting to get Gunnar's hands off Jay, but Gorrin caught me by the nape of my neck as if I were some unruly child.

I brushed him off, again only because he let me since he out-classed me when it came to strength by one hell of a measure, but I didn't go after Jay again. "Are you okay?" I asked her.

Jay nodded, but her expression showed her fear. At least I saw no injuries, no signs of anyone having hurt her. She walked with nervous but even steps and she didn't flinch or favor any place on her.

Which let me narrow my eyes and look at Gunnar. "What the fuck are you doing here?"

"Is that any way to say hello to an ex?"

"I would have preferred something more traditional, like a stake through your heart, but I didn't bring a stake and you don't have a heart."

He let out a soft laugh as if amused by my outburst but unworried. Clearly, he still had no idea what I was or what I could do if I wanted, and boy was he poking at my last fucking nerve. "It was hard to believe when you told me you sold your soul for me. In fact, it charmed me a bit, made me wonder if I'd been backwards about you. Maybe we *do* have a future. I mean, I'll be here in a few decades, and so will you, so why not?" He peered around the room as if it were normal for him to be here, but I could spot the tension.

He hadn't been here before, no matter how comfortable he wanted to act. He also didn't understand a fucking thing about this place.

"Let me make myself *perfectly* clear—you and I won't ever happen. Usually I'd say, 'not in this life,' but I can confidently say 'not in this afterlife or any other.'"

Gunnar chuckled as if he found my resistance adorable before he turned toward Gorrin. "Here she is."

Jay cowered away from Gorrin—not that I could blame her. Gorrin didn't look friendly at the best of times and the anger in his expression now was far from his best.

Still, Gorrin didn't approach her or give her more than a moment of attention before turning back toward me. "Make the deal."

"What? No. Kindly fuck off—or, better yet, fuck off in the least kind way possible. You don't have Brendon, so you've got nothing to bargain with. She doesn't need to make a deal with you, so why would she?"

Gorrin stood straighter, his honey-colored eyes swirling as he stared at me. "You misunderstand your leverage and the situation. Yes, you have Brendon—however, Gunnar never told Charles about that. Where Brendon is doesn't matter—as far as the Kannors know, the Sand Snakes still have him. That means the handover is still set up. At that meeting, the Sand Snakes will remove Charles, thus sending the family into chaos, as was the plan from the start."

My gaze moved to where Gunnar held Jay's arm and it all fit together into a sickening image. How had I missed the truth for so long?

"You were behind this all," I whispered, turning to face Gorrin. No matter Gunnar's part, he wasn't nearly smart enough to come up with this all on his own. No, this *screamed* Gorrin's hand. "With Brendon and Charles gone, the family would look toward the second-in-command—Gunnar. If he could secure a marriage with Jay, he would take over the entire family, and without Charles, who was going to oppose you marrying Jay?" I let out a long breath, forced to admit I was as dense as Gorrin had always said. "Which means you knew who Gunnar sold his soul to from the start— it was you."

"Not me—it was rather far down the line—but yes, he belongs to my line, thus ultimately to me."

"Why involve me in this at all? You had it set up without needing *me* to be a part of it. You could have done this all without forcing me to endure it!" I took a step toward Gorrin as if I could do a damn thing to him. I just couldn't help it—I had too much energy arcing around inside me and no outlet.

"You need to understand the way the world works," Gorrin said. "Which means you needed to put your past to bed, and you couldn't do that unless you confronted it. You want to hold on to the person you were, but that isn't possible. You must choose a side or you will tumble down into the abyss, and I will not allow that to happen."

"You can't force me."

"Of course I can. I had hoped you would come to this understanding on your own. When I saw what Jay wanted, when I realized how perfect this was, I created a situation where you would have to face the person you used to be, the life you used to live, and let it all go. You, however, failed to do as I expected. You didn't complete the task and chose instead to fight against it, but still, I let you do so. I gave you the space to come to terms with reality on your own, even when Gunnar told me of your plan, when you lied to my face, I still let it go so you could learn on your own. I never expected you to be stubborn enough to remain willfully ignorant."

"Never underestimate my ability to be ignorant," I muttered, the joke stupid but all I could come up with as my heart pounded. It was the way Gorrin looked at me, the confidence in his arrogant eyes, the certainty he had that he'd won already.

He kept going as if I hadn't spoken. "Since you were unable to come to the right conclusion on your own, I will ensure you see reason." He turned his gaze to Jay, who cringed at having his full attention. "Your father *will* die in thirty minutes if you do not make a deal with Loch. If you offer her your soul, in exchange, your father and brother will be safe. You will go back to how you lived before and will not need to think upon this or us for the rest of your life."

Gunnar lifted his chin. "What about me? If they're alive, I don't get what I want. Bitch won't marry me if they're still around and if the brat lives, he'll take over."

Gorrin peered at Gunnar as if he were little more than a piece of gravel stuck in the tread of his shoe. "You made your deal with a subordinate, not me. Had I been consulted, I would have flayed you alive for what you did to Loch, so do not think to negotiate or demand with me. Besides, you sold your soul for the power to seek revenge. As far as I understand, you did that and killed those who had targeted you—that means you have been duly paid. Had you done as you were bid by me properly, you would have secured your position in the Kannors. This failure rests on your own shoulders, so cease your complaints." With that, Gorrin looked away from Gunnar in dismissal.

"Wait a fucking minute," Gunnar said. "You can't just take shit back like that. Who do you think you're fucking with?"

"A lowly human who does not appreciate the things he was lucky enough to be given."

Gunnar didn't seem to like that answer, because he pulled a pistol from the holster on his hip and pressed the muzzle against Jay's temple. "Yeah? Well, I'm pretty sure this little plan of yours won't work if Jay here ends up with a hole in her head. Maybe you want to belly back up to the negotiation table, huh?"

Gorrin stared at Gunnar as if he didn't matter at all, as if his threat were at best a nuisance. "Stop," Gorrin said, his voice steady.

And as if those words were connected directly to Gunnar's body, he immediately dropped his hand, his eyes wide, his mouth open in a wordless scream. Then again, I *knew* that horrible feeling in my brain when I tried to resist an order, the agony that overcame me entirely. The first time a person went through that, it was shocking. When Gunnar stopped moving, stopped fighting, his body went lax. Had he passed out?

He'd be lucky if he had. Gunnar said enough stupid shit that being unconscious was no doubt his best chance at surviving.

Gorrin turned his gaze back to Jay as if he didn't give a fuck about Gunnar anymore. "Do you understand now? Are you prepared to make the deal in order to save your family?"

"This isn't fair," I blurted out. "You can't push her into it like that—it's against the rules. You told me a person has to make the deal of their own freewill, that we can't force them into it."

"I am not forcing her. I didn't order the Sand Snakes to abduct Brendon. I didn't make them want to kill the Kannors. I didn't remove Brendon from the Sand Snakes' care. Gunnar made and carried out his plan—I only made use of it when I saw Jay willing to make a deal. If I do nothing, the Sand Snakes will meet with Charles and kill him. That is the reality. If Jay wishes for that to change, then she will make the deal."

I clenched my molars in frustration at his loophole. He wasn't wrong, and if anyone understood the rules of the Chasm best, it would be him.

"Okay," Jay said, her voice quiet and frightened. "I'll do it."

"No," I snapped. "You don't have to do this, Jay."

"I can't just let my dad die, not if I can do something about it. If that something is selling my soul to save my family, well, I'll do that."

"But we saved your brother already."

"But without my dad, do you really think we'll have any chance to keep the family going? That anyone will listen to Brendon or me?" She peered over at Gunnar. "We don't even have Gunnar anymore, so there isn't a second to help take over."

I paced, trying desperately to come up with another option, to figure out some way to make this all work out. Nothing came to me, though. No matter how hard

I worked, how I struggled through it, I couldn't see a path forward.

I couldn't leave, not from this room, not with Gorrin here. It meant even if I could do a damn thing to keep the Sand Snakes from meeting up with the Kannors, I had no way to get there. Gorrin had made it so my phone didn't work, so I couldn't call Hale or Charles, couldn't warn anyone.

I was entirely powerless…

"Make the deal," Gorrin said, his words impossible to take as anything other than a clear order. Sure enough, that sensation in my head told me to obey, to do as commanded by the one who owned my soul.

Still, I shook my head, ignoring the way it increased the pain. "No," I said. "I won't damn her."

"You'll allow her father to die, then?"

"We don't know for sure what will happen. For all we know, the Kannors could come out on top, or maybe they'll hear about the attack ahead of time. You can't see the future, so you have *no* idea what will happen if we do nothing, but I know what will happen if I make that deal. Jay will be damned for eternity, and I won't do that to her."

"You are letting foolish human emotions blind you," Gorrin said, his voice not so calm or collected anymore. He advanced on me, driving me backward step by step until he trapped me between the wall and his imposing body. "You know better than to think you can resist me. I *own* you, little fish. You can struggle all you wish, but you will do as I say in the end. You will learn your place and the order of things. The only question is how much you have to suffer before you give in. This does not need to hurt you so." He lifted his hand.

I flinched, unable to help it with the pain in my head, with realizing just how much he'd played me.

He hesitated, a rare moment of indecision, as if he didn't like my reaction. Still, a breath later he set his hand on my cheek. "You need not suffer for nothing. Just give in. This is what Jay wants, so why deny her? It is not your job to bear the pain of others."

I looked into his eyes, wondering when they'd become so familiar, when they'd changed from the eyes I'd hated, the ones I blamed so much of my pain on, to ones that mattered to me? Even now, I hated how they calmed me.

But...no matter what he thought, no matter how he wanted to prove some point to me, I couldn't let that happen. I couldn't make another choice that I would have to live with forever, that I would hate myself for.

So I shook my head. "I won't do it." Each time I refused, that pain in my head increased, growing and spreading and twisting.

"You will." He said it with such absolution, then pulled away and grabbed my arm. He dragged me over so I stood in front of Jay. "Do it."

"No."

"You can't resist me forever."

"I can resist you for as long as it takes." I wished I sounded as confident as he did, but then again, I was against a wall with this. It was like hanging off a cliff and saying I'd hold on as long as I needed to. It wasn't true, but I didn't have another choice.

"You are suffering for nothing!"

"*You* are making me suffer for nothing!" I twisted and shoved hard against Gorrin's chest, feeling that other part of me, the demon I usually ignored, growing and gaining a foothold inside me.

I hadn't taken on my demon form since I'd first died, since I'd gotten attacked and had been forced to defend myself. It had terrified me since then, the idea that I had something else inside me, something dangerous and bound to the Chasm.

Shoving Gorrin only managed to make my head hurt worse, the pain echoing through my skull like a high-pitched scream. Was it my anger or my demon side making it easier to ignore that pain?

Whatever it was emboldened me to take another step toward Gorrin and shove him again.

"Don't be foolish," he snapped. "You can't defeat me."

"I won't be your pawn. I don't care if you own me, I won't just do what you say, won't hurt others just to save my own skin."

"You will follow my orders and you will accept your place here!" He caught my fist when I swung at him, the movement easy and proving just how much stronger and faster he was.

Fuck it. I didn't have to think anything clearly before I lost control, before my body shifted to my demon form. It felt as if I'd held it back for the past five years, as if it had been waiting to escape and couldn't wait any longer.

A glance at my fist, still clutched in his hand, showed the long black nails. I didn't need a mirror to see the rest, to remember the last time it had happened. I recalled the wings that hung heavy on my back, the black eyes and black lips.

Jay jerked backward, the sound of her frantic steps loud against the tile. I glanced her way, surprised that a part of me wanted to go after her. It sensed her fear, her desires, knew I could make a deal with her and own her soul and it *wanted* that. It craved it so deeply that it terrified me. She pressed against the far wall, as if to make herself as small as possible, then froze.

I directed all those complicated feelings at Gorrin, however. *He'd* set this all up, so he deserved to be the focus of all my anger and hatred.

"Even in your demon form, you have no chance against me. I have ruled as a Demon Lord longest of all and I could wipe you off the face of the Chasm without breaking a sweat."

"So do it," I snapped and pulled my hand back before lashing out again. I swiped out at him, my fingers outstretched. He yanked backward, but not fast enough. The clawed tips of my fingers sliced through his cheek, drawing blood and making me want to lick my nails clean for a taste.

He reached up to his cheek, then brought his red-covered fingers out to stare at them. I'd bet no one had dared to do such a thing in so long he probably no longer remembered. His eyes were wide as he stared at me, as though seeing me for the first time. His wariness soothed that dark part of me.

Yet he didn't give in. Instead, his gaze hardened. "Make the deal," he repeated in a firm voice.

"No."

He lifted his hand and a wave of power struck me, knocking me backward until I slammed into the wall. It pinched my wing, and a snap made me wonder if I'd broken something.

Do wings even have bones?

It wasn't the time for a biology lesson though, so I focused instead on getting back to my feet. Gorrin moved toward Jay, and that got my head in the game.

I rushed forward, faster than I could have in my other form, my feet barely touching the ground. My wings moved, the pain nothing compared to that screaming in my head as I refused to obey what he wanted.

I slammed into Gorrin's side before he reached Jay, sending us both to the ground. Gorrin let out a frustrated sound before knocking me off him as if I were nothing more than an insect.

I hit the ground hard yet again but rose even faster. The fight energized me, a part of me I'd kept caged finally free. It scared me, made me worried about who I really was, but I didn't fight it — I couldn't.

"I'm not going to make her suffer like I have," I snarled as I leapt at Gorrin. We went back and forth, with him deflecting each hit or taking it easily. He retaliated, but never to the point where he caused real damage.

Even still, that pain in my head frayed my nerves, made me quick to respond — anything to make it stop.

Well, almost anything.

"Just do as I say and this is over," Gorrin said, his voice low, his body wrapped around me, his lips against my ear. It might have been romantic in any other situation, with his broad chest against my back, his strong arms holding me close.

It was hardly romantic, though, especially with the way we both bled.

"Stop," Jay cried out, tears in her voice. "Please, just stop!"

But I couldn't. I struggled against Gorrin's hold, my wings pinned between us. "If you make this deal, you will *never* be free! Don't you get that? You will be bound forever, never able to leave this place after you die.

You'll have to do things you never wanted to. *Nothing* is worth that!" I tried to make her understand, to realize that she was offering so much more than she could comprehend.

What human could understand it? No person had any real view of what eternity meant, of how long it was. I'd spent five years here and that was more than enough to come to terms with how endless time was in the Chasm. Jay could offer all she wanted, but she couldn't make an informed decision.

It was like a child offering their firstborn in exchange for candy — they didn't care at that point because their future children meant nothing to them.

So no matter how Jay begged, I couldn't give in.

Gorrin wrapped his hand around the front of my throat, holding me still, his breath warming my ear as he spoke softly. "This is inevitable, little fish. This is the world. I fought against it once before and learned it was for nothing. That is why I don't want you to suffer the same."

"You're the reason I'm suffering."

"I would rather you suffer for a short time now than endure it for centuries as you struggle against the order."

"I will change the order if that's what it takes," I swore.

He laughed as if my words were those of a child, giving me the same dismissal I had to Jay. "You won't. That isn't how the world works. You follow along or you get dragged. This is me dragging you, and I will not stop until you submit."

"You'll never give up? Never accept that I won't be who you want me to be?"

"I can't. You will either fall in line or you will end up dead and the latter is not acceptable to me. So yes, no matter how much you kick and scream, I will ensure you do as is required of you, even if we both have to hate me for it."

"What the fuck is going on?" Hale's voice made me sag slightly, as if I had a friend finally.

When I looked up, it wasn't just Hale. Yazmor, Tyrus and Hale all stood in the room, their eyes wide as if none had expected the sight.

Then again, there I was, engaged in what was clearly a rough fight with Gorrin, me in my demon form. They'd seen that before, but this time was different. This time my anger was locked on Gorrin, on one of their own, and that was likely something not seen all that often.

"This doesn't concern you," Gorrin warned them. "This is between myself and a soul bound to me."

"This little lovers' quarrel you are having is sending waves through the entire Chasm," Tyrus said as he took a step closer. "Your fighting is being felt everywhere because she is in her demon form and you are throwing a massive amount of power around. That drew us here and it makes it our business."

Gorrin gripped me tighter, and a part of me felt like a bone the four of them fought over. I never figured myself that interesting a toy, but the way Gorrin held me made me question that. He spoke to me, his voice low. "Make the deal, *now*." The last word came out as a growl.

"I'll make the deal," Yazmor said in his normally cheery voice. "That resolves this, yes? I will make the deal and hand her soul over to you. Everyone wins." Despite Yazmor's voice being as carefree as ever, his smile held sharp edges, showing the tension in the room.

"No. Loch must do it or she will never accept her place here."

"You can't change people," Hale said. "You can't fucking expect they'll fall in line just because you want them to."

"You did. All of you took over the positions you now hold and you ensured the system remained in place. You changed and adapted and survived. If she doesn't do the same, she will fall. Do any of you want that?" Gorrin threw that out like a challenge to the other Lords there, and worse, no one said a word at first.

The tense quiet was filled with my panting breaths and nothing else.

Tyrus finally spoke up. "Even if everyone eventually gives in, you can't force that change on others. It is like a stick. With enough slow pressure, it will bend, but go too quickly, try to force it, and it will snap. Do you want her to snap?"

Gorrin's grip loosened a hair, as if the words had gotten through to him.

As quickly as that happened, however, the moment of softness disappeared and Gorrin tightened his grasp. "No. None of you truly understand what is at stake or the danger involved to those who fight the system. None of you have seen it. Loch, no more chances, no more delays. Do as I order or the command will tear your mind apart."

As soon as he finished speaking, that pain in my head intensified, making a mockery of anything else I'd experienced. It was as though he took the training wheels off.

I closed my eyes for a moment, everything from the past years hitting me.

No, longer than that. Not just my time in the Chasm but my entire fucking life.

I'd gotten thrown into a system that wanted to grind me down beneath the boots of so many powerful people. The families in charge, the enforcers, the people who thought they could determine the course for everyone else because of their strength and power.

I'd had to tiptoe through life, avoiding those who would hurt me for their own twisted pleasure, forced to do things I never wanted because I didn't think I had a choice. I'd been trapped by a system that harmed me, one that determined I had little worth beyond how others could use me and had locked me in that position all my life.

That *same* system existed here in the Chasm as well, one that expected me to fall into place and behave myself based on the rules others made.

I was done playing by their rules.

My wings spread out as if instinct allowed me to control them. They knocked Gorrin's arms away from me, freeing me from his grasp, but my movements were slow and clumsy because of the splitting pain in my head. It made the world hazy, and I struggled to see anything. It felt like I was underwater, like the world sloshed and I couldn't breathe through the crushing pain.

Words echoed around me but I couldn't identify the speakers, couldn't even understand them.

"You are going to kill her!"

"I'll make the fucking deal, you asshole, just stop it."

"If you harm her, I'm not going to be pleased."

My body moved but I couldn't fully control it. Or perhaps it was better to say my thoughts were so fragmented from the pain that I couldn't understand what I did or what I planned. Maybe I didn't plan anything and moved on instinct alone.

Something rested in my hand and I curled my fingers around it, gripping it to focus myself.

Familiar gold filled my vision. I stared up and into Gorrin's wide eyes, as if I could explain by that look alone what I wanted. I wanted to go back to the way I felt when he'd healed me, when I'd fallen asleep against him. I wanted that again, to feel that odd sense of security and stability he'd given me before.

It had felt like no matter what happened in the Chasm, Gorrin never changed. He was steady and solid and forever, and yet now, I'd been set adrift. This was a side of him I'd never known, something deeper and more volatile than I thought him capable of, and it had come out because of his worry over me.

He'd done all this to save me, and even if I hated him for it, I couldn't pretend that it hadn't been because he believed it was right, because he thought this was his only choice.

His eyes softened in a way I'd never seen before, nothing beyond his face visible because of the pain in my head. He leaned in and brushed his lips against mine, the kiss unexpected and gentle and so damned sad.

It stopped, though, and the pain in my head let up so abruptly that I collapsed to my knees. The world came to around me, and something lay on the ground next to me. I shifted, blinking to try and get my bearings, only to find that it was a body beside me.

Gorrin.

He didn't move, and when I reached for him, I realized I held something in my hand. My fist clutched the dagger he'd given me, red coating both the blade and my hand. My gaze moved from it back to Gorrin to find red spreading out, turning the blue fabric of his coat a deep purple.

I only had a moment for the horror to hit me, to realize what I'd done, before something so much worse than the pain in my head washed over me. It was power, so much of it that I feared it would tear me apart. It overwhelmed me until everything seemed to blink in and out. Just as quickly, however, it settled inside me, binding to me until I couldn't ignore it.

I twisted to find Yazmor, Tyrus and Hale standing there, their gazes locked on me as if unsure how to react or what to do. Worse, others filed into the room, damned who belonged to Gorrin, ones I'd lived with for the past five years.

It took only a moment before it seemed the room was full, and all those eyes rested on me. I forced myself to my feet, no matter how unsteady my legs felt, my body still aching from the power that poured through me.

The moment I rose, nearly every person in the room dropped to a knee and bowed their heads, all except for the Demon Lords who remained frozen in place.

One of the kneeling damned lifted his gaze to mine despite remaining bowed before me. "We are yours."

"What?" My brain didn't seem able to keep up, to understand her words.

"You felled Gorrin, so you are the new Demon Lord."

I looked over at Gorrin's body, but it had started to dissolve as if it had become hollow. The blood didn't disappear, neither on the ground or on my hands. It stayed there like a stain I knew I could never get rid of.

I'd told him I'd change the order, but I hadn't meant like this. I'd never meant like this. All I'd wanted was peace, but now —

I was a Demon Lord, one of the four who ruled over the Chasm, but to get it, I'd just murdered a man I loved.

Want to see more from this author? Here's a taster for you to enjoy!

The Devil's Luck: Devil May Care
Jayce Carter

Excerpt

I took a deep breath as I stared at the closed door. No matter how much I wanted to turn back, to forget this whole thing, I knew I couldn't.

I wasn't just Loch Lacey anymore. Those days, much like miniskirts and a lack of back pain, were long behind me. Now everyone saw me the exact same way—as a Demon Lord.

Who I'd been before no longer mattered. The power that filled me now had erased that all.

Which was why I hesitated at the sight I made, dressed in a suit that would have made even Tyrus, the well-dressed bastard, proud.

I closed my eyes and gave myself a pep-talk about moving forward, about doing what I needed to do no matter how I felt about it all.

It didn't work, much in the same way that when I'd still been alive, telling myself I didn't actually *want* that pizza while on my diet never really convinced me.

I still wanted that pizza, and I still wanted to run the fuck away.

Instead, I grasped the handle and twisted. With my shoulders pulled back and my chin held high, I strolled in.

And was immediately struck with something small and hard in my forehead.

"Boo," Hale called out, a large bowl of popcorn in his lap and a smirk across his lips. Somehow, his piercings made him look even more like a bad boy. Well, being covered in tattoos and dressing like a biker helped, too.

And I'd made the colossal mistake of having stripped him down to nothing, so I knew first-hand that those piercings went *all* the way down.

"Boo?" I asked.

"Why're you dressed like that?"

I peered down against at my outfit, then smoothed it as if that would make it suddenly suit me. "They're just clothes."

"Stop pestering her," Tyrus said as he stepped out from a back room, a large wooden board with snacks on it balanced on his hand. It was strange to see him doing something so domestic, especially because he actually looked right in his suit. "She finally came — why torture her?"

"You baby her too much," Hale complained as he tossed a handful of popcorn into his mouth.

"And you never moved past the age where you think the way to a girl's heart is to pull her pigtails."

"Yeah, well, Loch is the sort of girl who doesn't mind a little hair pulling." Hale narrowed his eyes until the blue of them barely escaped through the slits as if challenging Tyrus by staking some claim on me. It reminded me that these weren't men — they were Demon Lords. They had no issue killing one another if it came to that.

Or even if it didn't need to come to that—fuck knew I'd seen them go to violence for no good reason beyond boredom.

And yet I didn't want tonight to go that way. Well, I hadn't wanted tonight to go any way at all, but since that plan hadn't worked out, the least I could do was not end up covered in blood.

I opened my mouth to tell them off, but it ended up not needed because another voice, an impossibly cheerful one, rang through the room and Yazmor walked in from behind me. "You're all early!"

Tyrus twisted his wrist to glance at his extremely fancy watch. "We were on time. *You* are late." The lift of his dark eyebrows made him look even more regal than usual. Then again, little flustered Tyrus, which helped him keep that unflappable cool no matter what.

"Well, I think you'll forgive me because I brought drinks!" Yazmor moved around me carrying a large pitcher full of an icy red liquid. The sweet scent of strawberries wafted up as he passed me.

"Is that margaritas?"

He beamed back at me, somehow managing to ride that line between harmless and terrifying as he often did. He wore a pair of jeans with holes in the knees and a large T-shirt with the name of an influencer I'd seen but never really watched. How Yazmor could seem so out of place everywhere but still keep up with all the trends kids liked I didn't know. Then again, he looked a lot like a kid, or rather that age where men started to fill out a bit but still retained that youthful face and height.

I'd *seen* the real him, though, and it meant I wasn't dumb enough to underestimate him or trust that innocent-looking face of his. He was a hell of a lot more than the college student he looked like.

"I can't believe you didn't bring anything better," Hale muttered though he sure eyed the pitcher with interest.

"Movies and margaritas go together so well," Yazmor argued as he set the pitcher down and waved his hand over the table to make four glasses appear. He poured the drinks then passed them out.

And despite Hale's bitching and Tyrus' hard stare, both men took the offered drinks.

Hale caught my wrist, then tugged until I toppled onto the couch between him and Tyrus, their large bodies boxing me in and making me feel small and suddenly breathless.

I went to move, but Hale placed the large bowl of popcorn in my lap. "Just stay put."

I turned a glare on him at how close he was, at the way I had him pressed to one side and Tyrus on the other. Their arms were beyond warm, as if they burned me where we touched, and the entire world shrank until it stopped just outside of where we sat on the couch in the large theater room in my place.

Maybe part of the reason it unnerved me so much was that it had been so long since I'd interacted with anyone.

A month.

A month of hiding away in my room, of refusing to do anything more than I absolutely had to. Thank fuck no one had managed to come visit, since I had no doubt I'd stunk to high heaven and had looked like some sort of stray mutt.

"You finally came out," Yazmor said before handing me my own drink. "I thought we'd have to dig you out if you burrowed in any further. How long has it been?"

"Not that long," I answered as I sipped at the deceptively sweet drink.

"A month," Tyrus interjected. "It has been a month of hiding."

"Thanks, Dad." I took another drink. Despite its sugary taste I had no doubt Yazmor had filled it with alcohol. That thought made me take another gulp, wanting to numb my nerves and my memory.

Yazmor took a seat on the floor just in front of me, resting his back against my shins. It pinned me in place, something that would have made me panic before.

Instead, the edge of fear had mostly disappeared. I was nervous for an entirely *different* reason.

"Relax," Tyrus said. "The point of this is to give you a chance to relax. That won't happen if you remain so tense."

"Well, I'm sorry. It isn't like Demon Lord Movie Night is something I'm used to."

"Well get fucking used to it," Hale said.

"Why? Pretty sure you didn't do this shit before me." My words made me go still, the ugly memories like a spider hidden in the crevices of my mind. I could try to ignore them, but every once in a while, they skittered back out and made themselves known.

My brain spawned a picture of Hale, Yazmor, Tyrus and Gorrin—the previous Demon Lord—all watching a movie like this. They'd been antagonistic at the best of times, so the idea of them together in any friendly way was like rewriting gravity.

Seeing Gorrin's serious face in my mind started a tremor through me. Red moved through his shirt, spreading out, the picture in my head mixing with the memory from a month ago, from when I'd buried a dagger in—

"Loch!" Tyrus' sharp voice woke me, pulled me back from the edge of that abyss before I had to remember what I'd done.

I turned toward Tyrus, his face filling my entire vision. He set a hand on my cheek, his lips moving as if he were speaking, but I couldn't understand the words. I couldn't even hear them.

Instead, that dangerous memory threatened to consume me.

I shook so hard, everything moved around me.

No, wait…

The world actually did move as if an earthquake rocked the Chasm.

"Enough," Hale whispered into my ear from behind me, his breath warm and his word coaxing. "Don't think about it. It's fine."

I let his words wash through me, and between him and Tyrus' face, the ground stopped shaking. It all calmed until only the sound of my rapid shallow breathing filled the room.

The memory retreated, that spider crawling back into its crevice, leaving me an empty shell.

"Loch…" Hale whispered once I gained my footing again, when I could shut my eyes to close out the world around me.

I shook my head, not wanting to hear anything more, not wanting to get dragged back into the memories I tried so hard to bury deep enough to never face again.

"Movie time," Yazmor said, the cheeriness of his voice so obviously forced. Still, I welcomed the distraction.

At this point, I either upped and left, making a much bigger spectacle of myself, or I sat there and pretended to watch a movie sandwiched between the other three who ruled the Chasm.

So despite the tense mood, the memories I struggled to not think about, the tears that stung my eyes, I turned my gaze to the television and pretended none of that was real.

Nope. I hadn't killed the man I loved. I hadn't stolen his power and position. I wasn't one of the four who ruled hell.

I was just a girl watching a movie with three guys — that was it.

The devil's in the details…

I really was.

* * * *

Earth really did just keep moving. It was something that amazed me each time I realized it.

No matter what happened, the world was just so fucking big that it kept going. No matter how horrible, how devastating an event, Earth just kept spinning.

Sure enough, as I peered into the well in my office, the one that showed me Earth, I watched people just living their lives, oblivious to everything that had happened.

"Loch?" The male voice made every muscle inside me tighten. Hell, I was pretty sure I locked up so fast I could have thrown my back out from it.

Still, I turned as if unbothered, even if we both knew it was a joke.

Standing there, in my office, was Gunnar. He stared back at me, a strange look on his face. It was something between fear and interest — the same expression he'd had each time he'd seen me over the past month.

Even though I tried so hard to avoid seeing him, outrunning one's past was a lot fucking harder than it should have been. If I were in charge of creating the world, I'd make it a law of nature that exes never had to see one another after a break-up.

"Yeah?" I asked, striving for nonchalance. The last thing I needed was for him to realize how much he unsettled me.

He approached, then peered past me and at the well. "Spying on Jay?"

I shrugged, unable to deny it since he could *see* the truth of the matter. There, in the water of the well, the blonde teen sat with her young brother, Brendon. Toys rested between them, and Jay smiled so widely it made my chest ache.

I'd done so much for her, but hadn't gone to actually see her, not since Hale had sent her and her brother back home after everything had happened. I'd wanted to, but it felt like facing something I just wasn't ready for.

So instead, I'd watched over them from here, peering into the water to catch a glimpse.

"Can't believe she survived," Gunnar muttered and crossed his arms.

"Jealous?"

He snorted but kept his gaze locked on the water.

Of course he was jealous. After all his attempts to manipulate things, to gain power for himself, he'd been the one to end up dead. It had been his own damned fault for underestimating others. He'd been so sure that Jay was nothing but a tool for him, that she was too weak and stupid to stand on her own, yet she'd survived, and he hadn't.

When he'd shown up in the Chasm, it hadn't shocked me. I'd known he'd been headed here, having sold his soul to Gorrin, and when his little attempted coup failed miserably — due in large part to me — well that felt like a rare time when fate had actually gotten shit right.

As it turned out, Charles — Jay and Brendon's father — was tougher than he'd seemed. When the fake hand-off started — fake because I'd already had their hostage safe and hidden away — and the Sand Snakes had tried to take the jump to remove Charles…well, it hadn't gone well.

Charles and his men had gotten the upper hand after realizing that Brendon wasn't there. They had removed those who had shown up, dealing a hell of a blow to that group. It had left the remaining Sand Snakes in chaos, but no longer a threat.

Which meant now the happy little family was all back together.

Some weird part of me liked that. When everything had gone so badly — and fuck had it gone spectacularly wrong — at least Jay, Brendon and Charles got to live happily.

And Gunnar was killed by Charles, so that's nice, too.

It seemed Charles didn't forgive betrayal.

Well, the Gunnar-dying part I was a fan of, other than the fact that it left him as *my* problem. Because Gorrin had owned his soul, and I now possessed all that Gorrin had before, Gunnar's soul was now mine. I'd considered selling it off just so I didn't have to deal with him. Each time I came face to face with him, a rush of unease hit me. We had too much history and too much of it was ugly.

However, if I'd learned anything thus far, it was to keep dangerous things closer. Gunnar knew too much, was too slippery, for me to entrust him to anyone else.

If I were lucky, maybe he'd be stupid and get himself killed again, thus ending his torture of me.

I peered at Gunnar's profile and sighed. He was arrogant to a fault, but he wasn't entirely stupid. He'd already started gathering power, not nearly as stuck as I'd been when I'd arrived.

He'd come as a damned, not a demon, but he'd made deals as soon as he'd arrived. He'd set himself up as a man who could get things done, gaining power and allies immediately.

Of course, compared to my position as a Demon Lord, he was little more than a fly beside to me.

"Don't you think it's some sort of fate that we ended up here together?" Gunnar asked.

"Yep." Before he could get excited, I added on, "I figure it's my punishment for my life of misdeeds. Fate sure is a cruel bitch, isn't she?"

He made a soft sound as if neither surprised nor amused by me. Then again, he was one of the only people under me who didn't treat me with fear. He probably should have—I had more reason to hurt him than anyone else—but we knew each other too well. After having dating on and off again since we were teenagers, there was no way to ignore our history.

"So, you going to hide here again?" he asked.

"I'm not hiding."

"What else do you call this? Haven't left this fucking place in a month."

"I call it a stay-cation."

"Uh-huh. And just how long are you planning on licking your wounds before you pick yourself up and get shit done?"

"None of your business. Last I checked, *I* am in charge here, not you. Pretty sure that means I don't have to answer shit to you."

"Good try," he said and backed away. "But sure, you want to bury your head in the sand? Go for it. Guess you really haven't changed all that much."

With that, Gunnar walked out, leaving me there in the room that still reminded me of Gorrin. I hadn't changed anything, not the office, not the private quarters, nothing.

In fact, no matter how gross, I hadn't even changed the sheets on the bed, convincing myself that I could still smell him on them.

He was everywhere in this place, and the idea of leaving it, of losing any of it terrified me. It felt like admitting he was gone, like letting the last of him slip away.

No, not just that he as gone, but that I had killed him.

My eyes burned again, and suddenly the walls all closed in on me. The air was thick and heavy and choking. I couldn't stay here, couldn't look around at this all.

I *had* to get out of here. I'd hidden away for a month, and while I didn't want to go, I couldn't stay. That fact left me all but running from the room as if I fled Gorrin's ghost himself.

It didn't matter how far I ran or where I went, I doubted I'd ever manage to escape that pain.

And I didn't deserve to, either.

About the Author

Jayce Carter lives in Southern California with her husband and two spawns. She originally wanted to take over the world but realized that would require wearing pants. This led her to choosing writing, a completely pants-free occupation. She has a fear of heights yet rock climbs for fun and enjoys making up excuses for not going out and socializing.

Jayce loves to hear from readers. You can find her contact information, website details and author profile page at https://www.totallybound.com

Home of Erotic Romance

Sign up for our newsletter and find out about all our romance book releases, eBook sales and promotions, sneak peeks and FREE romance books!